NONE

OF

THE

ABOVE

NONE

OF

THE

ABOVE

I. W. GREGORIO

BALZER + BRAY
An Imprint of HarperCollins*Publishers*

Balzer + Bray is an imprint of HarperCollins Publishers.

Library of Congress Control Number: 2014949521
ISBN 978-0-06-233531-9 (trade bdg.)

Typography by Jenna Stempel
15 16 17 18 19   PC/RRDH   10 9 8 7 6 5 4 3 2 1
❖
First Edition

For Joe, because I know you would love me no matter what my chromosomes were.

And for O and G: I hope that you are never afraid to fall.

NONE
OF
THE
ABOVE

CHAPTER 1

Dawn is my favorite time of day. There's something sacred about being awake when the rest of the world is sleeping, when the sky is just turning toward the light, and you can still hear the sounds of night before the engines and conversations of the day drown them out. When I start out on an early-morning run, there's a clarity to the world, a sense that it belongs to me.

The morning before Homecoming, I met Sam at the bottom of my driveway as usual. He had started to warm up, his breath coming out in puffs visible in the chilly late autumn air. He looked serious, almost solemn as he stretched, but when he saw me his face lit up and he leaned in for a kiss. For a moment everything felt perfectly still.

Then we were off. Over hundreds of runs, Sam and I had established a rhythm, a pace that we no longer had to think about, as if we were running to the same internal song. Sam pulled back his stride a little to match mine, and I stretched out just a bit to match his. On some days, it seemed like we even breathed in sync.

We didn't talk much at first, not until we got to our one-mile mark—the entrance to Gordon Park. Normally, Sam's as much of a stickler about routine as I am. So it surprised me when he kept on the paved trail instead of running through the uneven paths in the woods.

"Last thing you need is to bust your ankle, too."

"Tell me about it," I said. It had been a week since my best friend Vee's injury, and every day I had to talk her off the ledge. She was convinced that her Homecoming was ruined. Plus, her mom had been telling all her friends that Vee was a shoo-in for Queen, so now she was worried about losing face. "I told her she'll still get enough votes, but she doesn't believe me."

"More drama that way."

"That's why we love her, right? Never a dull moment."

"Something like that." Sam had never been Vee's biggest fan, but he tolerated her because he knew we were like sisters. "One way or another, it'll all be settled tonight. We're meeting at six, right?"

"Five thirty," I corrected him. "Faith wants to get pictures of us in our dresses and tuxes while the sun is still up."

"Shit!" Sam exclaimed.

I nearly tripped over a crack in the road. "Oh my God, what?"

He looked over at me, hands held over his mouth in horror. "I was supposed to get a *tux?*"

I almost choked on my laughter and lunged to my right to side-check him. We ran pressed up against each other for a few seconds before settling back into our run, grins on our faces. Over the months that we'd been dating, there wasn't much Sam and I hadn't shared. We'd debated the merits of State versus the Big U ad nauseam, and we knew each other's workout playlists by heart. He knew about my family's dogged obsession with the New York Rangers, and had come with me the last time we'd made our annual visit to my mother's grave. But sometimes I felt closest to him when we weren't saying anything, when we were both just concentrating on the soft percussion of our footsteps, the rhythm of our breathing, and the road in front of us.

By the time we got to my neighborhood and could see the oak tree that we'd measured to be fifty yards from my house, my legs felt like molten lead and my lungs were screaming.

Time to run faster.

When we passed the oak tree, Sam and I didn't even look at each other. As if a starter gun had gone off in our heads, we accelerated into a sprint. My body became a blur of straining muscles, and for the umpteenth time, I repeated my team's mantra: "Pain is weakness leaving the body."

Nine times out of ten, Sam beat me to my house, but that morning one of my neighbors' kids had left their bike standing in the middle of the sidewalk. While Sam swerved to avoid it, breaking his stride, I sized the bike up and hurdled instinctively. Takeoff. Transition. Touchdown. Coach Auerbach would've been proud.

I slapped my mailbox two seconds before Sam caught up to me, and shimmied a victory dance in my driveway. Sam dropped his hands to his thighs and bent over, wincing.

"Nice finish," he panted.

"You could've won if you'd just jumped the bike," I said as we jogged a cooldown lap around my block.

"Maybe. Or I could've wiped out." Sam looked over at me and grinned. "I don't have your form."

The wind had picked up, and now that we weren't running I had started to feel the cold, but Sam's praise warmed me down to my toes. I grabbed at his T-shirt and pulled him into a kiss, my heart still pounding, my skin flushed from the adrenaline.

We had stopped running, but the rest of the world was just getting started. A car door slammed. My neighbor's cocker spaniel barked. A boy on a bike sped past us, yelling, "Get a room!"

"Get a life," Sam shouted back.

Reluctantly, I pulled away, the salty taste of his kiss lingering on my lips, but before I could head back to my house Sam bent over to whisper in my ear.

"To be continued."

I shivered with anticipation.

Ten hours later, I stood in front of the full-length mirror in Vee's room, thinking that I'd rather be running.

"Krissy, you know I love you. But did you have to wear sleeves?" Vee asked as we got ready for the dance, her voice a tug-of-war between admiration and horror.

As Faith zipped me up, I checked to make sure the seams I'd tailored weren't noticeable. The dress had been my mom's, and it didn't have real sleeves, just wide triangular straps to hopefully de-emphasize my javelin shoulders.

"What's the matter with sleeves?" I asked.

"I'm pretty sure everyone else is going strapless," Faith said sympathetically. Her own dress had a sweetheart neckline that perfectly showed off the jade necklace her grandmother had given her for her sixteenth birthday.

"Even the people who shouldn't are doing it," Vee added. "It's, like, a Homecoming law." When she saw me lifting up my arms and twisting down to peek at my underarms, she relented. "Come on, are you seriously worrying? You look good in every-thing."

I glanced up at the edge in her voice, and caught her running her finger against the rough fiberglass of her ankle cast, which Vee had had specially tinted to match her skin.

"I can't wait to see you in your dress," I said, changing the subject.

"Let me go get it," said Faith, going over to Vee's closet, where the four-hundred-dollar ankle-length dress she'd rush-ordered the day after her accident hung like some holy relic.

Vee tossed her dirty-blond hair like a horse swatting off a fly. Just like that, the moody snarkmistress was gone, replaced by the girl who had set me up on a double date with Sam after I told her how cute I thought he was. The girl who held my hair back and gave me a Sani wipe when I threw up my first tequila shot. The girl who helped me sort out my mother's clothes the day my dad left them on the front curb because he couldn't deal with having them in the house anymore.

Faith and I helped her slip her dress on, and the three of us stood in front of the mirror. We'd literally been friends since we'd been born, when our mothers bonded in a postnatal yoga class. In grade school, my mom would comment on how well Vee and Faith complemented each other as friends. "Sweet and spicy," she said. "They balance each other out." Even then, Vee had an edge, while Faith was the sugar.

"But what am I?" I asked.

"You, my Krissy?" my mom said. "You're the steady."

I didn't think that was too exciting, but my mom just smiled, stroked my hair, and said, "It may not sound exotic, but it's the best thing to be."

I smoothed down Vee's dress. "See?" I said. "You can't even see your cast."

Vee leaned against me and turned to her side, cocking her head. "Still wish I'd listened to Ms. Green when she said we should have people vote the week before the dance."

"Don't worry," I said. "It's in the bag."

As Faith and I helped Vee down the stairs, the camera flashes went off like fireworks. My dad was waiting at the bottom of the steps with Faith's parents and Vee's mom, his eyes bright with tears.

"God, you're an angel," he said, "just like her." He pressed me into his shoulder and I closed my eyes, fighting off embarrassment but finding myself tearing up anyway. Even though he wasn't wearing his warehouse uniform, he smelled faintly of metal and wet cardboard, which isn't exactly perfume but always smelled like home to me.

Faith's mom asked me to take a picture of them. They were almost exactly the same height, and could've been sisters with their identical dimpled smiles and straight jet-black hair. Out of the corner of my eye, I saw Vee's mom inspecting her dress, moving layers of the skirt around while Vee stood stiff as a mannequin, her hand gripping the banister for support.

"Your father's sorry he couldn't be here," her mom said, "but you know how busy things are this time of the year. We bought you this to match your dress." She handed over a blue satin purse studded with pearls and crystals, and lowered her voice. "I made sure to put in some protection. Wouldn't want you to be pregnant for prom."

"Mom!" Vee hissed.

I stifled my grin. Obviously, Vee's mom didn't know that she'd gotten the birth control shot earlier that month. Vee had convinced me to get one, too.

"But I haven't gotten my period in years," I'd protested, which was a lie, because even before I'd started hard-core training when I was thirteen, I'd never gotten my period. Ever.

The three limos pulled up with the boys. Even though I thought it was totally over the top, Vee had insisted that we get separate cars. When I asked her why, she'd just raised her eyebrows at me until I blushed. The limos lined up along the Richardsons' driveway in a row of gleaming black, and a morbid part of me couldn't help thinking that it looked like a funeral procession.

I got one more tight hug from my dad, who whispered in my ear, "Have fun, and be safe," which was the most disorienting thing that happened to me all night, if it meant what I thought it meant. My dad never really talked to me about Sam—he left that stuff to Aunt Carla, for better or worse. In fact, one of the reasons I'd never let Sam get past third base was my terror at the thought of my dad ever finding out.

But did he accept it? Maybe even expect it?

It was hard to get the thought off my mind in the limo while making out with Sam, who'd already had half of a Sprite bottle filled with champagne. He looked like a different person in his tux. Distinguished, almost. He'd put some gel in his light-brown hair, and I caught the whiff of a new cologne.

"You look killer in this dress," he said, one hand trailing down my arm and making my skin tingle.

"Better than a tank top and a sports bra, huh?" I took a sip of champagne and leaned into him again, running my hands beneath his tux until I could feel the muscles underneath his dress shirt. His fingers moved up my thigh, warm and strong. Before, I'd always put on the brakes at this point. But that night, I pushed closer into him and he reached beneath my underwear.

Abruptly, his hand stopped. "Holy shit, did you go to Brazil?"

"Yeah," I lied. It had bothered me for years that I'd never grown hair down there, but when my teammates noticed it I'd always just pretended that I'd gotten waxed.

Sam grinned his *GQ* grin, and leaned in for another kiss.

When we got to the dance, I spent a minute straightening out my hair and dress. Just as I was about to get out of the car, Sam reached out to stop me.

"Wait—I forgot your flowers." He fumbled in a side compartment and brought out a green orchid wrist corsage. "I thought it matched your eyes." The shyness in his voice made me feel strangely protective.

"It's beautiful."

"And one more thing . . ." He pulled a little velvet bag from his pocket and handed it to me. "Madison helped me pick it out."

I smiled. Some people would find it funny imagining a three-sport athlete asking his twelve-year-old sister for gift advice. Then again, most people didn't know that the twelve-year-old in question had her big brother wrapped around her little finger. I gasped as the contents of the bag slid into my hand with a sparkle: a ring, two hands clasping a crowned heart studded with emeralds.

"Sam. It's gorgeous."

"You sure you like it? It's called a claddagh ring or something."

"I love it." I gave him a kiss to prove it.

They'd decorated the entrance to the American Legion with white Christmas lights and votive candles, and I felt truly aglow as I walked in to the strains of Harry Connick Jr. crooning about love being here to stay.

Inside, we set up at a cocktail table strewn with rose petals and found a chair for Vee. Before long, she was holding court. I couldn't keep track of everyone who kept clustering around our table—members of the Events Committee, class officers, and random underclassmen looking to get brownie points. I caught sight of one of my track teammates and peeled off to say hello, then slipped over to the finger-food table. Reaching for the cheese spread, my arm bumped against someone's elbow, sending a pile of wheat crackers flying.

"Sorry!" someone said, as he fell to the floor to pick up the broken crackers. I wasn't sure if I could lean over in my dress, but I managed to bend my knees and get down low enough to pick up a few crumbs with a cocktail napkin. Our fingers touched, and when I looked up to see who it was, I grinned.

"Hey, Darren!" I said when we stood up again. I looked up at him—he was one of the tallest guys in our class, but barely filled out his rented tux.

Darren Kowalski's face flushed when he recognized me, and he ran his hands sheepishly through his brown mop of hair. "What's up?"

I pointed at his plateful of cheese. "I hope that's not your dinner. Your mom would have a heart attack. Is she still trying to feed you alfalfa-hummus sandwiches?"

Darren's mom and my dad had dated when we were in seventh grade, about a year after my mom died. I was sort of sad when it didn't work out, because Darren's mom was an amazing cook who ran a healthy-eating catering business. We hadn't really kept in touch for the past few years, what with the awkwardness of our parents being broken up, but he was a distance runner, so I usually saw him a bit more during track season.

"Nah, Mom moved on to quinoa earlier this year," Darren said.

"Keen-what?"

"Exactly. Like anyone in Utica gives a crap about how much protein is in their grain if they don't know how to pronounce it." He flicked his head to get his hair out of his eyes, and scuffed the hardwood floor with his shoe.

"I like your tux," I offered. "It's sharp."

Darren shrugged. "I feel like a stuffed penguin. But you look awesome. I totally voted for you."

For Homecoming Court. "Aww, thanks." Vee had been saying that Faith and I would get Duchess spots, at least. I had to admit, it'd be nice to be up there with my friends. "Who are you here with?" I asked.

"Becky Riley. Jessica's sister."

Jessica had helped out with the HPV-vaccine campaign I'd organized last year. She was into drama and was a glee club star. But before I could ask about his date, a hand snaked across my shoulder.

"Hello, lovely lady," Sam murmured. He grabbed my hand, pretending to smell my corsage, and kissed it. I mouthed a silent good-bye to Darren as Sam pulled me away.

"Everyone was wondering where you were," he said. I could barely hear him above the music. He dragged me onto the dance floor to join Faith and her boyfriend, Matt. Vee sat things out, of course, listening to a sophomore chatter on about something or other while her boyfriend, Bruce, stared into the crowd. After a while the DJ switched it up with some

Madonna, and a flood of my track teammates pulled me over to do the Vogue with them. Then the strobe lights went off, the disco ball started turning, and they played a slow dance—a cover of that Beatles song "In My Life." Bruce actually carried Vee out to the dance floor without her crutches, and they swayed together. Sam and I found a spot on the dance floor next to them. I laid my cheek on the smooth satin of his lapel, feeling the beat of his heart.

I pressed close against him and his hands started inching downward. "Later," I said, feeling eyes on us. But I kissed him to let him know it was a promise, not a brush-off. If tonight wasn't going to be the night—one week after my eighteenth birthday, with a limo to ourselves and no curfew—when was?

Before I knew it, the music stopped and Principal McCafferty got up behind a microphone to announce the Homecoming Court. Faith and I brought Sam and Matt over to where Vee was sitting again, and we each took one of her hands. Her back was ramrod straight as she watched Principal McCafferty.

"The two Duchesses of the Court are Faith Wu and Jessica Riley."

I whooped and gave Faith a huge hug, surprised to find that I was just the slightest bit disappointed. Princess usually went to a junior—that's what Vee had been last year. So I didn't make Court. I almost wished that people hadn't mentioned voting for me, because as Aunt Carla always said, low expectations were the key to a happy life.

But I didn't have much time to think about it all, because suddenly Principal McCafferty announced the Dukes. And one of them was Bruce.

WTF?

Vee's hand squeezed mine in a death grip as Bruce went up to collect his sash. I looked over at her in the disco-ball light, and saw her face freeze. "It's okay," I whispered. "King and Queen aren't always a couple." Even though Bruce was QB1, most people thought he was kind of a jerk. I never quite understood what Vee saw in him.

As expected, Prince and Princess were both juniors. As they went up to be crowned, they seemed so happy I felt a little catch in my throat. I leaned into Sam, who pressed a kiss into the top of my head.

"You're up next," I whispered to Vee, and the side of her mouth went up a fraction of an inch. I noticed a tiny little bit of her hairdo coming out, and I reached up to tuck a strand back into place. So I actually felt her freeze when Principal McCafferty announced in a delighted, booming voice:

"Ladies and gentlemen, I'm happy to announce your Homecoming King and Queen: Mr. Samuel Wilmington and Ms. Kristin Lattimer!"

My first thought was: Did she read the index card wrong?

But then my track teammates all went crazy, yelling, "Go,

Krissy! Go, Krissy!" As Sam pulled me up to the stage, I looked out at the sea of smiling and cheering people, and felt awesome and as if I wanted to puke all at once, kind of like the high I get at the end of a race when I know I've won my heat and I'm still flying inside.

Then there was a special song for the Court only, and as I watched Bruce dance stiffly with a bemused Jessica Riley, I glanced back to our table, where Vee sat wearing a stuck-on smile.

"Do you think they only elected me because Vee broke her leg?" I mumbled into Sam's neck as we danced.

"No way. They voted for you because you're awesome. And you actually act like other people exist when you're walking down the hallway. Why are you friends with her again?"

"Sam!" I gave him a little elbow. In some ways, Sam couldn't really understand. He hadn't moved to our school district until high school, and never saw the way people walked on eggshells around me after my mom's diagnosis. Vee and Faith had been the only ones who made me feel normal. "This isn't right. I should abdicate." The initial high was fading, and I was starting to feel the wrongness of the moment, like the little aches and pains that settle in after a race is finished.

"What, you think she's going to feel better about it if you give her that tiara out of pity?"

He was right. When Faith came over after the Royal Dance, I burrowed my face into her neck, not wanting to come up for air. "We'd better go see Vee."

As we made a beeline back to our table, I lagged behind, not sure what to say. Faith, however, was the sympathy queen. "Oh, Vee. It's so unfair. Why couldn't they have had the vote last week?"

Vee's stuck-on smile was back, or maybe it had never left. "Don't make such a big deal," she said. "I mean, it's not like it's prom or anything."

"You should be wearing this tiara, not me," I said.

"Don't be silly." She laughed, and it sounded canned. "I'm just happy for you. It's not like you get to dress up very often."

Bruce came over with a sour look on his face. He yanked his sash over his head and left it in a crumple on the table. "All right, we got that crap done with. When can we go get the real party started?" Our school had set up a dry post-Homecoming bash in the gym, but the real fun would happen at Andy Sullivan's house. Rumor had it he'd gotten four kegs and the keys to his parents' liquor stash.

The rest of the dance was a blur of congratulations and sweaty dance numbers. When Sam and I stepped out just before midnight, the cool night air felt like heaven. Sam flipped his phone to find Andy Sullivan's address, but I put my hand on his arm. I didn't want to face Vee. Or the people who had voted for me. "Can we wait to go to the party?"

I didn't have to ask him twice.

We had another helping of champagne in the limo, and then Sam convinced the driver to park at the golf course.

"Alone at last," he said, when the privacy window went up. A few seconds later, the door slammed and we heard the driver outside, talking on his cell phone.

"I wonder if he does this a lot," I said, momentarily self-conscious.

"What?" Sam murmured, and then his lips brushed against my ear and the world contracted.

"Never mind," I whispered.

Sam nuzzled my neck and his boutonniere brushed up against my nose. I took in a deep breath to smell the rose, but it was the kind bred for looks and shelf life, and all I got was a mix of booze and aftershave.

Sam fumbled with the zipper on my dress, only getting it halfway down before it stuck. He pushed his hands up the bottom instead, and I had a burst of anxiety that he would rip my mom's dress.

"Careful," I said. My hands shook as I helped him.

"You're cold," he said, draping his suit coat over my shoulders.

I let the coat drop to the floor and leaned into his chest, sighing at his warmth. "No," I said. "Not anymore." The memory of Vee and her mannequin's smile faded as I felt Sam's chest rise and fall.

＊ ＊ ＊

The first time Sam and I ever spoke, I looked like I'd just gotten in a fight with an alley cat. It was sophomore year, and I was on a high after winning my first race ever. My teammates had celebrated by dumping blue Powerade over me, and I hadn't even had time to dry off completely before I ran my second race, where I clipped a hurdle and ended up crashing into the infield. But there's no crying in track, so I brushed myself off and went with my friends to watch the men's 4x100 relay with bruised, bloody knees.

There was this new boy running anchor, a guy with a stride so effortless it looked like silk. After he broke the tape—of course he came in first—a couple of my teammates went to scope him out and get the story. Was he a transfer? I hung back, watching him as he brushed his sweaty hair out of summer-blue eyes, and when my friends finished congratulating him he looked up and gave me a smile that made me shiver even as I felt a blush creep over my cheeks.

"Nice job," I said shyly. I might have given a little wave, or something.

"You, too," he said, holding out his hand. "You're Kristin, right? Hundred-meter hurdles? I'm Sam."

I was too stunned that he knew who I was to answer. But I reached out my hand anyway, and he shook it. For days all I could think about was the comforting strength of his grip, and the way his smile made me feel like a goddess even when I looked like a bedraggled rat.

We didn't start dating until more than a year later. By Homecoming, it'd been five months. We hadn't gone all the way yet, but in the limo, with the champagne bubbling through my system, I couldn't remember why not. I guess I had been scared. Concerned about STDs or something.

Whatever it was I was nervous about, it didn't exist in the limo. Blanketed by darkness, protected by tinted windows, the only sound besides our breathing was the soft piped-in jazz. Sam traced his finger up and down my neck before letting his hand stop just under my shoulder blade. He kept it there for a long time, and for the first time all day I relaxed. As soon as we started kissing I felt the need tingling down my spine, making the jumbled-up mess of thoughts about my accidental tiara evaporate. I reached for Sam hungrily. This time, I wanted more.

"You sure?" Sam whispered. I nodded, afraid that if I spoke my voice would shake. Sam untangled himself to get a condom, and when he turned back the feel of him on top of me was headier than any champagne.

And then, oh my God. Pain.

It felt like someone had taken an electric drill to my insides. I gritted my teeth and tried to power past it, but it was too much. Sam shifted, trying to go deeper, and I whimpered.

His weight lifted. "You okay?"

I nodded, and tried to blink away the tears. I was an

athlete. I was used to pushing through pain. "Yeah. Just give me a minute."

"Want me to try to . . . help get you ready?"

I nodded again, my eyes closed. A second later, my hips jerked. "Aaagh."

Sam swore. "I'm so sorry. I barely . . . Usually—" He broke off.

I froze, wondering how many other girls Sam had done this with. He must have felt me shrink away, because he got up and sat on the seat, pulling his coat over his crotch.

"It's okay," I whispered, already feeling cold. I took a deep breath in, and let it out slowly. He'd been so patient. "I'm fine."

So we tried again. He'd barely started before I made him stop. Sam wouldn't try a third time.

After we'd cleaned up, Sam just held me for a little while, stroking my arm over and over.

"It'll be better next time," he promised.

I nodded, because that's what I wanted to believe.

CHAPTER 2

In seventh grade, about a year after my mom passed, my aunt Carla decided to reinforce my understanding of the birds and the bees. My dad and I had left the church by then, to her great disapproval, so she stayed away from any biblical references. Instead, she just told me that the most precious thing a woman could offer a man was her virginity. Back then I was still in my Ugly Duckling phase, all skinned knees and straggly hair, and I couldn't even imagine having a boy kiss me, let alone *that*.

"It's like you were the keeper of the only diamond in the world, and when you gave it to someone, it disintegrated. You can never get it back, Krissy. And after that, you can never look at the world in the same way again."

At the time, Vee and I had laughed about how stupid it was to describe a diamond disintegrating, because they're, like, the hardest thing in the universe. But in the end it turned out Aunt Carla was right.

The morning after, things *were* different. Uncentered.

I called Vee first thing. Right away, I regretted it.

"What?" she answered, cranky as all get-out. It was eleven o'clock, but I must've woken her up.

"If you're busy, I can call you later."

"No." I could practically hear her rubbing her eyes. "I'm not doing anything. What's up?"

I told her that Sam and I had done it. I didn't tell her that it hadn't seemed quite . . . right. "It still hurts when I pee," I said instead.

"It'll get better. It's about time the two of you did it. So how was the Homecoming King?" she asked in a voice that was half honey, half salt. "He any good?"

I hesitated. "Yeah. He was nice."

"Nice, huh?" I could see her eyebrow arch in my mind. I hated it, the way she always knew what I was trying not to tell her.

"You said yourself the first time always sucks. Didn't your mom take you to a doctor after you and Bruce did it?" I asked. Vee had enjoyed telling me about the exam. Making me squeal. "Do I need to be, like, tested?"

"You guys used protection, right?"

"I'm not stupid. Besides, I got the Depo shot, remember?"

"You shouldn't be preggers, then."

"I just said I'm not stupid." She drove me crazy when she was like this. "I mean . . . you know, HPV. I don't think the vaccine always works."

"I know," Vee said, her voice finally serious. I was quiet, thinking about my mom. Vee sighed, and gave me her gynecologist's number.

"Want me to come with you?" she asked.

I could tell she was being sincere, and I wanted to say yes. Instead I said, "Nah, I'm a big girl."

"'Kay, then." Her tone lightened. "It's not like I'm dying to spend my free time watching someone look at your vajayjay."

"Ha-ha." I went over to thumbtack the doctor's number onto a sliver of free cork on my bulletin board. The board was covered with pictures of our junior class trip, and Vee smiled out at me from the center of every group.

"So how was your night?" I asked.

She paused a second too long before responding. "Oh, you know. We had to come up with some new positions." *Because of the cast*, I thought. She tried a little too hard to sound casual, but before I could ask her what was wrong she launched into an OMG-have-you-heard about Mandy Woodson's date, who'd been so wasted that he peed on someone's lawn and had gotten arrested.

After we hung up I lay on my bed staring up at my broken ceiling fan, thinking about how Vinnie McNab had taken Sam's Homecoming King scepter and gone around pretending to "rule" the Court. First thing he'd done was thwack Bruce's butt with his scepter.

"Get your King a drink, lordy-boy," he had shouted. "If you do, I promise to put this up your ass, just the way you like it." A bunch of their football teammates had laughed. Bruce had been so pissed you could see the muscles in his jaw jumping up and down. When they were done with all the Court photos, he'd stormed off the stage without saying good-bye to anyone, and he and Vee had left soon after that.

Sam and I hadn't made it to the after-party. I was too traumatized. When I thought about it, it was strange that Vee hadn't mentioned my absence. Then again, maybe she had been glad not to have me there as a reminder of the election gone wrong.

The dance already felt like a distant memory. My dad had finished his breakfast by the time I stumbled downstairs. He handed me a cup of tea, which I downed gratefully.

"Good night?" my dad asked with a grin. He nudged my tiara. I'd left it on the kitchen table last night with my keys and cell phone, next to a stack of mail.

I looked down into my mostly empty mug; decades of spoon stirring had created a network of gray rings on the inside. My mom had always been a big tea drinker, practically a walking Celestial Seasons ad: Irish Breakfast every morning, Black Cherry Berry after dinner with dessert, and Lemon Zinger whenever anyone was sick. I breathed in the peppermint tea my dad had made me, and closed my eyes, steadying myself.

I mustered as much enthusiasm as I could, and lied.

"Yeah, it was great."

The next Monday was maybe the first time ever that I dreaded a morning run. Sam and I had texted a little over the weekend, but mostly as part of a group convo about how Kimmie Perkins wore her bra and underwear into the hot tub at the after-Homecoming party, and went commando for the rest of the night. We hadn't discussed what we'd done. What we'd barely done.

I still had twinges of pain when my running shorts rubbed the wrong way. As I jogged across my lawn to meet Sam, he stopped his stretching to stare at me like he was trying to read the fine print at the bottom of a sign.

"Hey," he said, touching my shoulder. "You doing okay?"

"Yeah, I'm fine," I said. Except I knew right away that *he* wasn't, because Sam never just touched my shoulder. He always draped his arm around me, establishing ownership. But that day he hovered just out of reach.

I stretched out my hand. "You still coming over tonight?" We had a standing Monday study date. On good nights, we got an hour's worth of work done before going down to the basement and making out on the sofa bed.

For a split second, my hand hovered in space, alone. Then Sam's hand tightened over mine. He pulled me to him and he planted a kiss on my forehead like a blessing.

"Course."

And it was summer again.

The relief that washed through my body almost took my breath away. I held Sam close. I pressed my cheek against his chest, feeling the familiar stubble of T-shirt print cracked with old age.

We started our run, and with each step the tension in my shoulders eased. I fell into the hypnotic rhythm of our matched strides, thinking that our Homecoming night hadn't been perfect, but so what? As long as we had ground under our feet and the wind at our backs, things were going to be okay.

When I called to make my ob-gyn appointment the next morning, the only time they had available was during my AP English class, which was a shame because it was the one class I actually enjoyed and was kind of good at. We were just about to start *The Merchant of Venice*, so I gave my teacher a heads-up that I'd be gone.

"You won't miss much," Ms. MacDowell assured me. "I'll have one of your classmates write up some notes for you. It's also the first day of extra-credit sign-up for acting out part of the play, though. You can give me a scene preference if you'd like."

"No, thank you," I said. "I'm not really an actress." That was an understatement. Whatever talent it was that allowed other people to step out of their skin to inhabit another character, I didn't have it.

"And congratulations on Homecoming," Ms. MacDowell added. "Your classmates have good taste."

I mumbled embarrassed thanks before heading to my desk, because with her hippie skirts and unshaven legs, Ms. Mac-Dowell didn't seem like the kind of person who cared about Homecoming. She seemed more like a person who'd start a petition against it.

So did Jessica Riley, who sat behind me. Jessica was more quirky pretty than pretty pretty: Long, aquiline nose. Bold mouth. Wavy dirty-blond hair that she didn't bother to straighten the way every other girl in my class did. She had a style all her own—grungy T-shirt and Levi's one day, vintage dresses the next—and her body type was super curvy, Kate Winslet instead of Kate Moss.

I was sure that part of Vee's crankiness that morning was the injustice of the jock and the drama geek getting positions on the Court instead of her. People like us weren't supposed to win popularity contests. The Queen should have been someone who cared about the tiara and the pictures in the *Observer-Dispatch*. I didn't even know exactly what Homecoming Queens were supposed to *do*.

I had a vague recollection of last year's Queen giving a speech at a pep rally or two, and had a sudden moment of panic. I turned around to Jessica, who smiled at me. "Hey," I whispered. "Do you know if this Royal Court stuff comes with, like, responsibilities?" She, at least, was used to talking in front of crowds—she won debate tournaments in addition to acting. But I was a total dud when it came to public speaking. "Do I have to give a speech or anything?"

"Beats me. We have to show up for the Christmas parade all dressed up, but mostly we're just figureheads."

If we were figureheads, it was kind of sad that it had been so important to Vee to be elected, even though I understood the pressure from her parents. Her dad was a big guy around town, the type of person who had a country club membership and did things like trade in his BMW for an Audi. Her mom was a real estate agent, and though she was always super nice, when she gave me presents it always seemed as if she was trying to upgrade me. Like my sixteenth birthday, when she bought me a Lancôme makeup kit and a pearl necklace. Aside from it being such an expensive gift that it made me feel uncomfortable, it was so not *me*.

Vee understood that, and even loved me for it. When we were younger, she was always over at my house, probably because when she had dinner with my family no one ever bugged her about what she was wearing, or reminded her how many carbs were in a bowl of spaghetti.

But maybe that's why Homecoming meant so much. Because what was the point of spending your whole life trying to be High School Barbie if you weren't even elected Queen?

After school, while I helped Vee into Faith's car, she clutched at my arm before slumping into the front seat, drained.

"You okay?" I asked. This wasn't like her.

"I'm fine."

"Have you thought about using one of those rolly things to get around?" Just last month a teammate had gotten a knee scooter to help her get from class to class while her ankle injury healed.

"Why? So I can look like a twerp whose mom won't let her get a skateboard?" Vee said bitterly.

Faith and I exchanged our "this too shall pass" look. The three of us had been through too much together to let snark get in the way of our friendship. My mom's death, Vee's parents' near-divorce, Faith's older brother's attempted suicide.

As we drove, I wondered if I should've scheduled my doctor's appointment for after class and had Vee come with me. Outside of school, with just the two of us, maybe we could sort things out. Restore the balance that Homecoming had disrupted. Because in the end, that's all I wanted with Vee. With Sam.

For things to be normal again.

CHAPTER 3

The ob-gyn's office smelled like an unholy marriage of baby powder and Listerine. After I found a seat, I tried to find something to read, but it was all *Better Homes and Gardens* and parenting magazines, so I just sat there and waited.

Some of the other patients were really pregnant. Like, waddling. One woman struggled so much to get out of her seat that the nurse got her a wheelchair to push her to the back hallway.

It'd been a while since I'd been religious; my dad and I had come to a mutual agreement to stop going to church in the months after my mom died. There were only so many sympathetic looks and well-meaning attempts to set my dad up that we could take. Even so, I still remembered the Sunday school classes that my mom had taught, and all I could think about that day in the OB's office was the book of Genesis—the part where Eve ate the apple and God told her he would multiply her pains during childbirth, and that she had to submit to her husband.

A woman who didn't look quite as pregnant as the others sat across from me. She had a car seat with her and the baby nestled inside looked so happy and warm.

"Aren't you the cutest thing?" I said. I leaned over and nudged the little pink bear hanging from the car seat handle. It jingled and the baby cooed and reached up.

I got my cell phone out and played some of the different ringtones. The baby gurgled and laughed, pretty much the best sound ever, and reached for my phone.

"You mind if she holds it?" I asked. "I've got some Purell in my bag."

"Go ahead." The mom shrugged. "You got kids?"

I laughed. "No, not yet. I'm a senior in high school. But I'm going to be a child development major next year at State." The day I'd signed my letter of intent and accepted my track scholarship had been one of the happiest days in my life; it was amazing to know my dad wouldn't have to worry about paying for college.

A nurse called my name, and I excused myself. She took me back to an exam room and handed me what looked like a stack of pink tissue paper.

"Dr. Johnson will be in soon. Everything off from the waist down, please," she said. "Leave the opening in the front," she added, and closed the door.

The pink thing the nurse gave me ended up being some kind of doctor's gown. I undressed, wincing as my bare feet touched the ice-cold linoleum. When I put the gown on and tried to tie it up, the little paper strap tore a bit. I felt like a really badly wrapped birthday present.

While I waited, I studied Dr. Johnson's Howard and NYU diplomas and her posters of the female reproductive system. Somehow, the pictures made girl parts look like an alien, with the uterus being the body, the cervix a bad hairdo, and the tubes and ovaries a pair of demented eyes.

I looked over at the exam table again. Where were the stirrups? Vee had told me about the stirrups.

When Dr. Johnson came in, she started out with a question about how high school was, I guess to make me feel comfortable. She asked me if I had a partner, and I told her that yes, I had a boyfriend.

"And are you sexually active?"

I blushed. "That's kind of why I came for all this." I made a vague gesture toward the poster on the wall.

"Of course. I saw from your family history that your mother passed away from cervical cancer."

It sounded like a question so I said, "Yeah."

"That must have been difficult."

The worst thing was that cervical cancer is so preventable. If my mom's insurance hadn't lapsed when my dad was laid off from his last job, they might've caught it sooner. I shrugged and looked at my toes. The nail polish from the pedicure Faith had given me was already starting to peel.

Dr. Johnson didn't say anything for a bit.

"So, when was your last menstrual period?" she said finally.

I shrugged again. "I don't get my period. I train for track pretty much all year around." Three or four of my more hard-core teammates had stopped getting their periods, too.

"Were you getting your period regularly before you started running?"

I shook my head. My aunt Carla had always said that I was a late bloomer, and it had always kind of bugged me, but then Faith would tell me how lucky I was that I didn't have to worry about tampons and maxi pads and stuff, which made me feel better.

"Hmmm. Okay." Dr. Johnson wrote something on my chart. She asked me a few more questions about my diet and birth control and stuff, and then stood up. "Well, let's go ahead with the exam then, okay?"

She listened to my heart and lungs. Then she had me lie down and kneaded my boobs and my belly while I stared at the ceiling. She made a little surprised sound and I looked over at her.

"Are you aware that you have a small hernia? Two, actually."

"What's a hernia?"

It shocked me that anything could be physically wrong with me. For the past decade, I'd been getting physicals from an old buddy of my dad's. Dr. Arslinsdale wouldn't even make me get undressed when he examined me—he just mashed on my belly over my clothes, said, "You're as healthy as a horse," and offered me a sticker.

"It's a very common thing," Dr. Johnson said. "You feel this little bump here?" She moved my hand to just above my crotch. "It's a small opening in your abdominal wall where your internal organs can come through. Give a little cough and you can feel it bulge a bit."

I pulled the crepe paper gown over myself. "Is that a problem?"

"It's not an emergency, but things could get strangulated, or caught, in the future. I'll give you a referral for a surgeon."

Strangulated was definitely not a word you liked to hear in a doctor's office. As my blood pressure started to rise, Dr. Johnson reached next to my legs and pulled something out of the exam table that clanked as it unfolded. The stirrups.

"Just put your heels here, scooch toward the bottom of the table so you're to the end, and lie back. I'm going to start with the internal exam. This is the speculum I'm going to use to see inside." She brought out a contraption that looked like a metal duck bill and presented it to me in the palm of her hand the way they showed off things on QVC.

When she went between my legs I pulled my knees together and Dr. Johnson had to push them apart. I stared up at the ceiling again. There was a water stain on the corner of one of the tiles.

"Try to relax," Dr. Johnson said.

That was pretty much impossible, but I closed my eyes and tried to think of other things. Cute puppies. Precalc. The new pair of racing spikes my dad had given me for my birthday. Coach Auerbach had told me that if I was really serious I needed three different pairs—one for racing, one for hurdling practice, and one for . . .

"Holy sh—!" It was like being torn apart from the inside. I gasped in pain and my knees came together, knocking Dr. Johnson in the forehead. I sat up and reached my hand out to apologize. "Oh my God, I'm so sorry."

Dr. Johnson slid her stool back and looked at me. There was a sharp furrow between her eyes. "No, that's okay." She pulled nervously at her latex gloves. "I'm sorry, I wasn't able to complete the exam. I'll have to try again."

I took a deep breath and lay down. The poking started again, and I clenched my hand on the paper covering the table.

"Huh . . . ," Dr. Johnson muttered to herself.

"What?"

"No, I'm . . . Was it very painful when you had intercourse for the first time?"

"Um, yeah." It seemed so obvious that I laughed through clenched teeth.

"There are a lot of lacerations. And your vagina is unusually short."

What the hell did that mean?

"I'm also having some trouble seeing your cervix for the Pap, so I'm going to bring over our ultrasound."

As I stared up at the ceiling, my heart started going crazy and I could feel my throat tighten. A couple of seconds later, before I could really start to panic, Dr. Johnson came in with a machine that looked like a rolling laptop. I winced as she put some ice-cold glop onto my stomach. As she swirled a little probe beneath my belly button, another furrow formed between her eyes. She frowned twice, and pressed harder.

It seemed to be hours before she finally gave up. "I'm sorry to keep you here longer, Kristin, but I'm going to have to order some extra blood tests."

That's when I started feeling numb, remembering how we'd take Mom to get her blood drawn after chemo and the phlebotomists would stick her again and again like she was a human voodoo doll as they filled vial after vial of sluggish, dark blood.

"What's going on?" I whispered as I got dressed.

Dr. Johnson didn't look at me at first, just tapped her pencil against my chart as if she was trying to figure out how much to tell me. Finally, she seemed to come to a decision.

"Why don't you sit down."

I shuffled over to the plastic chair by the door, heart pounding.

"So, Kristin," Dr. Johnson said, "in that ultrasound I just did, I wasn't able to find your uterus—your womb—at all."

"What do you mean?" I stared at her blankly.

"I want you to think back to all your visits to doctors in the past. Did anyone ever mention anything to you about something called androgen insensitivity syndrome, or AIS?"

"No," I said, panic rising. "What is that? It's not some kind of cancer, is it?"

"Oh, no," Dr. Johnson said. "It's not anything like that. It's just a . . . a unique genetic syndrome that causes an intersex state—where a person looks outwardly like a female, but has some of the internal characteristics of a male."

"What do you mean, internal? Like my brain?" My chest tightened.

Dr. Johnson's mouth opened, but then she paused, as if she wasn't sure whether she should go on. I was still trying to understand what she'd said, so I focused on her mouth as if that would allow me to understand better. I noticed that her lip liner was a shade too dark for her lipstick. "Kristin. Miss Lattimer," she said. Why was she being so formal all of a sudden?

"I think that you may be—" Dr. Johnson stopped again and fingered nervously at the lanyard of her ID badge, and at her awkwardness I felt a sudden surge of sympathy toward her.

So I swallowed and put on my listening face, and was smiling when Dr. Johnson gathered herself and, on the third try, said what she had to say.

"Miss Lattimer, I think that you might be what some people call a hermaphrodite."

CHAPTER 4

I blinked. A distant roaring filled my head, like the sound of a seashell pressed against my ear.

"You're kidding, right?" If I opened the door, would I see Vee pressed up against it, holding back laughter? Or maybe it was one of my track teammates. They were always playing pranks, like the time they tricked Lana Weissmuller into thinking that our assistant coach had the hots for her.

But no one jumped in yelling, "Surprise!" The only sound in the room was the hum of the forced-air heating, until I heard Dr. Johnson take in a deep breath. "Kristin, I'm so sorry. This is a lot to absorb. And I don't mean to imply that this is definitely what you have, but your exam and history all point to it. . . ."

I still didn't understand what "it" was. "What do you mean?" The roaring sound grew louder, and I raised my voice so I could hear myself. "What do you mean that I'm a hermaphrodite?" Saying the word, my voice broke off into a whisper.

Dr. Johnson winced. "I'm sorry, I shouldn't have used that term—it's quite antiquated. The better term to use is *intersex*." She reached over to the ultrasound machine and tore off a little strip of paper with a picture that looked like a fuzzy black cloud.

"You see this here? Usually you can see the uterus behind your bladder. But I can't see anything. And those hernias you have? I think there may actually be male gonads—testes—in them. Of course I'll have to do more labs. A karyotype—that's when we look at your chromosomes to see whether you are XX or XY—blood hormone levels and things like that. And Kristin, do you mind if I call in a family member, just so you can have someone else here with you?" She looked through my chart, where I had put my emergency contact information. "I'll have my nurses call your dad."

I nodded, and closed my eyes, hoping that when I opened them again I would wake up, but when I did, Dr. Johnson was still there, frowning at me under the unforgiving fluorescent lights.

I closed my eyes again.

"Kristin, are you okay?" Dr. Johnson touched my arm and I twisted away, wincing at the pain between my legs as I moved. Dreams weren't supposed to hurt, right?

But real life did. Oh, did it ever.

Dr. Johnson's nurse came in with some test tubes and a tourniquet and drew my blood. After that, I don't know how long I sat around in a daze while I waited for my father.

My cell buzzed and I looked down to see a text from Sam.

What's up? Didn't see you during lunch.

My panic rose up like a tidal wave. What was I going to tell him? What was I going to do? I could feel the muscles in my throat tighten, felt a sour taste at the base of my tongue the way you do just before you throw up.

After a while one of Dr. Johnson's nurses came in to see if I wanted a magazine while I waited. What I really wanted was to know how the fuck I was going to tell my boyfriend that I had testicles.

On the chair, my phone buzzed again. I didn't want to, but I picked it up.

You okay? said Sam's text.

My hands trembled as I keyed in the vaguest response I could think of:

Had a Drs appt. CU later?

Okay. Love you.

For a second I was able to hold it together. Two seconds. Then all the love and guilt and the fear that things would never be okay again overcame me, and I sobbed alone, in a cold room that smelled of antiseptic, with nothing but a crumpled-up paper gown to hold on to.

I was curled up in the fetal position when my dad came in, and I could hear him right away as he yelled in the hallway, "Where's my daughter? What's wrong with her?" and all of a sudden my brain went into overdrive. Was I still my dad's daughter, or should he start calling me his son?

I stood up when he came in. As soon as he saw me, his face collapsed with relief, like he had been worried that I'd been paralyzed or something.

"You didn't tell me you had a doctor's appointment," he said breathlessly.

"I just had some weird bleeding, that's all." That was the best story I had come up with while I waited.

"God damn it," my dad groused. He got irritable when he had to deal with anything medical. "The doctor said it wasn't anything serious. But it's obviously serious if she had to interrupt my work."

Then Dr. Johnson came in. It took her half an hour to explain things to my dad.

And that was the worst part of the whole day: seeing the parade of expressions that marched across my dad's face as he heard the news. First confusion. Then shock and revulsion. And then all the emotions seemed to neutralize each other and he just looked empty. Shattered.

When everything was said and done, Dr. Johnson reached over to put her hand on my dad's knee. "Mr. Lattimer, I just want to reiterate: the bottom line is that Kristin is perfectly fine. And while I'm relatively certain about the diagnosis, we still need to get the results of some blood tests to confirm everything. I'm also going to send Kristin to a specialist to see whether any surgery needs to be done about those hernias."

"Why would she need surgery?" my dad asked suspiciously.

"Well, in some cases, the gonads are more prone to developing cancer. . . ."

"Cancer?" My dad's voice cracked.

"It happens in fewer than one in one hundred people," Dr. Johnson said, as if that were supposed to make me feel any better, "and usually only in much older individuals. But some doctors do recommend a gonadectomy, or removal of the testes."

"If there's a risk of cancer, shouldn't we do it right away?" asked my dad. "Can we see this specialist tomorrow?"

"We'll have to check with her schedule," Dr. Johnson said.

"What do you mean, you'll look at her schedule?" my dad said, his voice growing louder. "This is an emergency."

"Well, it's not technically an emergency, Mr. Lattimer," Dr. Johnson started, but when she saw my dad's face getting red, she backpedaled. "However, I'll place a call to Dr.

Cheng." She picked up my chart and headed toward the door. "I'll be right back."

After she left, my dad slumped into his seat, and put his hand up to his forehead. I hurried over to his side, knowing that if there was anything that could break him, it was the thought of another cancer. "It's okay, Dad," I said, my face pressed up against his coarse brown hair.

"But what if it isn't?" His voice caught. "I couldn't handle it again, sweetie. I just couldn't."

"She said the tumors only develop when people are older," I reassured him. It felt weird to be the one comforting him, like somehow I was the adult and he was the teenager.

A few minutes later Dr. Johnson came back in and told us that the specialist had an appointment the next Monday at four o'clock. "Dr. Cheng will be able to talk to you about surgical options," she said. "She'll be able to give you more details about cancer risk."

At the *C* word, my father's face sagged again. But to be perfectly honest? Even knowing what cancer did to my mother, sometimes I think it would've been so much easier if things had been as simple as cutting out a tumor.

CHAPTER 5

When we got home from Dr. Johnson's office, I collapsed onto our couch, sinking into a cocoon of worn cushions and hand-made afghans. The shock and fear had worn off, leaving me empty. Dazed. Numb.

None of it made sense. I didn't understand how I could be part boy. Did it even mean anything, if I still looked like a girl on the outside? I had boobs and hips and cheekbones and lips that Sam loved to kiss.

Sam. Just thinking his name made a ripple of pain go through my body. I would have to tell him. Except . . .

Maybe I wouldn't.

I didn't have to tell anybody. For months after her cancer diagnosis, my mom kept it secret except for my immediate family. The only way for someone to know that I wasn't a girl was if he had ultrasound vision, or was able to look at my cells under a microscope.

Or was it more obvious? I stared at the childhood pictures on our mantel. Was it just that all babies look alike, or did I look like a boy in that nine-month-old portrait? All of a sudden, I remembered the time when I was eight and cried when my aunt Carla got me a pink pair of sneakers instead of the blue ones I wanted. Then, the day my mom gave me a spanking when I made a mess in the bathroom because I wanted to see if I could pee standing up like the boys in my summer camp.

Had these all been hints of what I might be?

"A hermaphrodite," I whispered. Saying the word out loud gave me the creeps. It made me sound like a bug, or something that belonged in a rock collection. I couldn't remember the name of the syndrome Dr. Johnson had mentioned. My dad would have remembered, was probably burning bandwidth looking it up now. But what was the point of looking it up when they weren't sure I had it, yet? All Dr. Johnson had done was do a quick ultrasound and mash on my crotch.

It's a mistake. I repeated it over and over in my mind until I actually believed it, the way Coach Auerbach had us chant mantras before meets to get the team into a winning mind-set. Say something often enough and you'll believe it.

I forced myself to pull out my copy of *The Merchant of Venice*. It was the perfect thing to get my mind off doctor's visits and blood tests, because deciphering Shakespeare took every ounce of my brainpower, when I did it right.

Act 1, with all the haggling and usury and blatant anti-Semitism was only okay, except for the part when Portia dissed all of her suitors, which was pretty enjoyable. Then, in act 2, scene 6, good old Will stabbed me in the gut.

But love is blind, and lovers cannot see
The pretty follies that themselves commit;
For if they could, Cupid himself would blush
To see me thus transformèd to a boy.

I knew it was stupid for that sentence to hurt. It wasn't like Shakespeare wrote it with me in mind—he was talking about how Shylock's daughter disguised herself as a boy to escape his house. Even so, I couldn't stop the tightening of my throat as I read it, or the acceleration of my heart.

Cupid himself would blush, I was such a freak.

I tucked *The Merchant of Venice* back into my knapsack and pulled out my precalc book instead. In math, there were no cross-dressers, no girls turning into boys. I lost myself in the numbers, and in the equations that I could actually solve.

Halfway through my problem set, our doorbell rang. It was Darren Kowalski. He had the faintest sheen of sweat on his forehead, and wore sweats and a long-sleeve cross-country shirt saying MY SPORT IS YOUR SPORT'S PUNISHMENT.

"Ms. MacDowell said you needed someone to take notes," he said. "There's a handout, too." He pulled a sheaf of papers from his CamelBak hydration pack.

"Thanks," I said. It made sense for Darren to have volunteered. He only lived a half mile away—the equivalent of a chip shot for a distance runner.

"No problem. You doing okay?"

I peered up at him, wondering when he'd gotten so tall, and tugged self-consciously at the afghan around my shoulders. I must look like some sort of invalid. "Of course," I said, my tone clipped. "I'm fine."

There's nothing wrong with me.

"Oh. Okay." Darren shifted the weight of his lanky body as if getting ready to run away.

Instantly, I regretted my defensiveness. My mom was probably rolling over in her grave at my manners. Darren had no way of knowing why I'd been absent. I regrouped, and gestured toward the kitchen. "Do you want something to drink?"

"No, thanks. I've got one here." He nudged his CamelBak straw with a finger.

"Oh, okay then." I was just about to reach for the door handle when my dad came down the stairs, carrying his laptop.

"Krissy, you should look at this website I found—"

He stopped short when he saw Darren, and the shame on his face was a second stab in the gut.

My dad snapped his laptop shut and managed a weak smile. "Darren! Haven't seen you in a while. How's everything?"

"Fine, Mr. Lattimer."

"How's the college search going? You still on the premed track?" Darren's mom had always talked about how good he was at math and science, and wasn't subtle about wanting him to become a doctor.

"That's the plan," he said.

"You looking at State at all?"

"Yeah, and Columbia. Maybe even Yale."

"A real brainiac, huh?"

Darren gave an embarrassed shrug and scuffed his shoe against our doormat, looking as massively uncomfortable as I felt.

"How's your mother doing?" my dad asked. "She seeing anyone these days?"

Oh my God. Could he be more awkward? According to Aunt Carla, Dad and Ms. Kowalski had broken up because Ms. K still wasn't over her ex-husband, who had announced one day out of the blue that he was gay. Our whole town had buzzed about it for weeks; rumor was he'd fallen in love with an elementary school teacher.

"Dad," I interjected. "Darren's in the middle of a run. He probably needs to get going."

"Of course. Well, good luck with colleges, Darren."

"Sure," Darren said. He shot me a grateful glance. "See you tomorrow, Krissy."

I watched him lope off into the twilight before hunkering back down to my problem set. It wasn't until much later, after I had gone to bed, that it occurred to me that my dad never did get around to showing me whatever website he'd found. But it didn't matter, I decided.

Because it's all a mistake.

CHAPTER 6

Sam met me at my locker Friday morning, like usual, and slung his arm across my shoulders while giving me a kiss on the forehead the way he always did. But all I could think of when he touched me was, *I may have testicles.*

"You never called me yesterday," he said. "Did you get my texts?"

"Oh, yeah." I tried to sound casual. "My phone ran out of battery and I didn't get them until late."

"As long as you're cool," said Sam.

"Yeah, I'm cool," I said, forcing a smile.

They say that the best hurdlers learn to compartmentalize. They break down each race into its components, and when they perfect the little things, the big picture comes together naturally.

So I focused on one piece of my life at a time. When I

was in the car with Faith and Vee, I made sure not to mention Homecoming, and concentrated so hard on laughing and keeping my smile planted on my face that my cheeks hurt when I got home.

When Sam came over on Saturday afternoon to "study" just like he always did, we fell into our make-out routine the way my feet slid into my worn running shoes. There were even a couple of moments when I allowed myself my usual fantasy where Sam proposed to me on graduation day. We'd go to college, of course (Sam was still waiting to hear from State), and then work for a few years before buying a house in the burbs and having kids who ran and played lacrosse and football.

I guess I'd forgotten about the part where I might not have a uterus.

The Monday of my specialist's visit, I got through the day class by class. The urologist had scheduled me for her last appointment. I sleepwalked through bio, and felt like a robot during math. In my child development class we watched a video about shaken baby syndrome and it was so horrifying that I lost myself in that. Then there was English.

On Mondays, Ms. MacDowell always did class "seminar style." As we moved our desks into a circle, she talked about how she always liked to teach *The Merchant of Venice* and *Othello* together because they were Shakespeare's most problematic plays. "Today, let's discuss how both plays unsettle assumptions and disturb the conscience with their portrayals of the Other."

"You mean by being racist and anti-Semitic?" Natalie Goldstein asked.

"And sexist," Jessica added. "Women in his plays are controlled by men and don't have power unless they cross-dress."

"Interesting. Why do you say that the play is racist and sexist," Ms. MacDowell asked, "rather than saying that it's a play *about* racism and sexism?"

"Because Shylock's the villain," Natalie said. "He's the one who gets punished in the end. Poor guy. He loses his ducats and his daughter, *and* they're going to make him go to church every Sunday."

"But was Shakespeare completely unsympathetic to Shylock's situation?" Ms. MacDowell pressed.

"No," Jessica said. "He gave Shylock the best monologue in the Western canon." She stood up straight and used her actress voice. "'Hath not a Jew eyes? Hath not a Jew hands . . . ?'"

"Yeah, and the Christians in the play are kind of asshats," Darren said. "They might win, but in the end they're the hypocrites. I mean, Portia goes on and on about the quality of mercy, but at the end of the trial she's just as vengeful as Shylock was.

"Plus," he added, "in the allegory of the caskets, Shakespeare basically says that people should look past the appearance of things. 'All that glisters is not gold,' you know."

Ms. MacDowell smiled at Darren, and looked around the circle at the rest of us. "What do you all think? Is Shakespeare subversively arguing for a world where, in the end, it doesn't matter whether we're black or white, Jew or Christian, man or woman?"

As my classmates piped up I stayed silent, my eyes riveted to the clock, my mind trying its hardest not to go there: maybe Shakespeare was preaching that it shouldn't matter if you were a man or a woman.

But what if you were something in between?

CHAPTER 7

When I walked into the specialist's office and saw all the old men sitting around, I was glad my dad had come, even if he couldn't look me in the eye anymore.

Most of the magazines were about golf and cars, and all the little brochures by the windowsill advertised Viagra and drugs for people who peed their pants. I stuck out like a sore thumb. One of the other patients, a man with white hair and brows so bushy they almost flopped over his eyes, kept looking up from his magazine in my direction. I wanted to say something to him about how it wasn't nice to stare, but I knew it would draw more attention, so I tried to focus on the paperwork I was supposed to fill out. On the top of the very first page it read:

NAME: SSN: DOB: SEX:

I stared at the posters on the walls, which were all colorful diagrams of kidneys and prostates. Each of them had cross sections of people cut in half—one male, with the penis sticking out like the mouth on a faucet. One female.

That was when I realized that life was a multiple-choice test with two answers: *Male* or *Female*. And I was *None of the Above*.

I was still staring at the posters on the wall when the nurse called me back to an exam room, where we waited for another fifteen minutes until a door swung open and a petite woman with black hair laced with gray came in. She reached out to shake my hand.

"I'm Dr. Cheng," she said. "So nice to meet you. I've got Dr. Johnson's notes, and I know that you must be totally overwhelmed by what she told you. Do you have any questions up front?"

I knew it was just her standard open-ended question to get me talking, but I almost started crying right then. *Can you make me into a girl?* I thought. *Tell me that I don't have balls.*

What I said was:

"Am I really a hermaphrodite?"

She winced. "We don't like to use that word anymore, because it isn't really an accurate term and carries a lot of stigma."

No kidding. I looked down at my blank form, and remembered the hours I spent memorizing the gender of certain nouns in French class. Hats and fish are masculine. Freedom and lemonade are feminine.

"So what am I?" I closed my eyes to remember the word my teacher had used when she told us that Russian actually had three genders. "Neuter?"

"Of course not," she said. "When speaking about your condition, we use either the term *intersex*, or *disorder of sex development*—DSD for short."

Like that was any better. When I didn't say anything, Dr. Cheng rolled her chair and leaned in closer, as if she were moving in to look through a microscope, and I was the specimen. "Not that it matters what we call you, Kristin. You're here because Dr. Johnson felt out of her depth and wanted you to talk to an expert about your condition and the types of treatment you could choose to have in the future."

"Treatments?" my dad interjected. "What treatments?"

"Can you do uterus transplants?" I asked hopefully.

But Dr. Cheng shook her head. "Transplants aren't really a viable option yet. I'm sorry." She opened the folder she was carrying. Calmly, she explained to me that the ultrasound and blood tests had confirmed that I did not have a uterus, that my body was pumped to the gills with testosterone, and that my chromosomes were in fact XY. "All this suggests that you have something called androgen insensitivity syndrome, or AIS. Have you done any research on this yet?"

My dad nodded, but I shook my head. I'd been so stupid,

burying my head in the sand.

"It's actually a very common form of intersex," Dr. Cheng said. She handed me an article that looked like it was written in Greek, and gave me a mini lecture on how embryos develop, using words like "mixed signals" and "defective receptors." It was mostly gibberish, but the bottom line was that I was a car that came off the assembly line all messed up. I was a lemon.

Dr. Cheng must've seen my eyes glaze over, because she finally stopped all the science talk and explained what all the mumbo jumbo meant in real life. I would never get my period. I could never have a biological child of my own. My vagina was only two inches long, which was why it hurt like hell when Sam and I tried to have sex—not that I mentioned anything about that in front of my dad. Finally, the testicles in my hernia might need to come out in the future because they could become cancerous.

"Why the future?" I blurted. "Can't we do the surgery now?"

"It's very controversial," said Dr. Cheng. "If you take the testicles out, you'll have to start taking estrogen for bone health. Plus, the risk of cancer in the gonads is very small."

"But not zero," my dad insisted.

"No," Dr. Cheng admitted. She looked down at my chart.

"I've done some reading online," my dad said reluctantly, not looking at me. "Sounds like surgical removal is the way to go. For psychological reasons, too."

Like not having to walk around knowing that you have testicles inside you. "I'd like to. . . . I do want to take them out."

Dr. Cheng leaned in. "Kristin, I totally understand that impulse. But why don't you go home and think about it before scheduling the surgery? There are side effects, and risks." She turned toward my dad. "There are a lot of issues to sort out, and if you want to talk to someone, I know some great therapists. This is a difficult, scary life change, and it will take some adjusting to."

"What, being gay?" I asked.

Dr. Cheng blinked. "I'm not sure I follow."

"That's what I am, right? I'm a man. But I've always liked boys, so . . ."

"No. Just having a Y chromosome doesn't automatically make you a man."

"Am I trans, then? Like, a man trapped in a woman's body?"

She shook her head. "I know it's really confusing, but chromosomal sex, gender identity, and sexual orientation are all separate concepts."

At my blank look, she took out a piece of paper and drew a quick sketch that looked like a gingerbread man. She put a circle around the groin area and wrote SEX. "Your biological sex is usually determined by your chromosomes, but in your case there's a disconnect—even though you're XY, externally you look female."

Next, she circled the gingerbread man's brain and wrote GENDER IDENTITY, underlining this twice. "Gender identity is one's internal sense of whether they're male or female. It often correlates to one's external sex, but not always; that's what being transgender is."

Dr. Cheng looked down at my hands, still clutching the stupid intake form. She took it gently from me and spread it. "This box here? You should put *female*. Because that is how the vast majority of women with the complete form of AIS identify themselves."

It took a moment for what she said to sink in. I was supposed to be a girl. A straight girl, even. But what kind of boy could ever love a freak like me? I didn't know if Sam was the kind—or if I was brave enough to see if he was.

"Kristin, in a way, you're very lucky," Dr. Cheng said. "AIS is a relatively straightforward form of intersex. There are other syndromes where the anatomy is more . . . complex, and all these issues of gender identity aren't as clear."

I didn't feel lucky, but Dr. Cheng didn't seem to notice.

"The next time you come back," she said, "I want to do a quick pelvic exam. I'll give you some sedatives to take before, and we can talk about dilation—stretching the vagina naturally. Here's a sample kit—you can take a look and read about it on your own." She handed me a nondescript white cardboard box and another pamphlet with pictures of what looked like plastic dildos.

"What do you mean, stretching myself down there?" I felt like I wanted to throw up.

"Kristin, I know it all seems very awkward. But with all of this—the medications and the dilation—most women with AIS live perfectly normal lives."

Yeah, right.

"So when can she schedule surgery? To get the . . . testicles removed that may have cancer?" My dad stumbled over the word.

"Mr. Lattimer, please be reassured that this is just a potential for cancer, and there are risks involved. . . ."

"I know there are risks," I said. "But I want those things out of me yesterday."

Dr. Cheng sighed. "Why don't I go print out some information on the procedure so you can review the risks and benefits and really ponder them. Ethically, I need to give you some time to make this decision. Okay?"

I sagged into my father's shoulder as Dr. Cheng left.

"I want those things out."

"I know, Krissy. So do I."

When Dr. Cheng came back with some handouts, I stared at the hieroglyphics before stuffing them into my purse. I looked at the time on my cell phone. It was getting old, and the paint was starting to chip from its hot-pink case. I wanted to go home.

"Are we done now?" I asked.

"It depends," Dr. Cheng said. "Do you have any more questions?"

"No," I lied. Of course I had questions.

I just didn't know what they were yet.

Right after we got home, Aunt Carla showed up. My dad had called her.

"Oh, Krissy," she said, wrapping me in her stout hug. She looked like she had been crying, her mascara making large raccoon stains under her eyes. "This must be such a horrible nightmare. Poor, poor Krissy."

On the one hand I knew she was probably right, and that my world might never be the same. On the other hand, nothing had really changed about me. I stood stiffly in her arms, self-conscious about her over-the-top pity. "It's okay. It's not a disease; it's not life threatening."

"But you'll need surgery? And your poor father. I haven't seen him this torn up inside since . . ."

Since my mother. I felt like I was in the middle of an earthquake, only it wasn't the ground that was splitting. It was my heart.

Aunt Carla clutched at my arm. "But I know you're strong, Krissy. And like your father said, no one needs to be the wiser. You know we'll love you no matter what. Remember when you were little and your dad always said that he'd love you forever and ever, until the sun fades?"

I nodded again. In the part of me that wasn't numb, I did know.

Though I wished she hadn't felt the need to tell me.

CHAPTER 8

The next day, the world was the same. Nothing about me had changed, either. Yet everything was different.

On the ride to school, I listened to Faith and Vee carefully. When Vee made fun of Larissa Jermain's blouse because it looked "mannish," I squirmed in the backseat. I felt a jolt go through me when Faith cooed over how she wanted to get the new MacBook Pro, the "girly" one. And when they mentioned Sam, going on and on about how many receptions he'd made in the last football game, my heart constricted in my chest.

I knew I needed to tell Sam. I vowed to myself that I would, soon, when I knew how.

But what would I say, I wondered, as he sat down next to me at lunch with his usual haul of two cheeseburgers, three Powerades, a salad, and a large basket of fries. He slid his tray over so I could share his fries.

I gave him a weak smile hello and nibbled at my tuna-fish sandwich. Aunt Carla had made my lunch. She always put too much mayonnaise in it, though I didn't have the heart to complain.

"So, Andy is gonna throw another party Friday night," Sam said, dipping three fries into his ketchup at the same time before shoving them into his mouth. "We should go, since we missed it last time. Remember to bring your bikini. The hot one? I think it was purple."

The purple one was a string bikini, and I'd worn it over the summer at the annual Spartan Car Wash. Had the thousands of drivers who passed me been able to see the faint bulge of my testes? I knew there was no way they could possibly know what was inside me, but my stomach did a somersault anyway.

Sam dug into his cheeseburger and downed it in three bites. "Man, do I need to let loose this weekend. Coach has been kicking our ass in practice."

A couple seats away, Bruce glanced down. "Stop whining like a pansy, Wilmington, and remember to bring your balls next week."

I blanched, and put my barely eaten sandwich back into my paper bag. I lurched to my feet.

Sam looked up at me. "You feeling okay?" He had just picked up his second cheeseburger.

"Yeah, I'm fine. Just feel like I might be getting a stomach bug, that's all."

"Want one of my Powerades?" he asked, holding up the still-wrapped bottle.

"That's okay. I'm going to run to the nurse's office and see if I can get Tums or something."

"'Kay. Later."

I never made it to the nurse's office. Instead, I went to the second-floor girls' room and sat in a stall until my stomach settled, listening to the rhythm of doors opening and shutting, of water running and the hand dryer blowing. I read the graffiti on the wall from top to bottom. I wasn't too surprised to see a big BRUCE TORINO = ASSHOLE in red Sharpie, but I was a little peeved to see that someone had written AND VR IS A BITCH underneath it in ballpoint pen. I tried to scratch it out, but the lines were too deep.

Now that we had a diagnosis, my dad had begun to troll the internet. When I got home from school Wednesday he was sitting in front of the computer with a half-finished cup of coffee. Next to him was that day's pile of printouts that he had specially highlighted for me.

"Krissy, did you email the support group yet?" my dad asked, tearing himself away from the screen with some difficulty.

"Not yet." I unzipped my book bag and hauled out my homework. One of the first things my dad had printed out for me was the AIS-DSD Support Group website. Supposedly they had an email list, and meetings. I couldn't imagine what they talked about. Hoo-hoo Dilation and the Care and Maintenance of Your Testicles?

"You should do it, honey. It'll be good for you. I already heard back from the parent support group."

"Dad!" It was so typical. He always forgot that he was not the one with the disease. Or syndrome. Or whatever it was.

"It's all right if you're not ready to contact anyone yet, though. Linda said that you just need to know that they'll be there when you need them."

"Who's Linda?"

"The doctor who's the leader of the parent support group. Her daughter, Maggie, is in her twenties. She just got married and is going to adopt a baby girl."

Because she couldn't have her own baby, I thought. It was selfish to think that adoption wasn't as good. I knew that. But it didn't change the way I felt, the gaping hole I could actually feel in my belly, as if I'd been the victim of some organ snatcher. Except I never had a womb to begin with.

"Krissy, promise me you'll at least look at the website. You don't have to email anybody. But they have a whole section for girls who have just learned their diagnosis. It'll help. I swear."

I looked up at my dad. Since I'd started high school, with both indoor and outdoor track, and year-round training, we hadn't seen much of each other. He'd been switched to a six a.m. shift a few years ago and always went to bed at nine, so when I had late track practice we were ships passing in the night. When I did see him, I never really looked at him. I was surprised to see that his wrinkles had gotten deeper, the creases around his lips there even when he didn't smile.

I could do this for him.

I closed my World History book, not taking my eyes from my dad. "I'll go up and look at it now."

It turned out that my dad was right. The internet was hope.

There was a group of women smiling at me from the landing page of the support-group website. I clicked on the JUST LEARNED tab with Frequently Asked Questions, the first of which was, "Am I really a girl?"

The answer was: "Yes you are, really!"

I know it's not possible to hold your breath for a whole week, but when I read that line, it was as if I released a breath I'd been holding ever since Dr. Johnson had broken the news. It was only when I saw the answer on the screen in plain black and white that I started to think that maybe my life wouldn't fall apart after all.

There were other questions that I hadn't even formulated in my mind, and more answers. I felt tears prickle in my eyes when I read the very next one:

What do I tell my partner, family, friends?
Nothing today; wait until you're fully informed, and then gradually share when it's safe and you're ready.

That part was less helpful. What did that even mean? How could you tell when it was safe? It wasn't like people went around with tolerance meters that you could monitor, or signs saying, "Welcome, hermaphrodites!"

Down at the bottom of the page, there was a picture of a girl holding a brown-and-black terrier. Or maybe it was a stuffed animal—I couldn't tell. The girl had blond shoulder-length hair, and a great smile. Underneath the photo there was a letter from the girl, from a real, live girl with AIS who lived in Maryland. Who had recently gotten married. Who was in medical school. And who welcomed me to her "sisterhood" and offered up her contact information if I had any questions.

My dad never asked for much. So I opened my email.

Subject: New Diagnosis

At that point I stopped. Who was I supposed to address the message to? There was no contact person listed. I finally decided to not even put in a salutation.

Hello!
My name is Kristin. I am 18 and was diagnosed with AIS a week ago. I saw your information on the AIS-DSD website and was interested in joining the support group. I live in Central New York and would

love to know if there are any other teens in the area.

Thank you for your time,

Kristin Lattimer

I read the message over once, twice, three times. Did it sound too formal? Was I supposed to give them my address? I typed in the Support Group website and scoured the "Contact Us" section, but it didn't say anything about giving them my address. So I put in my phone number just in case they wanted to contact me. And with a deep breath, I pressed Send.

For the next hour, I hit Refresh every five minutes, until I got bored and started looking through the mountain of research that my dad had collected.

When I used to babysit a lot, before track became a year-round training thing, my favorite activity to do with kids was puzzles. I loved getting down on the floor with them, teaching them what a corner was, and what it meant for an edge to be straight. There'd be that aha moment when things clicked, when they'd start getting that you could rotate pieces, match colors and patterns.

My life had been one big puzzle, except I never knew it. As I flipped from page to page, reading about AIS and what it meant, everything started to make sense: Why I never got my period—I didn't have a uterus. Why I never had a problem with acne, and why Sam had thought that I'd gotten a Brazilian wax—something about how my messed-up hormones prevented zits and pubic hair. Why it had hurt so goddamn much my first time—my vagina was too short because my organs didn't develop right.

My body missed an exit.

So I was stranded in no-man's-land.

Or more accurately, no-woman's-land.

I got about halfway through my dad's stack before I started feeling restless. It was dinnertime, anyway, so I bounded down the stairs with more energy than I'd had in a couple weeks—since Homecoming, really.

"Dad! I did it! I emailed the support group."

My dad was still hunched by his computer. When he turned around there were tears streaming down his face.

"What's wrong? My God, is something wrong with Aunt Carla?"

He shook his head, and I was shocked to realize that the expression wasn't one of fear, or anger, or sadness. It was an emotion that I would've never thought to have seen on his face.

Relief.

He waved me over to his computer. He was reading what appeared to be a magazine article, with a really detailed picture of AIS anatomy. I looked at the diagram, wondering if I was missing something, and then looked back at my father.

"Dad?" I said.

He opened his mouth to say something, then closed his eyes.

"You don't have a cervix."

"Huh?"

He pointed to the diagram with a trembling finger, and I looked closer. No uterus. No cervix.

I was never going to die of cervical cancer like my mom.

And that's when I started to cry.

CHAPTER 9

The first couple of days after my diagnosis, my alarm clock would go off like it always did and I'd stumble to the bathroom half asleep. Then there'd be a moment—as I was brushing my hair or going to the bathroom, for instance—when I remembered that I was a hermaphrodite, or intersex, or whatever people chose to call me.

The day after I realized I would never die of cervical cancer, though, I woke up knowing what I was. It had settled into my bones, heavy and uncertain.

It wasn't supposed to be a running day, but I pulled on my tracksuit anyway. Some people eat comfort food; I take comfort runs.

Sam was probably already awake, doing strength training in his basement, but I didn't call him. Having him there running beside me would only muddle me up even more.

If there's anything more head-clearing than the air at five in the morning in late October, I've never experienced it. I've always loved running in the cold, loved how my sweat evaporated right away when I ran. The way the wind made my cheeks rosy and smooth, and how I could see my breath scar the air. The cold always made the track faster. Harder on the knees, but quicker on the rebound. I never lost races in the cold.

You also tended to overthink less when it was close to freezing outside: Don't look at a problem from so many angles that you lose sight of the real issue. Don't worry about how your boyfriend will react to your being a hermaphrodite, when you might never be ready to tell him what you really are.

As I ran back home toward my neighborhood, the early birds started coming out. Mrs. Davidson was a nurse, and her silver Camry was the first car I saw, rear lights glowing like demon eyes in the blackness of predawn. My dad wouldn't be far behind—he usually got ready for work while I was doing my cool-down stretches.

I jogged up to our front porch, stepped inside, and in the warmth suddenly things felt less clear.

The coffee table was still a mess of highlighted printouts. The handout that Dr. Cheng had given me on vaginal dilation lay on top, along with the unopened kit. I'd finally read it the night before. It assured me that dilation "can feel a little strange at first, or unpleasant, but after a short while most women and girls can dilate quite easily." It gave a link to a YouTube video that demonstrated the dilation process, and described a specialized stool called a "bicycle seat" so you could do it hands-free, in case you wanted to do schoolwork or email while you were growing your own vagina.

The whole thing made me feel queasy. I shuffled the pamphlet to the bottom of the pile when I heard my dad's footsteps on the stairs.

"Morning, Dad," I said, reaching above the fridge for the cereal and putting it on the table. I sat down in front of my laptop, opened up my mailbox, and saw:

Subject: Fwd: New Diagnosis

My heart stopped. I clicked on the email.

Hi Kristin,
I am so glad that you emailed me! I would love to speak with you and answer any questions you might have about your diagnosis. When is the best time to talk?
Yours,
Maggie Blankman

"Dad! I got an email from someone in the Support Group!"
"How about that?" he said, brightening.
I wrote Maggie a quick email telling her it'd be fine to call

anytime after seven at night.

All of a sudden, I didn't need any coffee. I wolfed down my Raisin Bran and did some thigh stretches while leaning against the kitchen counter. "Dad, is it okay if Sam and I go out tomorrow night?" I knew it'd be fine, but I always liked to tell my dad my plans ahead of time.

"I'll see if any of the guys want to come by and watch the Rangers game. You go have fun."

"Love you." I pecked him on the cheek and sprinted up the stairs to take my shower.

"We're on for tomorrow," I told Sam at lunch.

"Sweet! It's gonna be awesome. It's Richardson's turn to be DD, and she's gonna bring her parents' van." Sam leaned down to whisper into my ear, and a flutter went down my spine. "I've been thinking about you every night."

The flutter expanded, settling nervously in my belly. I faked a smile. "Me, too, baby."

It wasn't a lie. I had been thinking of him, too. One of the Frequently Asked Questions on the AIS-DSD Support Group website was:

Can I be sexually active?
Yes, and we're here to help give you support on how to be healthy, active, and fulfilled in and out of your bedroom. . . .

They didn't go into specifics. Maybe the people in the Support Group knew that I was *this close* to running away from the whole thing, screaming, "TMI!"

There was way too much information, but I could understand how my dad could get addicted to all the research, because the alternative was to be adrift.

Alone.

"Earth to Krissy?" Sam said impatiently.

"What?" I'd zoned out.

"So Vee's gonna start the circuit around seven, so maybe seven fifteen at your house? Don't forget the hot tub."

The flutter curdled into a ball of dread. I hadn't.

As I waited for AP English to start, I swiveled back in my chair to ask Jessica Riley if she'd been to Andy's post-Homecoming party.

She shrugged and twirled one of her curls around her finger. "Quincy and I stopped in for a little while, but we ended up meeting my sister and Darren at Carmella's. I promised my mom I wouldn't take her to a party with alcohol."

"That's nice of you." I pressed on to the real question I wanted to ask. "How big was the hot tub? Could a lot of people fit?" Maybe if I waited long enough, there wouldn't be room for Sam and me. Then I wouldn't have to worry about the bikini after all.

Jessica laughed. "I'm pretty sure it's only supposed to hold eight people, but there were at least a dozen in it when we were there. It was a total group grope."

Not what I wanted to hear. Before I could respond, Darren leaned in from across the aisle. "Did I hear my name taken in vain?"

"Yeah, I was telling Kristin that my sister thought you danced like a Muppet on crystal meth."

Before I could tell Darren that she had said no such thing, he flashed a smile. "Sweet! Exactly what I was going for."

On the way home that afternoon, as Vee and Faith debated whether to wear jeans or miniskirts to the party, or just wear a dress over their bikinis, I wondered how they would react if I told them. After all, there was almost nothing we didn't know about one another. I knew that Vee couldn't stand it when people laughed at her and wasn't above white lies to protect her reputation. I knew that Faith was so afraid of hurting other people's feelings that she never made decisions except by committee. And the two of them? They knew that I was horrible at keeping secrets, and that I had the fashion sense of a blind nun.

That summer's Spartan Car Wash had, in fact, been the first time I'd ever worn a bikini. My mom would have sooner slit her wrists than parade her prepubescent daughter around wearing a two-piece, and after she died it wasn't like my dad and I spent quality time bonding over what kind of swimwear I'd have each summer. The suit that I brought to the car wash at Hanna's Quick Stop had been a freshman-year summer-vacation gift from Aunt Carla, who had used some Kohl's Cash to buy it when she realized I'd outgrown my previous suit. It was a black two-piece, but not the sexy kind. The tankini top covered my entire midriff, and the bottom was cut like boy shorts.

Vee wrinkled her nose when I pulled out my suit in the back office that was our impromptu changing room. "Seriously? Boy-cut is so, like, five years ago. Why don't you try one of mine?" She had brought four bikinis. I'd chosen the purple one because it had a little more *substance* than the others. At least the top part was padded. The one that Vee wore looked about as thick as a sheet of two-ply toilet paper, and wouldn't have worked for me because I had a little more going up top than she did.

Until I stood at the side of Route 30 during rush hour, I hadn't actually thought about how wearing a bikini is basically like being in public in your bra and panties. But we got a lot of donations. We also inspired an op-ed piece in the *Observer-Dispatch* decrying "the objectification of impressionable young women under the pretense of school spirit."

"Hey," Sam said when he read the piece. "There were some hot cougars out there objectifying *me*. Why didn't they write about the poor, impressionable young men?"

"Whatever," said Vee. "If you've got it, flaunt it." She let me keep the purple bikini.

Stressed out as I was about Friday's party, it took me a while to dig through the summer clothes stored under my bed. Eventually I found both Vee's suit and the one from Aunt Carla. I shut my door and put on the bikini. I stood in front of my full-length mirror and stared at my groin. With the right lighting, you could see two little shadows that didn't quite belong there—my hernias. I coughed just like Dr. Johnson had told me to, and something just above my bikini line jumped under my skin, like that moment in horror movies right before the alien pops out of the person's stomach.

I tore off the bikini, disgusted with myself. It was just a matter of time before I disgusted Sam, too. Instead of trying on Aunt Carla's suit, I pulled on a pair of sweats and a thermal top. Then I curled up in my bed, and thought up some excuses for not going to Andy Sullivan's party.

Somewhere in between "I've got the stomach flu" and "My dad grounded me because I flunked a math test," my phone went off. I panicked, thinking that Sam was the last person I wanted to talk to, but it was an unfamiliar number.

"Hello?" I said.

"Hi, is this Kristin?" a woman's voice asked. It was a good voice.

"Yes. May I ask who's calling?" I answered automatically. My mom had drilled that one into me when I was five.

"This is Maggie Blankman. From the AIS-DSD Support Group?"

Holy crap, I'd forgotten. "Oh, wow. Thanks for calling."

"Of course; my pleasure."

There was a moment of silence as I panicked. Was I supposed to have prepared questions?

"Nice to meet you," Maggie said after what was probably only a few seconds, though it felt like hours. "You said in your email that you just found out last week?"

"Yeah. My ob-gyn figured it out when I went in for my first appointment. How about you?"

"My family found out about my AIS when I was six. Of course I was really young, so they didn't tell me all the details of AIS right away. My mom's a doctor, so she spent a lot of time when I was little slipping in stuff about different types of anatomy, and how adoption wasn't unusual. She finally told me the truth when I was sixteen. I was lucky I was able to find out about it gradually. It's rough having to find out everything at once like you did."

"Yeah." I felt a pang of jealousy. She'd known for so long. There was another silence. Over the line, I could hear the strains of a Sarah McLachlan song.

"How's it going?" Maggie asked. "Do you have any questions?"

Did I have any questions? My mind roiled with them, but it was like shooting a moving target—I couldn't pin one down.

"So . . . what am I?" I asked finally.

She knew what I meant right away. "You're a girl. You can do everything every other girl can do except get your period and give birth."

I wasn't sure about that. Everything? I had to screw up every ounce of my courage to ask the next question. "What about sex? I tried a couple of weeks ago with my boyfriend, and it was a disaster."

Maggie made a sympathetic sound. "I'm really sorry about that. When you know about it beforehand, you can do things to get yourself ready."

I grimaced a little at her euphemism. "I know. My doctor, she . . ." I struggled to say it out loud. Over the phone. To someone I'd never met, even if she was in medical school. "I've read all about . . . dilation. But it seems so creepy."

"I can totally understand, but you get used to it. Supposedly, it's not that different from using a tampon. "

I stifled a giggle. My mother would roll over in her grave.

"Remember," Maggie said, "you might not even need to do it for long. Some of us don't have to do it at all."

My cheeks flushed, and I felt a wave of warmth throughout my body, but not because of the subject matter. Because she had used the word *us*.

It was one of those times when you don't realize how lonely you are until, suddenly, there's someone by your side. My eyes prickled, and I started sobbing, my breath coming out in shuddering gasps.

Maggie misunderstood my tears. "Kristin. I know it seems strange, but a lot of perfectly normal XX women have to dilate, too, for a ton of reasons. . . ."

"No, no," I said, laughing. "I'm not sad-crying. I'm happy-crying. It feels so amazing not to be alone."

"I know what you mean." She took in a deep breath. "This really is a sisterhood, you know? You should always feel free to call me, but there's a senior at the U, Gretchen Lawrence. She only lives an hour away from you. I'll email you her information."

After we hung up, I blew my nose and rifled through the stack of papers that my dad had brought up to my room. I drummed the little white cardboard box with the dilators, and read Dr. Cheng's handout one more time.

I booted up my computer and typed in the URL for the YouTube link from the pamphlet. A still shot popped up of a middle-aged woman with short blond hair sitting on a couch in what looked to be her living room. You could see her dining table in the background, and a family photo on the end table.

It was all very civilized.

The video was fascinating, in a disturbed kind of way. They had found the woman with the most reassuring voice on the planet to demonstrate their product. She had classy hands, too, that made the dilator look less like a sex toy and more like, well, actual medical equipment.

I watched the video twice, then sat back in my chair. I opened the white cardboard box and took out the individually wrapped dilators, which were just clear plastic rods with rounded tips.

I took the smallest dilator. It went in about two inches before it hurt. The second time, I lay in bed as the pamphlet described and it went in a little farther.

It felt gross. It felt dirty, and I could picture—no, practically feel—my mom rolling over in her grave, but I repeated Maggie's phrase like a mantra: *It's not that different from using a tampon.*

After half an hour, I stopped. But instead of putting my sweats back on, I had the impulse to put on my black two-piece, which Aunt Carla had made a big deal about being a "shaping" suit. I'd never been so grateful for someone's obsession with cellulite. The bottom was made from a heavy spandex that hid my hernia bulges completely.

And I remembered what I told Maggie: No one had had a clue. Not my mom, my dad, or Dr. Arslinsdale. Not even me.

I went to bed with that hope in my mind.

CHAPTER 10

The third time I dilated, I got to three inches, which sounded like a bad locker room joke waiting to happen, but seemed like progress. The sample kit from Dr. Cheng had three sizes, and gave information on a more complete set, which I almost ordered online. But then I imagined my dad coming across the line item for MiddlesexMD.com, and I used what I had. I ached a bit afterward, but it was a good ache, like the burn of a deep stretch. The pain focused me, and kept me from thinking too much, because when I really thought about what I was doing—what I was putting and where—another part of me withered from shame.

Each time I dilated, it got a bit easier. But the morning of the party, I knew it wasn't enough.

When Vee drove up in her mom's minivan just after seven, she looked surprisingly chipper for 1) being the designated driver and 2) driving her mom's minivan instead of her Jetta. But she'd been much less bitchy since her doctor had switched her to a soft cast and told her she didn't need to use crutches anymore.

"All right, girls—are you ready to paaar-TAY?" she crowed as I got into the backseat.

"You *do* know that the whole point of being designated driver is that you don't do any drinking, right?" Faith asked. As SADD secretary, she had been the one who'd organized our car pool. After extensive soul-searching, she had decided junior year that the Bible did not specifically support laws against underage drinking, and that God would forgive her for doing something technically illegal as long as she wasn't hurting anyone else.

"Of course, Miss Prissy Pants," Vee said, giving me her patented love-Faith-so-much-but-OMG-can-she-be-a-buzzkill eye roll. "Can't you see that I'm just high on LIIIIFE?" She put down her window and whooped into the frigid night air, setting some neighborhood dogs barking.

"Sweet Jesus, girl," Faith's boyfriend, Matt, yelled. "Turn the damn heat on. And the stereo."

"Sorry, Mattie," Vee purred, flipping him the bird, "I don't have any Hannah Montana for you to listen to tonight." But she switched on the radio and found something loud and bassy.

When we picked Sam up, he pulled himself next to me and gave me a deep, hard kiss. Involuntarily, my knees pulled together. I felt a phantom throb between my legs and forced myself to breathe in and out. I willed my thighs to relax.

"Everything all right?" Sam asked when he came up for air, and to put his seat belt on.

"Of course," I said. I had to get my act together. "It's just freezing in here."

"Here, take my coat. I've got the perfect thing to warm you right up. . . ."

My hands were ice-cold, but he slipped them underneath his waistband.

"Jesus, Wilmington. At least wait until we get to Sullivan's house?" Bruce, sitting shotgun, peered back through the rear-view mirror at us. "You've got dibs on the master suite. We get it."

I blushed, and used it as an excuse to pull my hands out of Sam's pants. He turned and leaned forward to grab Bruce in a headlock. "What, lordy-boy? You giving up your territory? We can wrestle for it."

When we got to Andy Sullivan's place, everyone else congregated at the keg in a parade of red Solo cups, but I spotted some people doing tequila shots at a back table.

"Hey, Krissy, you want?" asked Craig Martinez, holding out his arm.

I didn't want. I needed. I took a lick of salt with lime in hand and tossed down two shots.

"Thanks," I said, my eyes watering. Craig grinned, and in

the light it looked like a leer.

I went back over to the keg. About halfway through my second cup, I was finally ready to face Sam. He was down in the rec room playing pool with a bunch of his teammates, and I brought him a couple of vodka shots, thinking that if he were drunk off his ass he'd be less likely to realize that something was wrong with me. I watched him for a while with Faith, until Vee came down and told us people were starting to go into the hot tub.

She made a face when I brought out Aunt Carla's suit. "Oh. My. God. Why did you bring that thing?"

"I couldn't find the bikini you gave me," I lied.

"Whatev. Good thing Sam's probably so horny he'd screw a horse."

My laugh sounded tinny even to myself.

Vee and Faith shrieked as they stepped out onto the freezing deck. When they dropped their towels and slid into the hot tub I tried not to stare, tried not to be that creep in the locker room who checked out the other girls.

I chugged the rest of my beer and let out a breath. It hung like a cloud in the frigid air as I let my towel slip to the floor and plunged into the hot tub.

Once I was in the tub I wondered what I had been worried about. It was so steamy that no one could see anything, and anyway I was safe under the water. Safe and warm and starting to get very drunk. Everything that everyone said was hilarious, the funniest thing I'd ever heard. My brain felt Saran-wrapped. I hardly noticed it when Sam came out onto the deck, didn't register anything until there was a splash next to me and hands reached around my waist.

"Have I ever told you how sexy you are when you laugh?" Sam nuzzled into my neck.

"You're just saying that because you're so horny you'd screw a horse." I giggled.

"Doesn't mean you're not sexy, though."

He thought I was sexy even in Aunt Carla's spandex nightmare. My drunken heart melted. "You're the best boyfriend ever," I slurred, dangling my arms around his shoulders. I kissed him, and our wet bodies rubbed against each other and everything was heat and muscle and lust.

"Dudes!" someone shouted. We ignored him, our tongues tasting of lime and beer. The voice got louder and I felt someone's hands on my shoulder, shaking us apart.

"Yo, Wilmington. Lattimer," Andy Sullivan yelled into our ears. "What did I say in my email? No cum in the tub. This is a five-bedroom house."

Sam gave him the middle finger, but stood up anyway and handed me a towel. The other people in the hot tub hooted, and I had a vague sensation that I should be embarrassed, that I should be a little afraid. And then Sam lifted me up over his shoulder, and my teeth were chattering in the freezing air, and all I needed was to be warm again.

Up in the master bedroom Sam stripped off his suit as soon as we shut the door, and grabbed at mine. Before I knew it I was naked, chattering. I groped at the bed in moonlight. We hadn't even bothered to figure out how to turn the lights on.

I slid under the cotton sheets. My hair was still wet, the sheets cool, and goose bumps formed on my arms. When our skin touched it burned so sweetly I closed my eyes. His body enveloped me, devouring me. I didn't notice the cold again. Sam's hands were everywhere.

And then they were *there*.

"Oh, God, baby."

I held my breath, waiting for the pain, but it didn't come. Not at first.

"Hold on a sec," Sam said, and all of a sudden he was gone. I heard him rustling around the gym bag we'd left our clothes in. "I knew I had one somewhere . . . there it is."

When he got back in bed my pulse quickened, and I wasn't sure if it was from lust or fear.

"Be gentle, okay?" I whispered.

He bent down, and I forced myself to take in deep, even breaths.

At first, my crappy attempts at Lamaze did the trick. Or maybe it was the tequila. Sam groaned.

I kept my hips still, afraid to move, and for a minute, things *worked*. I almost laughed out loud with relief.

I was having sex. With a boy. And he was warm and he

thought I was sexy when I laughed and he didn't notice that my body was a lemon.

I started moving my hips, sliding my hands along the light hairs on his back. I could feel his glutes tighten as he moved and when I reached down to touch them they were so delicious that I pulled him against me.

Mistake.

I closed my eyes with the pain but managed to stay quiet. When my fingers clenched, Sam must've thought it was because I was so into things, because he went faster. I gritted my teeth, and turned my head. Just before I couldn't take it anymore, Sam shuddered and collapsed on the bed next to me. I turned my head away to wipe my tears on the pillow and when I turned back Sam's eyes were still closed.

"Oh, baby," he said, still catching his breath. "Oh, baby."

After a few minutes, Sam started snoring. I pulled my legs together and rolled off the bed. The pain made me stagger to my knees. I could feel it in my belly, a burning deep inside, in a place that shouldn't be allowed to hurt. Somehow I managed to pull my clothes out of Sam's duffel bag and drag them on. Why had I decided to wear skinny jeans? I crab-walked to the door so my jeans wouldn't rub against my already raw skin.

Out in the darkened hallway, I shut the door and leaned back with my eyes closed. The party rumbled on, and I could hear at least one of the other bedrooms at the far end of the hallway getting some use. For several minutes, I stood there frozen, wondering if Sam and I had sounded like that.

No. I hadn't been making any cries of pleasure.

I stumbled toward the stairs, wincing with each step. I told myself what Coach Auerbach always told us before each meet: no pain, no gain. I'd done what I'd set out to do. We'd had sex, and Sam hadn't noticed anything. Wasn't that what I wanted?

I only got two steps down the stairs before I started crying.

I turned back into the darkness. There was a bathroom at the top of the stairs, but it was locked. I jiggled the handle so they'd know someone was waiting. I heard someone puking, and wiped away my tears.

"Everything okay in there?" I said.

"Yeah, yeah. It's all peaches and cream," a familiar voice yelled back.

"Vee? It's Krissy." The door opened a crack and Vee waved me in. Faith knelt, praying to the porcelain gods. The room reeked, and I felt queasy myself.

"I told her not to mix a screwdriver with a mudslide." Vee shrugged. "You okay?"

By the way Vee stared at me, I knew my mascara must be a mess.

I covered my mouth with my hand, suddenly overwhelmed by nausea and pain. "Oh my God, I need to sit down."

She cleared the way for me to sit on the edge of the bathtub, but when I sat it drove the crotch of my jeans up, bringing new tears to my eyes. I gasped and fell onto my knees.

"God, Krissy. What *happened*?" Vee looked closer, took in my sex hair and my new hickey. Her lips flattened. "Did Wilmington do this to you? That son of a bitch . . ."

And that's what did me in. After holding it together through all the doctor visits and the awkward conversations with my dad and the fucking advice from Aunt Carla, the thing that tipped me over the edge wasn't the world's most painful vaginal dilation. It was Vee being sympathetic.

I was so sick of being strong, of keeping it all bottled in.

So I let the floodgates open.

"It's not Sam," I said. "It's me. I found out last week that I'm intersex."

Vee's furrowed brow told me she did not compute, so I swallowed and tried again.

"I'm a hermaphrodite."

For a moment Vee's face went completely blank. Then she laughed.

CHAPTER 11

Back in eighth grade, when the typical thing we did on Friday nights was have a sleepover at Faith's house and stay up all night singing "Girls Just Wanna Have Fun" until her parents made us shut up, Vee, Faith, and I spent months perfecting our ability to lie with a straight face. Let me tell you this: there is nothing in the universe that is half as funny as seeing your prim-as-a-parasol, Bible-studying friend Faith go up to the douchiest member of the boys' basketball team and tell him with a straight face that the extra-small condoms he ordered accidentally got delivered to her house, and where would he like her to leave them?

More recently, we'd moved on to an epic game of bluff wars. One of Vee's more successful dupes ended with me dressed in a slutty nurse's outfit in one of the stalls in the boys' locker room.

I got her back, though, when I managed to convince

her—with the help of some "articles" that I'd gotten from the internet—that laxatives were an aphrodisiac. Vee didn't speak to me for a week after that. But I'd proved that, in the right circumstances, I could pull off a lie. Which was maybe why she thought I was trying to pull a fast one when I told her I was a hermaphrodite. Because who in the world would possibly believe that? Certainly not Vee, who'd helped me buy my first bra, who'd seen me naked in the shower after swim class every Friday during sophomore year. She'd set Sam and me up, for God's sake.

So she laughed, and I wanted so badly to smile and say ruefully, "Damn it, I thought I had you for sure." But I couldn't.

"It's not a joke," I said. *I am not a joke*, I thought.

Vee's face scrunched up in confusion. Faith had stopped puking, and rested the side of her head on the rim of the toilet seat. Her eyes were glazed. "That you, Krissy?" she slurred. "I think I'm sick. I don't have the enzyme you need to drink, you know. It's my parents' fault. Everything's my parents' fault."

"Shhh," Vee said, stroking Faith's long, straight hair. "We're both here. Everything's gonna be okay."

Was it? I hoped so badly that it would, so badly I allowed the truth to stumble out.

As if from far away, I heard myself say, "That visit to the ob-gyn? I found out why I've never gotten my period. When my mom was pregnant with me, something went wrong. I'm not . . . I'm not exactly a girl."

Vee's hand, still intertwined in Faith's hair, froze. "Shit. You're serious, aren't you?"

I got up, wincing, but this time I held on to the pain like a touchstone. With fire burning in between my legs, I told Vee about my chromosomes taking a detour. About not having a womb. About having testicles.

At the word *testicles*, Vee let out a nervous giggle.

Being laughed at once was bad. Twice was unbearable. My face flushed, and I could barely breathe from the humiliation. How could I have been so stupid? I lurched up and headed for the door, but before I could run out, Vee reached over and grabbed my arm.

She covered her mouth with her other hand, and I could feel her stiffness, like she was trying to control herself. "I'm sorry, Krissy . . . I . . ." She groped for something to say, and I felt the shame start to dig into my bones.

Vee put a hand up to her head. "Jesus, Krissy. I totally don't know what to say."

The silence in the room pressed in from all sides, suffocating me. I stared at Faith's hand splayed against the Sullivans' impeccable grouting. She always had the best nails.

Finally, Vee said one word. "Shit."

I looked up at her, saw the crease in between her eyebrows. She was in the confusion stage. Had I already missed the revulsion, or was it still to come? "You can't tell anyone," I told her, feeling the panic rise in my throat.

She just shook her head. Then she asked, "Have you told Sam?"

I leaned against the door and closed my eyes, still feeling slightly fuzzy. "I will. I just need some time. There's a lot I don't know. I might have surgery."

Vee grimaced. "What, like he'll deal with it better if he thinks you had a sex change?"

"It's not like that!" I insisted, stung. "I'm a girl. Dr. Cheng said that people with androgen insensitivity syndrome should be considered girls."

I saw the reflection of my words on Vee's face: *should* be. Meanwhile, Faith, always a happy drunk, started singing. She got up and tried to dance, and tripped on the bath mat. Vee caught her. "Okay, I think it's time to make my first drop-off of the evening." She looked over at me. "You wanna go home, too?"

I nodded. I did, more than anything in the world.

The minute Vee turned the engine on, the metal station we'd been listening to pulsed through the car at max level.

"Turn it *off*," Faith moaned from her position curled up in the backseat.

So we drove home to country music dialed down to a murmur. Somehow, even though I couldn't understand the words, I still got their misery.

I sat shotgun, of course, and looked over at Vee every once

in a while, but she kept her eyes glued on the road as if she were taking a driver's test.

At the Wus' house, Vee spritzed some breath freshener into Faith's mouth and we walked her into her house and up to her room. We made sure that she was lying on her side in case she puked while she was in bed. Her parents were already asleep.

From when we walked out of the Wus' until we were almost near my house, Vee didn't say another word. The silence, the not knowing what she thought, felt like a bowling ball in my stomach. Finally, I blurted out, "Aren't you going to say something?"

Vee let out a frustrated puff of breath, and pulled over. "Oh, Krissy. I just . . . What the fuck?"

"Tell me about it. Promise you're not going to treat me like a freak?"

That got her to grin. "Oh, Krissy," she simpered, like she was quoting from a second-rate chick flick, "don't you know I love you just the way you are?" She switched to her normal voice. "Seriously, haven't we been through enough shit in our lives that you trust me not to drop you just because of some . . . hormone thing?"

I blinked at the unexpected tears in my eyes.

"Hey." Vee reached over to grab my shoulder. "We'll get through this, just like we've gotten through the rest of it."

I took a deep breath and nodded, suddenly so, so weary. "I think I've got to just sleep everything off. Night." I fumbled to open the door. "Drive safe?"

"Like I have a choice. I'm more sober than a nun in outer space."

"Wish I could say the same." I stumbled into my house and sat on the couch, planning to pull off my knee-high boots before heading up to my room.

Then I made the mistake of closing my eyes, and before I knew it, I drifted off to sleep.

CHAPTER 12

I dreamed that I was eight, and an evil witch had transformed me into a beast that was part girl, part bear. When I left in the morning to catch the school bus, a mob of angry neighbors and PTA members threw batteries and cans of tomato sauce that exploded on the ground next to me, spattering me with crimson. But I was lucky: it was all just a nightmare within a dream, and when I woke up sweaty and trapped in my sheets my mother was already in my room, brought in by my screams. I hugged her and burrowed my head into her neck. I could smell the Pond's cold cream lingering on her skin as she stroked the back of my flannel pajamas and whispered into my ear.

"Nothing to be afraid of, my love. It was just a dream."

"But the witch turned me into a bear!"

"Even if you were a bear, you would still be my baby. You'd still be my Kristin Louise Lattimer."

Then my mom's voice rose, and sharpened to a needle point that sent shards of pain through my head. "Kristin Louise Lattimer!"

My eyes opened and I felt a hand shaking my shoulder. Aunt Carla's hand, to be exact.

Back to the real nightmare.

I opened my left eye. My right eye was mashed into one of the velour throw pillows on our living room couch. A pillow that happened to reek of chlorine and vomit.

I craned my neck to face Aunt Carla and got blindsided by a headache the size of Texas.

I turned and stifled another groan at the pain that caused. My dad sat on his La-Z-Boy, slapping the TV remote in his hands over and over again. "Krissy, I know it's been a tough time," he said in a voice strung tight between anger and compassion. He paused, and I could tell he was trying hard to give me the benefit of the doubt. "I'm glad that you went out with your friends, but this . . . you know there's no place for this. Not in our house." He waved at the puke stains. "You're grounded for the next week."

"I'm so sorry, Daddy," I moaned. "It won't happen again. I'll go clean up." I reached down to grab my purse and jacket.

"That's not all. Cell phone," my dad said flatly, holding his palm out. "You'll get it back on Monday morning."

Seriously? "Dad, I know that what I did was wrong. You don't have to treat me like a baby."

My dad shook his head. Looking at him, I was struck for the first time by how heavy his eyelids were, how sad, like a stray dachshund. "You know the deal, Krissy. Actions have consequences. Especially actions that involve alcohol."

My guilt swallowed up my indignation. I handed over my cell phone. My dad handed me a Tylenol.

Dragging myself to my bathroom, I did the best I could to shower off the smell of hot tub and booze and sex. When I came out and tried to check my email, though, I couldn't connect to the wireless.

"Dad, the internet's down!"

"No, it isn't. I turned it off. You're grounded, remember?"

"Dad!"

"Consequences, Krissy. I'm taking your car keys, too."

"What about running?"

My dad thought for a second. "You can take a half-hour run today and tomorrow."

That would be just enough time to run to Vee's or Faith's house. But not to Sam's. It'd have to do. Not until later on in the day, though, when I'd stopped feeling queasy if I moved too quickly, or if I thought about what I'd told Vee.

Just like my mom would've wanted me to, I sat in my room and thought about what I'd done, and the thinking was ten times worse than losing my cell phone, a hundred times worse than not being able to check Facebook. Because when the Tylenol kicked in and the throbbing in my head faded, a simmering fear replaced it. Not a boiling-over fear, not quite yet, because the back-and-forth in my hungover brain sounded something like this:

OMG, she's going to spill everything.

No, she isn't. Remember how she kept the secret about Faith's crush on Danny Evans for a year and a half?

She told Bruce that Jill Sorrento was cheating on his brother.

That's different. It was, like, the ethical thing to do.

What if she lets it slip?

No one would believe her anyway.

When Aunt Carla called me down to prep for dinner, I was grateful for her chatter. I fixed the green beans, taking care to snap the ends perfectly so the fibrous seam peeled off like a piece of green dental floss. Then I mixed the ingredients for a loaf of whole wheat bread, wiping the layer of dust that had accumulated on our bread maker. After starting the mixing cycle, I washed my hands and cleaned up the counter as best I could.

"You good now, Aunt Carla?" I asked. "I'd love to go for my run before dinner."

She sniffed. "You and your runs. Would it kill you to skip one?"

I had an answer to that. It was Coach Auerbach's favorite (and only) Bible quote. "First Corinthians: 'Do you not know that in a race all the runners run, but only one receives the prize? So run that you may obtain it.'"

The late-afternoon sun cast my shadow far ahead of me, and I chased it to Vee's house, trying to ignore the fear that bubbled up to the surface again. The flood lamps were already on at the Richardsons' house when I got there, and when I walked up to the front porch I felt as if I were in the spotlight. Before I rang the doorbell I made sure to wipe the sweat off my face and redo my ponytail. Vee's father answered the door, his BlackBerry at his ear.

"Hello, Kristin," he said, looking irritated.

"Hi, Mr. Richardson. Is Vee here?"

"Hold on for five seconds," he said into the phone, putting it on mute. Mr. Richardson turned to me. "I'm sorry, but Vanessa went to the Carousel Mall with her mother in an effort to decimate my last paycheck. I'll tell her you stopped by."

"Could you tell her that my cell phone isn't working? She can come to my house."

"Of course," he said, pressing the Unmute button. The door wasn't even closed before he resumed his conversation.

I sprinted home, trying to console myself with the fact that Vee's father hadn't reacted to me with more than his usual polite distance, so he couldn't have heard anything. I also figured that if Vee had wanted to spend the day spreading rumors about me, she wouldn't be driving to Syracuse to go shopping with her mom. She'd be holed up in her room going down her speed-dial list, subtweeting and vaguebooking, like she did the Sunday after junior prom.

The next morning, I felt more like myself and went out for an early run so I could catch Faith before church. The fear from the night before had died down, replaced by an anxious curiosity. Of all the people I knew, Faith was the one who could keep a secret the best; her family had kept her brother's mental illness hidden for years.

The Wus lived in the opposite part of town from the Richardsons, in a development where the houses were a little closer together, but not so close that people had to build fences like they did in my neighborhood. The light frost on the Wus' immaculately landscaped lawn was just beginning to melt when I walked up the path to their front door. Angie, Faith's younger sister, answered and yelled up the stairs to announce me.

"I saw some pictures of you in your dress," she said shyly. "You guys all looked so beautiful."

"Well," I said, feeling self-conscious in my faded green tracksuit, "your sister really works magic with that makeup."

"Krissy, that you?" Faith called from the top of the stairs. "I'm getting ready. Come up to my room?"

I took off my shoes and walked up to Faith's room, bracing myself as always for the onslaught of pastels. Except for a set of gorgeous brush paintings she'd gotten on their last family trip to China, Faith's room looked like it'd come out of a special edition Pottery Barn catalog.

Faith shut her door and started putting on some mascara.

"Krissy, I'm so glad you came. I tried to call you all day yesterday."

"My dad took my cell phone. Grounded."

"What a drag!"

"No kidding. I can only stay a few minutes because he's expecting me back soon."

She turned to me, lipstick in hand. "Okay, then. Before you leave, you have to tell me what happened Friday night. Pretty much all I remember is lying on some bathroom floor."

"You don't remember anything?" I hesitated. "Have you talked to Vee yet?"

"She was shopping all day yesterday." She frowned, her forehead creasing. "Why, did I do something totally embarrassing?"

"No." I sat down on her bed, and looked around her room. On the back of the door hung a wooden sign saying I CHOOSE TO BE HEALTHY, HAPPY, AND FULL OF LOVE, a sixteenth-birthday present from her mom. There was a section of her bookshelf dedicated to Chicken Soup for the Soul books. And taped to her vanity was a postcard that she'd picked up at the Mark Twain Museum when her family did a Mississippi River cruise the summer after eighth grade: *ALWAYS DO RIGHT. This will gratify some people, and astonish the rest.*

I made my decision. If I could trust anyone in the world, I could trust Faith. I took a deep breath.

"I need to tell you something," I said. "You know how I've never gotten my period?"

"Yeah." Faith had always been the one telling me how lucky I was that I didn't have to deal with tampons. "It's because of all the training you do, right?"

"Remember when I went to Vee's OB? It . . . it turns out I don't have a uterus."

"Oh, honey." She put her brush down and reached for my hand. "Does that mean you can't have kids? How did this happen?"

I shook my head, tears forming in my eyes, and I was just about to spill the part about my chromosomes and testicles and my stupid syndrome, when her sister poked her head in. "We're leaving in five, Faith. Mom needs to pick up some fruit for the meet and greet. Can you do my hair now?" She waved a bag of hair ties and bobby pins, oblivious to the horror on her sister's face. And the shame on mine.

"I'd better go," I said, blinking as Angie sprawled on Faith's bed.

"Krissy . . ." Faith reached out after me. "Give me a call if you need me, will you?"

I shook my head. "No cell phone."

"Then . . . email?"

"Internet's cut off, too. But maybe my dad will let me use it just once. If I need it."

Back at home, I asked Aunt Carla if Vee had stopped by, but of course she hadn't. She wasn't an early bird. Her dad had probably flaked out and forgotten to tell her I'd dropped in yesterday. If Vee hadn't even rehashed the night with Faith, it almost certainly meant that she wasn't going to talk about it with anyone.

Vee didn't tend to let things percolate—not like me. She either made a big deal out of something, or dismissed it to clear her bandwidth. I imagined Vee thinking of the randomness of my Y chromosome, asking herself, "WTF?" and forgetting about it.

That night, as I got ready for bed, I realized that, all in all, it had been pretty peaceful spending the weekend without my cell and internet. I did wonder whether Sam had called, or if Maggie had emailed again, but I'd know soon enough.

Just one more night, and I'd be back in the game.

CHAPTER 13

My dad didn't give me my cell phone back on Monday until I literally walked out the door. As I reached for it, he gave it a warning shake. "Don't let it happen again," he said, the crack in his voice almost too small to be noticeable. I paused to give him a hug, even though I could see Faith's car waiting at the curb.

I thumbed on my phone as I cut across our lawn, and saw my seven missed calls and ten text messages at the same time I registered there was only one person waiting in the car.

"Where's Vee?" I said, opening the shotgun door for the first time in months.

"She's hitching a ride with Bruce today," Faith said. "She needed to get there early to put up some posters." She wasn't smiling. Faith always smiled, even at 6:50 on a Monday morning. She put the car into gear and started driving, sneaking a peek over at me after a few seconds. "So, uh, I guess you never got in touch with her?"

"No . . . but it looks like she called me," I said. Twice, it seemed. "Why, did you two talk?"

"Yeah," Faith said. I felt a little jolt in my chest, a shot of adrenaline like the feeling I got when the starter would tell runners to get on their marks. Just like at the beginning of a race, though, Faith made me wait for the gun to go off. As I held my breath, she kept her eyes on the road, pacing herself a perfect two car lengths behind the Chevy in front of us.

"So," I said finally, "what'd you two talk about?"

"Well . . . after church I called her because I was so sad about your news. And she filled me in on some of the details you left out."

I couldn't look at her, and stared straight ahead. The Chevy in front of us had a large, rusting dent in its rear fender.

"Krissy," Faith said. "Why didn't you tell me?"

"Your sister was there. I couldn't say it in front of her."

"That you're . . . partly a man?"

I flinched like I'd been slapped. "Is that what Vee told you?"

"No. Yes. I mean, that was kind of the take-home message."

"Oh my God." Stumbling, I tried to explain to her about how it was all just a chemical misunderstanding. "Dr. Cheng said that I was basically still a girl."

"Okay. I'm sure . . . I mean, I hope people believe you."

My heart stopped.

"What do you mean?"

"I mean, now that people know . . . you know how rumors spread, Krissy. We'll have to do some damage control."

This time my heart didn't stop. It *exploded*. "People? Plural? What people know?"

As if in answer, my phone pinged. I looked down and saw an unfamiliar number, and out of habit I clicked it open. There was no message, just a picture. An old-style movie poster with my face Photoshopped onto the body of a pudgy figure with eighties clothes, and the words:

It's Kris—the Hermaphrodite!

It was as if someone had grabbed me by my throat and twisted.

No. No no no no.

My lungs didn't seem to work. I felt like I was underwater, could barely hear Faith ask me over and over again if I was all right. If I had been able to breathe, her question would've made me laugh, because I was pretty sure that things would never, ever, be all right again.

When I showed Faith the tiny photo on my phone, she shook her head. "Why are people so small?"

That wasn't the right question. "Who told everyone?" My

words came out in a gasp. I didn't have enough air to scream. "Does Sam know?" I whispered.

She looked away, biting the inside of her lip. Even she couldn't sugarcoat this. I crushed my book bag into my chest as if I could squeeze out all the pain.

Faith reached over to hug me, her face a mess of emotions. "Krissy, you will get through this. Sam's crazy about you. You just have to explain the situation, like you did to me."

The last few minutes of the ride to school were a blur. After Faith got out of the car, I sat there for a few beats, reminding my lungs how they were supposed to work. Trying to tamp down the feeling that catastrophe was just around the corner.

"I don't know if I can do this," I told her.

Faith looked anxious but determined. "Come on. We'll do it together." She came around to open my door. I kept my gaze on the ground as I walked up to the front entrance, but out of the corner of my eye I could see flickers of movement as heads turned.

The kids on the stairs moved aside to let us through. Just inside, a guy bumped into me with his shoulder, almost knocking my bag off.

"Watch it, Kristopher!" he said, and laughed like he'd just said the funniest thing in the world.

When Faith stopped at her locker, she turned hesitantly toward me.

"Krissy," she said as I walked past my own locker. "Krissy, just wait for me. We can go to homeroom together." But I kept walking, past the library and to the other side of school. Toward Sam's locker. I had to get to him, tell him my side of the story.

He'd just opened his locker when I reached him. When I called his name and touched his arm he jerked away so hard he dropped his books. It was worse than a slap.

"Get away from me," he said, without even looking up.

"Sam," I whispered, even though it hurt so hard to say his name that I wanted to scream. "Can we please talk?"

"I've got nothing to say to you, you homo," he said loudly, his eyes darting back and forth to people behind me. Bruce and a couple of football players came over and I sensed them closing in. Fear dried my throat.

"Yo, Kristopher," one of the guys said. "You here to give Sam-I-am another rimjob? He's got the lube ready for you."

Sam slammed his locker shut and I jumped.

"Can it, Luke," Sam said. Then he turned to me, pointing his index finger at my mouth. "You stay away from me, you hear?"

"Oh no, are you breaking up with your boyfriend, Sammy? Maybe I can make it up to you tonight." Bruce gave Sam the goose and Sam elbowed him in the neck. "Oooh, come on, baby. . . ."

His friends walked toward the gym, and as Sam turned to follow, I grabbed at his arm again. This time, when he pulled away, a thread of his sweater caught in my fingernail. He rounded on me. I could feel the muscles in his arm spasm.

"Sam, please . . . ," I begged. "Let me explain."

"What the fuck is there to explain?" Sam said. His eyes were bright, like there were tears hovering in his eyes. He leaned in, and I allowed myself to hope that he was going to listen. But instead he just whispered, "I thought I loved you, you fucking man-whore. And you've been lying to me. I have nothing to say to you. Ever. Again."

He turned and left before I could explain that I hadn't known for that long, that I hadn't been lying. But what would have been the point? Because how could I ever convince him that I was telling the truth?

I collapsed against the lockers, and slid down into a crumple. Above me, people turned to stare as they hurried to class. I couldn't see their faces through my tears, but I could feel the pounding and shuffling of their feet as they walked past.

The bell rang. The ground went silent. And I began to process how deeply I had been betrayed.

CHAPTER 14

I spent first period in the girls' bathroom, using a paper towel soaked in cold water to bring down the puffiness in my eyes. Then, after the bathroom cleared a few minutes before the bell rang, I dragged myself to the north-wing stairs and waited.

In less than a minute, I heard a pair of uneven steps echoing through the empty hallway. Even after she'd transitioned to a soft cast, Vee's teachers still let her out of class early so she could get a head start on the crowds. I'd been her bag carrier long enough that I knew her schedule by heart.

She froze when she saw me, and stared at me as if I were a stranger, not the person who physically carried her part of the way to the school nurse the day she broke her leg.

My hands clenched as I turned toward her. "How could you do this to me, Vee?"

"Do what?" she asked, seeming surprised, but that was

Vee. Always an incredible actress.

"You told," I said, my voice still stuffy with tears. "Everybody knows. Sam, too. How could you? I had the right to tell him myself. I would've been able to make him see that I'm the same person. I'm still Kristin. Not a freak."

"Wait a second, wait a second." She put her hands out as if she were stopping traffic. "Calm down. I told Faith, but you'd already told her part of it. I did *not* tell Sam."

"Then how does he know? Who else did you tell?"

"Only Faith, I swear!"

Something about the tension in her shoulders and the set of her jaw told me she was lying. "No one at all?" I pressed. "Really?"

Vee squirmed. She actually squirmed, and it should have been a victory, but instead it was a disaster. "Okay, fine. I told my mom—"

"Oh. My. God. You told your mother?" I wanted to throw up.

"I mean, what was I supposed to do?" she said defensively. "I had to tell someone. It's all so fucked up. I mean, I was so traumatized—"

"*You* were traumatized?"

"Whatever, I was in shock. So I told my mom. And she said that someone should tell Sam. But I didn't, I swear!"

"You expect me to believe that?" Never, not in a million years. It was exactly what she would do to someone who'd stolen the thing she'd dreamed about for three years. "It's because you were jealous that they voted me Homecoming Queen, wasn't it? You bitch!"

"You have some nerve, calling *me* names, after what they've been calling you," she said hotly.

"Oh sure, turn it back on me," I said. My jaw hurt from gritting my teeth. "It's always my fault, isn't it? I'm the one who always has to apologize? Well, I'm sick of it, Vee. The world does not revolve around you. When you say things, people get hurt."

"I *told* you that I didn't tell him."

"You told your *mother*. Isn't she in Junior League with Sam's mom? How else could he have found out?"

"Beats me. Do you really think my mom would go out of her way to tell him? She thinks you're a fucking saint. Which clearly you aren't."

"Maybe she only thinks I'm a saint compared to *you*."

Vee rolled her eyes, and in that one gesture—so careless, so familiar—I saw the fault line in our friendship, saw the crack develop. Then Vee asked, "Why are you getting so bent out of shape, anyway?" and made it into a chasm.

I stared at her, this horrible, clueless person I considered to be my best friend in the whole world, and my simmering hurt boiled over into anger. I screwed my face into a smile and did the one thing I knew could hurt her:

I laughed.

"They're right," I said, in my best imitation of her ruthless-ness. "You really are evil. No wonder no one voted for you."

Vee flushed. The side of her mouth quivered. As her eyes hardened, I stepped back involuntarily.

"And look what they got," Vee said, her voice pure venom. "The Homecoming Hermaphrodite. Well, they can have you. I wouldn't be caught dead with such a freak. Excuse me, I have to get to my next class."

She clunked down the hall.

The bell rang.

And after I stopped shaking, I ran.

CHAPTER 15

I ran the three miles home, hearing Vee's voice in my head. *I wouldn't be caught dead with such a freak.* The bitter late-autumn air stung my face and slicked my tears into the wind. Half of the time I could barely see the ground in front of me. Thank God it was a workday and the streets were empty.

When I got home, I went straight to the bathroom and puked, knocking over half the stuff on the counter on the way to the toilet. After I washed myself with Listerine I knelt down to clean up the mess: A couple of hair clips. Some lipstick. The claddagh ring Sam had given me Homecoming night. When I had shown it off to Aunt Carla she'd gotten all excited, saying that in the old days it was practically an engagement ring. The heart was for love, the two hands were for friendship, and the little crown over the heart meant loyalty.

What a load of crap.

I turned the ring around and around between my fingers, and thought about flushing it down the toilet too, but that seemed spiteful and wasteful. So I stuffed it into my travel bag to get it out of my sight. Maybe, just maybe, after Sam calmed down he wouldn't be so mad, and he'd realize what an asshole he'd been and apologize and everything would be okay.

All I wanted was for everything to be okay again.

I went to my room, and lay on my bed. I looked around at my track trophies and the posterboard collages of my friends. Nothing in my room had changed. Yet everything was different. I'd only ever felt that way one time before: the day after Mom died.

I ignored the first three text messages I got. After the fourth one, I turned my ringer off, and stared up at the ceiling, a prisoner in my bed. I couldn't run because of the people outside. I couldn't check my email or my phone for fear of another Photoshop masterpiece. So this was how shut-ins were made.

My thoughts didn't so much swirl as swarm as I rehashed the conversations with Vee and Sam over and over again in a masochistic loop.

Later, when I heard my dad's car door slam, I knew I should get up to go down and greet him, but my legs felt like they were made of Play-Doh.

Instead, he came to me. "Krissy, you in there?" he asked after knocking on my door.

"Yeah, just getting back from a run." Not *exactly* a lie.

"I'll put something on, maybe the lasagna in the freezer?" I listened to his heavy tread down the stairs, then my thoughts swarmed again. I relived the pain, the humiliation and the fear, and then one thing that Sam had said made me sit up straight in bed, my hand to my chest as if I'd just been stabbed.

I thought I loved you. . . .

Past tense.

My whole life, I'd only told four people that I loved them. One of them was dead. Now another one of them hated me. I went a little crazy. That's the only way I can explain why I opened up my phone, trying to ignore the other texts, and typed a message to Sam:

> I am a girl. Please talk to me so I can tell you the truth. You know I love you, and would never, ever try to hurt you.

Maybe I was a glutton for punishment. But this I believed: it shouldn't be possible to stop loving someone so quickly.

As my dad and I ate, I kept my phone on my lap. It didn't ring, but our doorbell did just as I rose to clear my plate.

It was Faith, with an anxious-smiley mash-up on her face.

"Hey. You haven't been answering my texts. I was just coming by to see if you were okay."

My dad hovered in the foyer. "Is something wrong, Krissy?"

Faith looked back and forth between me and my father, her smile faltering.

"Oh, I'm just here to see if Krissy's okay with all her Homecoming Queen duties. You know how it is—photo shoots and speaking responsibilities and everything."

"Huh. You girls have a good chat."

My dad wandered back into the kitchen, and I waited until I heard the clank of dishes in the washer until whispering to Faith, "You didn't have to come."

"I waited for you for half an hour after school! How could I not worry? What was I supposed to think?"

I shrugged, and picked at my cuticle. "I don't know . . . that I'd gone underground. Isn't that what you're supposed to do during a natural disaster?"

Faith put her hand on my arm. "We'll get through this, Krissy."

I pulled away at the pity in her eyes. How could she understand? Everyone loved Faith the instant they met her. In fifth grade, she and I had sold cookies together outside the local Walmart, and that'd been the first time that my dad hadn't had to buy a dozen boxes so I could meet my quota.

Even she couldn't sell hermaphrodites, though.

"Should I pick you up tomorrow morning?" she asked.

I shook my head, thinking how nice it would be not to

have to hear the whispers, not to have to worry every second about whether Vee or Sam would be around the corner. Then I remembered the suffocating vortex of my bed. I worried that if I stayed home I wouldn't be able to keep the whole blowup away from my dad. And I heard my mom's voice in my head. *A lady always holds up her head and smiles, even in the most trying circumstances.*

"I'll be ready," I promised Faith.

Glutton for punishment.

I went back into the kitchen to the sight of my dad crouched over his laptop with his hand to his temple, muttering something under his breath.

"Do you need some Excedrin?" I asked.

"No, no." He shook his head. "I'm fine. It's just . . . Did you know that AIS may be what that runner Caster Semenya has?"

"Who?"

"Don't you remember? That teenage girl who came out of nowhere and broke all those records in the eight hundred meters a few years ago? They accused her of being a man. Ended up suspending her. She was from South Africa or something."

"So?"

"If State ends up taking away your funding . . ."

"No." My voice came out strangled. *Please don't let them take this away from me, too.*

My dad rubbed his hand up and down his face like he was wiping off sweat. He took a deep breath, and schooled his face to look calm. "It's okay. . . . I can always take out some loans if they take it away."

"What . . . my scholarship? Can they do that?"

"Honey, I'm sure it'll be fine. I'll make some calls tomorrow." He fiddled with a napkin, and I stared at the liver spots on the back of his hand. His comb-over had gotten thinner and thinner. When had my dad gotten so old?

I went up to my room, but couldn't fall asleep. Instead, I lay in bed for an hour listening to the sound of the wind battering the trees against my bedroom window. Longing for the past. Dreading the future. And drifting in the present like a ship lost at sea.

CHAPTER 16

Faith picked me up early the next day so we could get in and out of our lockers before the morning stampede. For the first time since freshman year, I got to homeroom before the warning bell had even rung.

Ms. Thomason looked up when I walked in, and waved me over to her desk.

"Kristin, how are you doing?" she asked gently. I recognized that eggshell voice. "Ms. Diaz left me a message for you. She wants you to stop by the guidance office whenever's convenient for you—here's a hall pass. You could even go now, you know. I don't have any important announcements."

I shook my head. "No, that's okay. I don't want to miss first period." More like, there was no way in hell I was walking anywhere during school rush hour.

As the other kids filtered in, none of them laughed or

pointed or anything, so I guess that was an improvement. I almost wished that I had a test so I could pretend to cram. Instead I listened to Faith go on and on about the winter-formal bake sale.

"You know how hard it is to get people to bake," Faith chirped. "Will you make Rice Krispie Treats? If you can, make sure to use some Fruity Pebbles on the top," she said as we heard a ruckus out in the hallway. A bunch of kids went over to the door to peek out, and I raised my head to see what the commotion was about, but Faith ignored them. "It adds color and makes them so much more—"

"What's he writing?" one of the other kids asked.

"Whose locker is that?"

"It's probably some stupid football hazing ritual."

That didn't make sense; I thought it was too far into the season for that stuff. I felt a flicker of dread. And I heard my name.

"Where're you going?" Faith asked as I stood up. "Just wait here, Krissy. I'm sure it's something stupid."

I had to push through people who were coming into the classroom, giggling. As I walked down the hallway toward the noise, I felt someone grab my arm. It was Darren Kowalski. He wasn't laughing.

"Hey, Kristin," he said a little too loudly. "I wanted to talk to you about that *Merchant of Venice* homework. Were you thinking of doing an extra-credit scene at all?" He tried to steer me in the other direction, toward my homeroom.

"No, Darren," I said calmly, despite my racing heart.

I pulled my arm away, and went down the hall to my locker to find out what Darren was trying to prevent me from seeing. When I got there I just stared at it, as if it was some other person's locker and not mine. It was so ugly. They'd chosen an awful dark green color, and half of the paint was dripping down because they'd done such a crappy job. Vinnie McNab, the guy who had the locker next to mine, was going to be pissed because they'd gotten some of the spray paint on his door, too.

STaY aWaY, TRaNNY FaGGOT

The first thing that popped into my head was that I wished they'd chosen a more girly color. *I'm a girl I'm a girl I'm a girl.*

The bell rang, and people started rushing to class. Staring at my locker, some people laughed. Other people looked disgusted. Either way, it was like I had this bubble around me that no one was willing to enter. Hell, I didn't want to be in it, either. I looked down to see if the people from my homeroom were still looking out at me, and they were. Faith hung half out of the doorway. She was waving me to come back in, and I almost went, but then I saw Vee standing one classroom down, her face stony. I wrenched my head away, back to the words on my locker. Was it me or did the *S* look like Sam's handwriting? The thought turned my heart into a block of ice.

Stay away.

"What's going on here?" Ms. Thomason peeked her head out at the commotion. I watched her face as she looked at my locker, her mouth twisting, and knew that there was no way I could go back to homeroom. But where could I run? Where could I possibly go to hide from what I was?

As I stumbled toward the back entrance, I passed the gym. I saw the USD seal on the floor and looked up at the SPARTAN PRIDE sign my teammates and I always hit on our way out to the track. Instinct took over.

I walked to the back of the gym, where the varsity teams had a weight room. It had that comforting Febrezed-over smell that I associated with track. I went to one of the leg machines and lifted until it hurt. Coach Auerbach liked to say that pain was our friend, and I'd always bought it. Physical pain meant that you were bending your body to the will of your mind, that you were stronger than muscle or bone or cartilage.

I kept going until I could tell myself that the tears in my eyes were from pain, not from shame and panic and dread of the future.

The door to the weight room opened.

"Krissy, that you?" Coach Auerbach walked in. It was strange seeing her in jeans. She must've just gotten to school. "You're getting an early start on training."

I pretended to wipe sweat off my face. "Gotta defend my indoor title."

Coach Auerbach's face fell. She sighed, and put her hand on my arm. "Krissy, why don't you come into my office for a minute? We need to talk."

"At least two of the other teams in our division have already filed complaints with the athletic board, accusing me of cheating and demanding an investigation," she told me. "I know that probably nothing will come out of it, but I'm sorry to say that we can't allow you to run until we get things straightened out.

"I know it sucks, Krissy. But I'm sure it'll blow over real soon."

I tried to hold things together, but I could feel pieces of myself crumbling, turning to dust. Vee and Sam. Now the team, and probably my scholarship, too. What would be left?

"It's not fair. I'm a girl." My voice came out in a whisper.

"Sounds like it's more complicated than that," she said sadly.

"You know that running is the only thing that . . ." I couldn't go any further.

"Krissy, no one is more heartbroken than I am about this." I believed her. Coach Auerbach had been my wingman on half a dozen interviews with recruiters, ridden at the front of the bus on who-knows-how-many road trips. She leaned over to touch my hand. At her kindness, tears started streaming down my face.

Coach Auerbach handed me a tissue and rubbed my shoulder. "It's okay, Krissy. It might just be a temporary thing. After all, the IAAF ended up reinstating Caster Semenya after she passed a medical eval."

"How long did it take for them to clear her?" I asked.

Coach Auerbach didn't look me in the eye. "It's not really the same situation, Krissy. She was competing in the world championships, and was shooting for the Olympics."

"How long?" I demanded.

Finally she sighed, and answered. "About a year."

Someone knocked on the door, and a girl's voice said, "Hey, Coach, I was wondering—"

I looked up, and through my tears I saw Rashonda Glenn, one of the juniors, who would probably be captain next year. She still had her hand in knocking position but her mouth gaped open like a fish's. I turned away from the shock in her dark-brown eyes.

"Never mind, Coach. I'll come back later." She always was one of our best sprinters.

Pain was my friend, my ass.

Coach Auerbach let me pull myself together in her office. Got me some hot tea and a cool washcloth. I lay down on her couch while she taught a phys ed class, but eventually all the yelling from the gym started bothering me and I snuck out.

I didn't want to go back to my locker to get my lunch, and I had a twenty that I always kept in my sneakers for when I was jogging, so I picked up the spare coat I left in my gym stall and went to the 7-Eleven.

What if I never ran another race in my life? I couldn't imagine it. Couldn't imagine never again living in that perfect endless moment before the starting gun went off, never feeling the ecstasy of leaning into a finish tape. Of course, I would run. I would always run. But what did hurdlers do when their careers ended? They didn't put hurdles up in their backyards just to remind themselves that they used to fly.

What was funny was that I never wanted to be an athlete. Then suddenly one day in phys ed—during all that Presidential Fitness stuff—I was the fastest. Faster than all the boys, even, except one or two. I joined the track team, and a couple of years later I had a college scholarship, a new posse, and a boyfriend.

Now I didn't even have someone to walk with to the 7-Eleven.

Because I didn't want to have any of the deli workers looking at me funny, I picked out one of the premade sandwiches even though they're always gross and soggy.

In front of me, a little girl and her father waited to pay for some soft pretzels. The little girl sidled up to the candy racks. When she fingered some Kit Kats she lost hold of her stuffed rabbit, and it tumbled to the floor. I picked it up before it got trampled on by customers rushing in from the cold.

"Hey, you dropped something," I said.

"Thanks," said the dad, but the girl just stared at me for a second. As her father paid for their stuff, she kept on turning around to look at me. I wondered if she could tell that I wasn't really a girl.

"Remember, Dee Dee, it's not polite to stare," her father whispered as he shuttled her out the door.

I bet if he knew the truth he'd stare, too.

"Five twenty-seven," the cashier said, glancing at something to the side of his register. He didn't even look at me as he palmed my bills and dished out the change. "Thank you. Next."

The wind picked up when I went outside. I looked up at the sky, muddy and gray. No sun to be seen, even though it must be around noon. Kids were starting to shuffle back to school. Mostly they had their heads down from the cold and didn't notice me, but one redhead with earmuffs recognized me from homeroom. She turned her back to me as she passed and whispered something to her friend, and I felt another wave of humiliation.

I walked up to the edge of the parking lot and watched the cars go by, catching little glimpses of the drivers' faces. They all stared ahead at the road, everyone in such a rush to get to their destination, barely registering things on the outside before they blew on by. I wondered if they were going on errands, or rushing to hot dates. I wondered what they thought of when they saw me. Did they see a girl? A boy? Could they tell something was wrong?

I teetered on the side of the road, unable to see an opening to cross. There were too many cars. I was too tired. Way too tired to run.

I stepped out into oncoming traffic and looked to the left, saw a car approaching. I was vaguely aware that it was far enough away that I should be able to cross if I sprinted, but my limbs felt leaden, as if I were sleepwalking. The other side of the road seemed so very far away. I heard the screeching of tires, a wordless shout, and then something hit me from behind.

CHAPTER 17

A pair of arms enveloped me. I knelt on the side of the road like a supplicant, staring at the wheels of a Ford SUV. I could still feel the sting of its love tap on my right leg.

". . . you okay?" I turned around and stared blankly at Darren Kowalski. He released me right away, but before he did he held his hands against my shoulders for a second as if afraid that I would topple over once he let go. We were close enough that I could see the individual strands of his curly hair flapping in the wind.

I nodded wordlessly. What had I almost done?

The owner of the SUV, a stocky middle-aged woman, slammed her door and came huffing over. She looked both scared and pissed.

"What the hell were you thinking? Didn't you see me coming?"

I stared down at my gloveless hands, pockmarked with gravel. "I must have spaced out or something." I rubbed the gravel off and stood up. "It's so cold. . . . I must have forgotten to look both ways."

The woman eyed me. "As long as you're all right. I suppose you want my insurance information?" she asked hesitantly.

"No, that's okay, I'm fine." I showed her that I could walk around fine. The woman looked relieved, but I felt a hand on my shoulder.

"Are you sure?" Darren whispered into my ear. "Why don't you get the information just in case something comes up. Things never hurt right away."

"No." I shook my head and leaned away from him. "You can go," I told the SUV woman. "Please. I'm sorry to have bothered you."

The woman started to say something, but another gust of wind blew and she hunkered back to her car and drove off. For a while I just toed the pebbles on the ground as the wind whipped my hair.

"You heading back?" Darren asked after I didn't move. His voice was full of unanswered questions that I was grateful he didn't ask. Behind him, a cluster of his friends from the AP/ Honors track were huddled, shooting occasional looks at me.

I shook my head as if waking from a dream, then nodded. It was either that, or run home again. But I was tired of running. "Just give me a minute to catch my breath."

"Hey, guys," Darren shouted to his friends. "You can go without me." They shuffled away. So I walked with Darren. We crossed the highway in silence—I was still in shock—but as we cut through the back alley of a gas station, he spoke.

"Do you ever just wish that you could find the guy who coined the phrase 'Sticks and stones can break my bones, but words will never hurt me' and smash his face in?"

I turned to stare at him.

"You know. Some words are just . . . they trigger actual physical pain. Like the word *faggot*."

I winced.

"See?" Darren said matter-of-factly. "You look like someone just sucker-punched you. Other words don't do that. I mean, the word *gay* is totally okay, even if it does sound kind of dippy sometimes. *Queer* sounds kind of cute, and *lesbian* is almost, like, classy sounding."

When I didn't say anything, Darren went on. "After my dad came out, I totally used to flinch whenever I heard the word *gay*. Even when it wasn't actually used to mean 'homosexual.' Like, I remember watching the movie *Camelot* with my sister when she was in her King Arthur phase. There's this song in it called 'The Lusty Month of May,' and one of the parts is something like 'It's wild! It's gay!' and I remember wanting to curl up and die.

"Once in a while some jerk-off on the bus would call me

a faggot, or say I was gay because my dad was, and my mom would tell me, 'Don't let other people's labels define you,' and make me a strawberry shortcake or something. But I'll be honest, it never helped."

As we neared the school, I asked, "What did?"

"Well, it helped that most people were cool with it. I mean, we're in the twenty-first century, and in a lot of places, you're more likely to be ostracized if you're homophobic than if you're gay."

But not all, I thought.

"The biggest thing that made me get over it, once I stopped hating my dad," Darren continued, "was that I realized what an insult it was to my father to think that my life had ended just because people thought I was gay." Another gust of wind blew, and Darren hunched his shoulders against the cold. "You never knew my dad, but he was a kick-ass father. He was the kind of dad who loved baseball and taught you how to play catch when you were in kindergarten, but didn't pressure you when you said you wanted to quit in fourth grade after batting 0.177 and almost falling asleep in center field during the last game of the season."

"I think I remember him," I said. "He always used to come to our elementary school concerts. A big guy, right?"

"Yeah, he's like six foot four, two hundred twenty. He always blamed my mom's cooking for the last forty pounds."

"Do you see him often?"

"Not as much, since he moved down to the city. Three or four times a year."

"It must have sucked when he left."

"Like, epic levels of suck," Darren said. I grinned despite myself. His smile back was shy, and I had a pang of regret that we had stopped hanging out after our parents broke up.

"I'm sorry," I said.

Darren shrugged. "Time heals all wounds, and all that crap. So, how about you? Are *you* going to be all right?" He turned toward me, and I couldn't figure out if he was asking about my AIS, or almost getting run over by a car.

I chose to assume it was the latter. "I'm okay. It was just a little tap. I can't believe I was so stupid. I must've missed that class in kindergarten when they taught us to look both ways when we crossed the street."

"Yeah, well." He brushed his hair out of his eyes and looked down at me with an expression I couldn't read. "You gotta take care of yourself, okay?"

"Okay."

Darren held my gaze for one more second, and loped off to his class.

As I walked to American History, I decided that I hadn't actually tried to kill myself. At least, not really. Maybe for the teeniest fraction of a second, I'd kind of thought that it would be easier if I could just go to sleep and never wake up, but I wasn't sure if that counted.

What hadn't been done, hadn't been done. And it wouldn't ever be. I could never do that to my dad, and I had to remember that no matter how dark things seemed, now it would get better. It had to.

I must've looked half frozen when I got to American History, because Jessica Riley looked at me funny when I sat down next to her. When I caught her staring at me, she jerked her head down quickly to look at her spiral notebook, and I thought that was the end of that. But a minute later, before class had begun, she turned to me and asked, "Do you, um, know when we're supposed to do the yearbook photos? For Homecoming? And are we supposed to wear our dresses?"

I blinked. I had forgotten that the Homecoming Court had a special spread in the yearbook. It seemed strange that they wouldn't cancel it this year; I mean, would Sam really want to have his picture taken with me?

"I think they do it in the spring, together with prom pictures, but maybe you should ask Faith. She's always on top of those things." I made an effort to make my voice sound normal.

Jessica nodded, and took a closer look at my eyes. "Are you okay? You look like you might be catching a cold or something."

It would actually be nice to be sick and have an excuse to stay home from school.

We were on a unit on women's suffrage, and I couldn't concentrate on my notes. I felt queasy the whole class. It wasn't until the middle of class, when Mr. Morris read an Elizabeth Cady Stanton quote out loud, that I realized what bothered me.

"'It would be ridiculous to talk of male and female atmospheres, male and female springs or rains, male and female sunshine . . . how much more ridiculous is it in relation to mind, to soul, to thought . . . to talk of . . . male and female schools.'"

I couldn't stand the word *female*. It gave me PTSD or something. When I heard the word, a jolt of electricity went down the back of my neck and turned into a ball of stress in my stomach. It was like, when Mr. Morris used the word, he wasn't just saying "female." He was saying "not Kristin Lattimer."

Finally, I couldn't stand it anymore and got up for a bathroom pass. As I walked out, someone stage-whispered, "Is that for the girls' bathroom or the boys'?"

Their laughter rang in my ears as I hurried to the bathroom. I rushed into the first open stall, which ended up being the same one where I had tried to scratch off Vee's name what seemed like years ago. I stared at the door, wondering how long it would take for my name to make it up there.

A toilet flushed in the stall to my right, and as the person went to wash her hands someone else walked in.

"So, what's up with the fishnets, Jenny?" I recognized the voice of Marissa Sweeney, one of the junior cheerleaders.

"I dunno," said Jenny coyly. "Maybe I'm just swimming around ready to bump into some newly available fish in the sea."

Marissa laughed. "OMG, are you talking about Wilmington?"

I felt like throwing up.

"Maybe, maybe not," said Jenny. "My mom always said you gotta get the hot ones when they're on the rebound."

"Wait, doesn't doing it with a tranny make him gay?"

Jenny thought for a minute. "No, I think it means he might be bi. But with a butt like that, who cares?" They laughed, and changed the subject to some other guys they had their eyes on, but at that point a buzzing in my ears overwhelmed me and I curled my knees up against my chin to stop the crushing feeling in my chest.

It took forever for the bathroom to clear out, so I stumbled back to my seat in history just before class ended. I dawdled while packing my book bag, and didn't get up to leave until everyone else had left. I put in my earbuds, the better to drown out the whispers, and slipped out.

As soon as the bell rang in study hall, I flashed my pass and walked the empty corridors to Ms. Diaz's office. I hadn't been there in ages. Because I'd been recruited, I'd gone through the whole college deal early, and Coach Auerbach had guided me through most of the process.

Ms. Diaz greeted me like an old friend. I remembered how we'd bonded my sophomore year because she'd been a discus thrower in college. She was pushing fifty now, and maybe a little thick around the waist, but you could still see the strength in her arms. It made me feel strangely comfortable.

"Kristin, so good to see you again. Sit down, make yourself at home."

Her office had two seats—a fluffy armchair set off to the side of her desk, and a wooden captain's chair directly across from her. I choose the wood, and rubbed my fingers against the smooth grain for a few seconds before looking up at Ms. Diaz.

She leaned in just the slightest bit. "I heard you had a bit of a rough morning."

I nodded, cringing at the understatement.

"Do you want to talk about what happened?"

I shook my head, still fingering the arm of my chair.

"I respect that," Ms. Diaz said, with the tiniest of sighs. "But I wanted to bring you in to remind you that if you ever need a safe place to talk things out, I'm here. Everything you say in this room is completely confidential. The more I know about the situation, the more I can help."

I looked up. My words came out slowly, driven by morbid curiosity more than anything else. "My situation. What *do* you know about it?"

Ms. Diaz took a deep breath. "Well, I gather that there is a medical issue such that there's a question about your gender."

Close enough. I nodded.

"I can understand how things must be very confusing right now," she went on. "And truly upsetting, too, the way your classmates have reacted. Kristin, it breaks my heart to see you the target of such cruelty."

Ms. Diaz's face blurred as the tears welled up in my eyes.

"There are a lot of things we can do to help. Regular counseling sessions, peer education. First of all, though, I want to make sure you have a good support system. Are there any other students you feel comfortable talking with?"

"Yeah," I sniffled. "Faith Wu."

"She's a sweetheart, isn't she?" She handed me a tissue. "How about adults? Are you okay with my calling your father to—"

"No!" I almost leaped out of my chair. Ms. Diaz gave a little start. "Please leave my dad out of this. He has enough to worry about. Please, please don't make him upset."

"Of course not, Kristin," Ms. Diaz said soothingly. "You're eighteen. We don't have to involve your father if you don't want to. But would you mind giving me permission to speak with your doctors so I can get more information on your diagnosis in order to . . . educate our faculty and staff at least?"

I agreed—I'd do anything as long as they didn't call my dad—and wrote down Dr. Cheng's information.

"Just, please . . . no pictures of naked girls with bars over their eyes." I thought of the pictures of "AIS physiology" on Wikipedia.

"Come again?" Ms. Diaz asked.

"Never mind," I said.

When I got home, I called Mohawk Valley Urology Associates. It took three minutes of navigating an automated telephone line, and another twenty minutes waiting for her to call me back, but I finally got hold of Dr. Cheng.

"Hello, Kristin," she said. She sounded harried. "My nurse said you have a problem?"

I almost laughed out loud, almost told her that yes, I had a problem: I had fucking testicles instead of ovaries, and when was she going to do something about it?

But instead, that politeness kicked in again, and I managed to ask a question that no teenage girl should ever have to ask, in a measured tone that would've made my mother proud.

"Yes," I said. "Could I please schedule surgery as soon as possible to remove my testicles?"

CHAPTER 18

I got lucky. Dr. Cheng had a last-minute cancellation and she squeezed me in for Wednesday the following week, but not before bringing me in to her office to tell me and my dad, face-to-face, what I was getting into.

"Once your testicles are removed, you'll have to take daily estrogen to replace your hormones."

A pill every day.

"While most girls do well with medication, sometimes testosterone deprivation after surgery causes hot flashes, depression, and mood swings until we get the dosing right."

Eighteen years old, and going through the Change. At least Aunt Carla and I would have something to talk about. I should have gotten a menopausal woman costume for Halloween, not that I'd be trick-or-treating tomorrow.

"For these reasons, a lot of people in the intersex world are very passionate against gonadectomy."

I'd seen a couple of articles, and couldn't really understand why some people were so militant against surgery. In little babies, maybe I could see delaying an operation until they were older and could make their own decision. But once you understood what you were . . . how could someone not want to be fixed?

I couldn't conceive of a world in which I wasn't broken.

"Finally," Dr. Cheng said, "on top of the potential complications from surgery—namely bleeding, infection, and pain—I'd be remiss if I didn't warm you that estrogen does have side effects. It can cause weight gain. Blood clots. Headaches. Fluid retention. And there's a theoretical increased risk of breast cancer."

At the *C* word, my dad flinched, and I felt my heart race. Dr. Cheng just sighed and brought over a form for me to sign. "I apologize if it seems that I'm laying things on too thick. But it's my job to make sure you're fully informed about the risks and benefits before you give consent for the procedure."

I thought back to that moment when it'd seemed easier to deal with cancer than with being intersex. Now, more than ever, I agreed. I couldn't cut the Y chromosome out of each of my cells, but I could cut out those balls that everyone seemed so fixated on.

I looked at the consent form, which listed two paragraphs

of complications, including brain damage or even death from anesthesia.

Without even glancing at my dad, I signed my name.

The nurse who called the night before surgery reminded me that I couldn't eat or drink anything past midnight the day before my procedure, so by the time they rolled me back into the operating room I wanted to keel over from starvation. One of the techs had me shimmy over onto a metal table covered with bright white towels, and strapped me in. Then someone put a mask over my face that smelled like cherry bubble gum and I went to sleep.

What felt like two seconds later, I woke up feeling like a quivering ball of Jell-O. Someone had thrown a blanket over me but it didn't cover my legs or my arms, and a man was saying, "You're waking up from anesthesia, Kristin. The procedure's all over. Everything went great."

My testicles were out. I had hoped, expected even, to suddenly feel like I was a girl again. But all I felt like was an empty jar.

When I got home, Aunt Carla was already there, ready to play nursemaid. "You just lie down and relax, young lady. I've got a pot of nice chicken soup on the stove and some tea with lemon." I didn't have the heart to tell her that those were cold remedies. Maybe they worked just as well for girls who'd been castrated.

Up in my room, I changed into pajamas and looked at my incisions. I had two of them, one on each side right at my panty line. I probably couldn't wear a thong, but I might be able to get away with a normal bikini.

I ran my fingers across the red, puckered lines. Dr. Cheng had told me that she'd used dissolvable sutures and skin glue, so I could shower as soon as tonight. The skin around where she'd cut felt sore, like a muscle strain, but not truly painful.

After dinner, when I went to say good night to my dad, he was at the kitchen counter hunched over his laptop. I caught a glimpse of someone in a track uniform and peeked over his shoulder.

"I'm researching that runner Caster Semenya," he said. "I can't really find many specifics about the case. I mean, from the medical point of view." He didn't look at me, keeping his eyes on the screen. "But if anything happens with your scholarship, I think we can fight it."

"You mean, in court?" I didn't know if my dad could afford a lawyer.

"We'll see if there's an issue," my dad said, still scrolling through an article. He clicked through to another article and there was a close-up of a runner. I couldn't tell if it was a man or a woman.

"Is that her?" I asked.

My dad nodded. We both stared at a shot of Caster waving

the South African flag after winning a race. She had tight cornrows that emphasized her thick eyebrows and the hair on her upper lip, and her toned arms and six-pack reminded me uncomfortably of Sam's. In her yellow-and-green skintight track uniform, you could see that she was flat as a pancake, and that she definitely did not have what my aunt Carla called childbearing hips.

My dad clicked on the little triangle at the center of the picture, and a video played.

"When she won the eight-hundred-meter dash at the 2009 world championships in a time of 1:55.45, Caster Semenya was just eighteen years old," a woman with a British accent said. "Because she had improved her personal best time by eight seconds in less than a year, officials decided that they were 'obliged to investigate' for performance-enhancing drugs. When they found a level of testosterone that was four times that of a normal woman, this sparked a gender-verification test and a year-long ban from competition. But Caster Semenya and her family insist that she is a girl. The controversy has sparked a firestorm of criticism against the International Association of Athletics Federations' handling of the matter, with some accusing the organization of being sexist, racist, and insensitive to privacy and human rights."

Next they had clips of an interview with Caster's father: "She is my little girl. I raised her and I have never doubted her gender. She is a woman and I can repeat that a million times."

They showed pictures of the South African town she grew up in, and interviewed her high school teacher and her grandmother, who told the camera, "It is God who made her look this way." And then they ran a clip of an interview with Caster.

Her head was bowed, except for when she took a swig of her water, and the guy interviewing her was offscreen so you could only hear his voice. You assumed it was a man, and he asked the usual questions about her time and whether she would set a world record. Then Caster talked, and her voice was deeper than his. My dad gave a start.

As I stood behind him, trying not to have a panic attack, my dad searched "intersex test," and I got to read about how in the seventies, before lab testing was developed, officials would have all the girl athletes parade naked in front of doctors to make sure all their parts were in order. Then he clicked on a link to a David Letterman skit about a "gender verification test" that involved hitting a person in the crotch with a baseball bat. My dad swore and closed the tab right away, but I'd seen enough to make me feel sick.

Together, we found another article about Caster where this women's magazine gave her a makeover. They'd put on hair extensions, stuffed her in a dress, and decorated her with earrings and dangly bracelets. LOOK AT OUR CASTER NOW! In some ways, that was the worst of all. How easily you could make someone look more "feminine." How easily you could turn a freak into a homecoming queen.

One thing Coach Auerbach hadn't mentioned was that, even though Semenya was cleared to race in the Olympics, some people thought that she had thrown the gold medal race because she didn't want to face any more controversy, and didn't want to be accused of having an unfair advantage. And who could blame her?

My dad surfed onto a video of Caster at a press conference a year after the controversy broke. While he watched Caster talk about staying positive as an athlete, all I saw were the YouTube user comments underneath. *God, it sounds like a dude*, said one. *It LOOKS like a dude too*, said another. Then: *OK here's the real test. What guy would want to stick his wiener there?*

And all of a sudden it was too much.

"Turn it off," I said loudly. My dad jumped. "Please turn it off," I pleaded.

He blinked and shut his browser. "Honey, why don't you go see if there's a game on?" my dad asked. "I'll be done in a second. I can make popcorn."

I swallowed. My dad's hand was still on the mouse. I might not have the stomach to read any more, but he did. When my mom was throwing up from chemotherapy, all I could do was hold her hand. But my father researched every kind of anti-nausea treatment and came home with ginger and peppermint oil and DIY acupuncture wrist bracelets. It's what he did to keep the powerlessness from eating him alive.

I shook my head and gave him a kiss on the head. "You

keep reading. I'm going to bed."

I trudged up the stairs to my bedroom, telling myself, *I don't look like Caster. I look like a woman. I am a woman. Dr. Cheng said so.* Just to prove it to myself, I dug into my closet and got the emerald-green Victoria's Secret nightie that Sam had given me for Christmas. I put it on and posed in front of a mirror. I told myself that if I took a picture and posted it on Craigslist personals I would get hundreds of responses.

I would. I knew I would.

But the only response that I wanted was one from Sam. With shaking fingers, I tore off the nightie. Even after I'd curled into bed in my flannel pajamas, though, all I could think about was Sam, and each memory was like a hot poker in my chest: The look of joy on his face when he saw how pleased I was with his gift. The way his lips parted ever so slightly when I modeled it for the first time. The feel of his biceps against my rib cage when he lifted me up for a kiss.

I had been staring at my alarm clock for almost half an hour before it dawned on me that I had lied to Sam and Faith. And to myself. Dr. Cheng hadn't said that I was a woman. She had said that most people with AIS "identified themselves" as women. Which wasn't the same.

Which wouldn't ever be the same.

After another half an hour of lying in bed awake, I turned my light on to go to the bathroom and tripped over my purse. The pain medicine Dr. Cheng had given to me fell out. I hadn't planned on taking it—the pain wasn't that bad—but then I caught sight of the little yellow warning label with a droopy eye. MAY CAUSE DROWSINESS.

A bonus side effect.

Before I could change my mind, two of the Percocet pills were in my mouth. They didn't go down easy, sticking in my gullet like concrete. Even after I went to the bathroom to get some water, it still felt like there was a knot in my heart, but before I knew it I had drifted off to sleep.

CHAPTER 19

I woke up the next morning in a Percocet haze. The whole world was fuzzy, and I couldn't move, as if I'd been cemented into my bed. My muscles had turned into stone, my blood into molten lead. Just turning my head to see my clock took all the energy I had. Reaching the snooze button was impossible.

It didn't matter if I went to school, did it? In the grand scheme of things. No one would be hurt. No one would die. The only people who'd care would probably be Sam and his jerk-off friends, because they wouldn't have their new punching bag. If I stayed at home it'd be one less piece of homework for my teachers to grade, and one less stop for Faith.

It was a win-win situation, really.

I lay there until I had to pee so badly I couldn't hold it anymore, and I rolled out of bed. As I walked to the bathroom my dad was coming upstairs to put his uniform on.

"Why aren't you dressed yet? Faith's going to be here any minute."

"I don't think I can go to school today."

My dad went instantly into alarm mode, which I should've predicted. "Is everything okay?"

"I'm just feeling sick from the pain meds."

"I'll get you some ginger ale on the way home. But we should make an appointment—"

"No," I interrupted him. "No more doctors. Please?"

He looked at me, and turned away quickly. "Okay," he said, taking a deep breath. "But I'll ask your aunt Carla to check in on you in an hour or two."

"Fine."

I went to the bathroom, texted Faith that I wouldn't be going to school, and crawled back into bed.

I woke up to a blinding light.

"Wake up, sleepyhead! It's a beautiful morning!" chirped Aunt Carla.

I tried to pull my pillow over my head, but she pulled it away and threw off my covers, which were damp with sweat. Aunt Carla gasped.

"Krissy, are you okay? Do you have a fever?"

"I don't know. I just feel hot." When I went back to bed that morning, I'd tossed and turned. One minute I'd be burning up, the next minute I'd be freezing.

"I'll get the thermometer. What you really need is some nice fresh orange juice and some hot biscuits." When I lifted my head I could smell something buttery and amazing. My stomach grumbled.

"Okay, okay," I said.

After the juice and biscuits, my stomach felt full but the rest of me still felt empty. Out of place. Aunt Carla took my temperature, which turned out to be normal.

I brushed my teeth. Took a shower. And when I started thinking too much about school and Vee and hernias I went into the kitchen. Maybe I could surprise my dad with dinner. I flipped through our recipe box, and stopped at my mom's baked ziti recipe. It had been my dad's favorite, but we hadn't cooked it in years.

I couldn't understand how staring at a recipe card could make me feel physical pain. My mom always used to say that my dad was proof of the old saying that the way to a man's heart is through his stomach, and I wondered what aphorism she would've used to get me through today. Probably something like, "What doesn't kill you will only make you stronger." I couldn't remember how many times she said that during her first few rounds of chemotherapy. By the end, though, her maxim became, "God doesn't give us more than we can handle in life."

My mother never saw me run, and that was one of the saddest things about leaving the church—giving up the idea that

my mom was up there in some cloudy-fluffy angel land, looking down on me for my first kiss, or the day I won the state
championship. I wished she could've seen me at Homecoming. Or even now. I knew she would've loved me even if she'd
known that I had boy parts.

I decided to make a pie, which had been our favorite thing
to make with each other. I loved cutting the butter into the
flour, and the satisfaction of making a perfect lattice. Flour
everywhere, soft and dusty like baby powder.

It would have killed my mother never to have grandchil-
dren, I thought suddenly. She would've pretended it was okay,
probably, but I knew she would've taken it hard. She probably
would've noticed that I never got my period and taken me to
an ob-gyn sooner. Maybe if she'd been alive, I wouldn't have
had to tell Vee.

And what would my life be like, if no one knew but me?
Would I still be running, or would I feel guilty that I was somehow cheating?

I'd never know.

I folded the crust into the pan and started to work on the
filling.

While the pie baked, I brought out my laptop so I could email
the secretary who was supposed to get homework assignments
for students who were out sick. There were dozens of new
messages in my account. I hadn't checked my email since the

locker incident. Half of it was spam, or the daily digests from the college track mailing list.

I would have ignored them all, just let them clog my inbox, if it weren't for the Facebook notifications:

Pat Hermaphrodite tagged you in a photo.

Bruce Torino commented on a photo you're tagged in.

Andy Sullivan liked a photo you're tagged in.

The kitchen was warm from the oven being on, so I shouldn't have felt so cold. My hand shook as I logged on to Facebook, where I had 846 friends. Where my status was still "In a relationship." Where I was still listed as being female.

It hurt so much to see my profile picture that I almost couldn't breathe.

Vee had taken the picture over the summer, at her annual pool party. Sam and I were cuddling with each other on a lawn chair, and God I looked happy. I remembered the day: the smell of coconut-scented suntan lotion, the brilliance of the pool reflecting the cloudless sky. It was surreal seeing myself like that, like looking at the school photo of a missing child.

Just below that was the picture I had been tagged in.

Whoever it was in real life, Pat Hermaphrodite was a pretty talented Photoshopper. He (or she) also had good access to porn, to find a penis that was just the right proportion and angle to splice onto the picture of me in my bikini at the car wash.

The picture had seventy-three "likes." Sixteen comments. I didn't want to read them, but it was as if I was going by a car wreck and couldn't turn away.

There was one comment from Jessica Riley saying, "So not cool, guys. Not cool," but five others that told her to chill out, that it was just for fun. Every post felt like a dagger thrust into my back, and still I scrolled through the list of people who "liked" them.

They were faces I had known since kindergarten, faces of teammates and rivals. A few people from my homeroom. One guy who'd sent me a singing Valentine during middle school. The girl who stood next to me in the alto section of our junior chorus.

I wanted to throw up. I ran to the bathroom, but when I got there all I did was dry-heave over the sink. When I lifted my head I could taste the acid in the back of my throat.

My brain could barely wrap itself around the hurt. These weren't mean people. I told myself they'd probably just seen a funny picture and clicked "like" out of habit, because that's what you do when you read something on Facebook.

But who was I kidding?

CHAPTER 20

When Faith called later that afternoon, she was totally shocked when I told her about my surgery.

"Oh my God, was it something serious?"

"It was just a hernia," I said, which wasn't exactly a lie.

"Why didn't you tell me?"

I had no excuse, and I knew it. But Faith forgave me, as always.

"You know I'm the chair of the Sunshine Club," she said. "We should at least throw together a care package for you. My mom just got some of those almond cookies you love so much. I'll send around a card tomorrow."

And what would people write in it? "No. Please don't make a big deal. I should only be out a few days." Dr. Cheng had actually said that I might not have to miss any school at all, but no one needed to know that.

"I'm pretty sure they covered 'Making a big deal about having a surgery' in Friendship 101. I'll stop by tomorrow to give you my bio notes," she said. "I can't promise that I won't bring brownies, too."

I really hoped she wouldn't send around that card. Could I tell her not to ask anyone who had liked that picture on Facebook? After we got off the phone, I turned on my computer.

I had untagged myself in the photo, but I couldn't help myself from going back to it like a moth to a flame. Pat's picture was up to 132 "likes."

Once again, seeing the profile picture of me and Sam together took my breath away, the reminder of old happiness cutting like a razor blade. I deleted the picture but couldn't bring myself to find another one, and left the generic drawing of an androgynous blue silhouette in its place.

Fitting.

That's when I noticed that just underneath my empty profile picture, where it said "In a relationship," Sam's name was missing. When I searched for his name in my friends list he was gone, too. I couldn't find him on Facebook at all.

I'd been blocked.

We were officially over.

It shouldn't have come as a surprise to me; it shouldn't have reduced me to a crying, shaking ball of misery. But there you have it: the power of the internet.

I cried at the memory of how warm and safe I'd felt when

he hugged me. I cried because I blamed myself for not telling him as soon as I got my diagnosis. But mostly I cried because I missed everything about him—his grin, his quiet sense of humor, and the steadiness of his footsteps as they kept pace beside me.

I knew I wasn't supposed to run yet. But my whole body itched for it, craved it like a junkie: the feel of muscles pulling, heart thumping, lungs filled to the brim with fresh air and *life*. I couldn't stay in my room any longer, couldn't sit still while the world crumbled around me. I pulled on my workout clothes. At the bottom of the stairs, I peeked into the living room, where Aunt Carla was ensconced on the couch.

"I'm just going out for a second," I told her, standing out of sight so she couldn't see my blotchy face.

"Make sure to be back in time for dinner," she said, barely looking up from her crossword puzzle. "I've got a roast in the oven."

I decided to run my three-mile loop, which took me through the older part of our development, the one with fewer kids in high school. As soon as I felt the pavement under my feet the cloud in my mind lifted, and my legs took over.

My incisions pulled as I ran, but the soreness was a sweet kind of pain, reminding me that I wasn't the same person—the same *thing*—that I had been the day before. The wonderful *tangibility* of it struck me for the first time. I would have scars to prove what I had done.

What I had done for Sam. Surely he would be able to see that?

With a subconscious eagerness, I found myself turning onto my five-mile loop. My eyes had dried; my nose no longer felt like a cherry tomato. In my mind, I ticked off the landmarks at each half mile:

The library.

The old farmhouse with the barn, once red, that had faded to a light pink.

Sam's house.

With a jolt of recognition, I stopped. The world spun.

The light in his room was on, a shining beacon. Was I imagining it, or could I almost make out the shadow of a person? Who knew how long I would've stood on the sidewalk in front of the Wilmingtons' house with a staccato heart and gasping breath, if a car hadn't pulled up into his driveway and brought me to my senses.

I turned to flee back the way I'd come. But then a door slammed, and I heard a woman shouting behind me.

"Kristin! Hey, Kristin!"

I turned around. Sam's mom walked down the driveway to meet me, her wide grin so similar to her son's it made me want to cry. As much I wanted to run, I couldn't.

"Kristin," she said, holding out her arms. "I haven't congratulated you yet for Homecoming! Tell me, have you come back to earth yet?"

As I sank into Mrs. Wilmington's hug, I realized that Sam must have been too embarrassed to tell his mom. It was almost worse than her running me off the property.

I plastered a pleased look onto my face, praying that it would be convincing. "Nope, it's still sinking in."

"Please tell me you'll come in and have something to drink. Sam's been holed up in his room the past couple of days. He and Bruce must've had some sort of spat."

"Oh, I'm only halfway through my run," I said, jogging back a couple of steps.

Mrs. Wilmington clicked her tongue and grabbed my hand. "Don't be ridiculous, Kristin. The season hasn't even started yet, and Madison misses you. She hasn't seen you in weeks." I allowed her to pull me toward their driveway, partly because I didn't want to be rude, but mostly because I couldn't help but dream that being brought in by Mrs. Wilmington would put me under a spell of protection. Sam would have to listen to me if I was with his mother.

Walking into the Wilmingtons' felt like coming home, right down to the spot in the shoe rack for my sneakers.

"Sam! You've got company," his mother yelled. When he didn't respond, she shooed me toward the stairs as she went into the kitchen. "I'll get you some Gatorade. Blue, right? You know where to go."

I hadn't even gotten to the bottom step when the door to the basement rec room flew open and a twelve-year-old whirling dervish flew out.

"Hey, who's here? Krissy, is that you?" Sam's little sister, Madison, threw herself at me with such force that I almost lost my balance.

"You never emailed me the pictures of your dress," she said reproachfully when she let go. "Sam just had one little teeny shot on his phone and the lighting sucked." I had to laugh at how stern she looked, even with her curly brown hair frizzing out in all directions from her run up the stairs. "And why aren't you wearing your ring?"

My grin froze on my face. "I had to get it sized a little. It was a bit too small. But it was beautiful. Sam said you helped him pick it out?"

"I did," she said proudly. "Sam wanted to get you this awful gold thing but I told him that silver and green would be better colors for you. Did he tell you about our Christmas pageant? I got the part of an angel. Promise you'll come to opening night?"

I tried so hard to keep smiling that it hurt. "Congratulations, sweetie! You know I'll do my best to make it."

"Okay. I'm going to look beautiful. Want to see a picture of my costume?" She was tugging me toward the rec room when her mom came in.

"Maddie, I know you're excited to see Kristin, but why don't you let her go up and talk to Sam for a little while?" Mrs. Wilmington handed me a cup of Gatorade.

Madison pouted. "But it's not going to take a *little while*. It always takes *forever!*"

"Then maybe you should think of something to do that'll take a long time," said her mom. "Why don't you give Allison a call?"

"*Okay.*" Madison slumped. "See you soon," she told me.

I nodded wordlessly as she went back downstairs.

My hand only shook a bit as I drank the blue Gatorade. "Thanks so much," I said, handing the cup back to Mrs. Wilmington.

She smiled. "Madison really thinks of you as her playmate first, and Sam's girlfriend second. Why don't you go upstairs? I'm going to start some dinner."

I took the first step cautiously, as if I were scaling a cliff. Though I'd barely broken a sweat in the cool autumn air, someone had cranked the heat up in the house. At the top of the stairs, I stopped to wipe off a thin sheen of sweat from my forehead. I redid my ponytail in a mirror on the landing, thinking about how I always used to make fun of the girls on my track team who ran with makeup in their little armbands instead of iPods.

Silently, I walked to the second room on the right, and listened at Sam's door to the strains of Eminem. As I raised my hand to knock, a track ended, and I could hear the faint sound of a keyboard clattering. I wondered if he was doing homework or IM'ing. Or posting on Facebook.

With a flash, I came to my senses. My hand dropped. What in God's name was I doing? What could I possibly say that would change his mind? I would never be able to take back his humiliation, or restore his ruined reputation.

I deserved nothing. Not his forgiveness, and certainly not his love. And he'd already made his wishes clear: *Stay away.*

I took a step back. Turned around.

But just before I reached the top of the stairwell, his door opened.

CHAPTER 21

"Hey, Mom," he yelled. "Do you know where my—"

Sam caught sight of me and stopped midsentence. His mouth gaped open slightly for a moment, then snapped shut into a thin, pursed line.

We stared at each other.

I noticed Sam's stubble first—about a day and a half's worth, I figured. When we were going out, for him to skip a day of shaving was unusual. He knew I liked him smooth.

Sam broke the silence. "What the *hell* are you doing here?" His voice was oddly subdued, and he pulled nervously at the white V-neck undershirt he wore over his sweatpants. Maybe he only kept his voice down because he didn't want his mom to hear, but it was better than him shouting like he had in the hallway at school.

"I was running. Your mom invited me in." I could've told

him that I was just about to leave, but I didn't. Because as much as I wanted to go before, now I wanted to stay. I took a step toward him.

But there was more to it than that—somehow I sensed something . . . *open* about the wariness of his blue-eyed gaze. A willingness, now that we were away from teammates and A-listers and teachers alike.

"You haven't told her yet?" I asked.

He looked away, picking at the paint on the doorjamb with a fingernail. The muscles in his jaw spasmed, and he seemed to come to a decision. Stepping back, he waved me into his room. Heart pounding, I followed.

The smell of boy made me ache; funny how you can be nostalgic for the scent of deodorant mixed with sweat. Sam's room looked exactly like I remembered, with one exception. Before, there'd been a ring of pictures circled around his desk. Now, the wall was blank. I didn't think it was possible for my heart to sink any further, but it did.

Sam straddled his desk chair, and waved me to the armchair by his stereo without looking at me.

"What was I supposed to tell her? Not just my mom—everyone? My sister? My *dad*?" His voice broke, and I understood. Mr. Wilmington's favorite nickname for Sam was "stud."

"I don't know. . . . That it's a medical condition." A wave of grief and anger overwhelmed me. "God damn it, Sam. It's not like I am what I am out of spite."

"I know, I know," he moaned. He put his hands over his face. His beautiful hands. I couldn't help it—I reached out and brushed his knuckles with my fingertips.

He flinched, and I closed my eyes at the sudden pain in my chest.

I retreated, and told him, "I had surgery. You don't have to worry about . . . my having boy parts anymore." I pulled down my tracksuit to show him my scars, two puckered-up pink lines running just below the level of my underwear.

I tried to explain to him about mixed signals and testosterone deafness, but the more I talked, the more his eyes glazed over. Finally he just raised his hand. Gave a long blink. And looked at me with clear eyes.

"Why didn't you tell me?"

My turn to look away.

"Why do you *think*? Because I was scared."

"You . . . you didn't trust me."

I shook my head. "Should I have?" I stood up and paced around, needing to move, needing to feel brave. "Show me that I should've trusted you. Show me that you don't care about these scars. That all you care about is who I am, not what I am." I stopped in front of Sam's chair and sank to the ground in front of him. I looked up at him, our faces inches apart.

Sam bowed his head so that it rested against the back of

the chair. He stayed there a long time, breathing heavily as the clock ticked. Behind him, his computer pinged two, three times with message alerts.

"Do you remember the first time we met?" I asked him.

"Wasn't it at some track meet or something?"

"Yeah. I was all gross from my race and had this awful jog bra on that made me flat as a pancake. I thought for sure that when Vee got you to come out on a double date you'd remember me as a total train wreck and run in the opposite direction. But you came."

Sam lifted his head. Our gazes met, and I felt it—that magnetism, that connection that we'd always had. Slowly I moved in closer until I could feel his uneven breath on my face. "You saw me for who I was," I whispered. "Can't you see it's the same thing now?"

Just as our lips were about to touch, Sam pulled back and shook his head with a faraway look. He turned to me. His eyes hardened.

"I'm gonna say this once, and only once," he said, his words brittle. "I. Don't. Date. Men."

I gasped as if he'd struck me, and I couldn't stop the tears from brimming.

"I am *not* a man." Why couldn't he see? Hopelessness burned into frustration. "You've seen me . . . *all of me*. How can you not accept that?"

Sam wiped his hand down his face with frustration, and shook his head. When he spoke, his voice had thawed a little. But not enough.

"Maybe someone else can, Krissy. But not me."

He got up from his chair and stared down at me, really looked at me, and the revulsion and pity in his eyes only made my tears come quicker.

"I'm sorry," he said, not offering me a hand up.

Somehow I made it to my feet on my own. I dried my eyes with my sweatband and sniffled to clear my nose. As he held his door open, Sam stared down at the worn patch of carpet at the entrance. "I promise I won't tell my sister if you don't want me to."

I paused at the threshold, and wondered if it'd be possible to shield a twelve-year-old from the truth, or if she'd hear the malice behind the whispers. It hurt to think of her blaming me for staying away, but so did the idea that she could hate me for what I was.

"You can tell her that we got into a fight over going to different colleges. Tell her that high school romances never last," I said, allowing a sliver of bitterness to creep into my voice.

"Whatever."

"Yeah, whatever," I said, as my last figment of hope shriveled up and died.

I turned to shuffle down the hallway. When I didn't hear Sam's door click, I turned around once at the top of the stairs.

He still stood there, leaning against the doorjamb, staring down at the carpet. I felt sure he could feel my eyes on him, but he didn't look up.

Halfway down the stairs, the door shut.

I let myself out of the house without saying good-bye to Mrs. Wilmington, who was still in the kitchen, humming show tunes.

Dusk had fallen, and I ran home in the twilight.

I welcomed the darkness.

Because really, at this point, being anonymous was what I wanted more than anything.

CHAPTER 22

The next day, Faith stopped by with the promised almond cookies and a Get Well Soon card. She'd gotten a normal-sized one, unlike the card for my birthday just a few weeks earlier, when she'd bought a huge thing that looked like a small poster. She'd even gotten some people to sign it: a few track teammates, a couple of choir members, and some of the girls from her youth group.

"I hope you get better soon," she said. "It sucks driving in alone."

"What, Vee isn't riding with you?" I tried to sound casual, but failed.

"I don't want things to get awkward when you get back. She's been hitching a ride with Bruce." She hesitated. "I know she doesn't show it, but I think she feels really badly about how things went down."

I snorted. Faith meant well, but she was kidding herself if she thought I believed that. Vee didn't do guilt, unlike Faith, who always seemed to feel responsible when someone was upset, as if all the sorrows of the world were somehow her fault, and the solution to all sadness was in her hands and her hands alone.

She looked guilty now as she asked, "Would you be willing to talk to her? Work it out? I hate seeing you two fight. We've been the Three Musketeers since *preschool*. This can't go on forever?"

"What would I possibly say to her?" I said. I hated acting irritated, but sometimes Faith was *too* nice, to the point of it being a fault. "She hasn't even tried to call me, or apologize. For God's sake, Faith—she *screwed* me by telling Sam. How could I forgive her for something like that when she doesn't even think she's done anything wrong?"

Faith was silent. I couldn't tell if she was hurt by my anger, or if her well of sympathy had just run dry. She opened her mouth to say something. Paused. Shut it again.

I went on before she could start her "turn the other cheek" mantra. "I know you're going to say something about forgiving other people's trespasses, but sometimes forgiveness needs to be earned. I'm sick of appeasing Vee. She's not the only person in the world with problems."

Faith looked uneasy, the way she always did when there was conflict. "But what if—" She stopped, and brushed a couple of cookie crumbs off her jeans.

"What?" I asked.

"Nothing. Just . . . I hate this."

"You and me both."

After Faith left, our doorbell rang again within a few minutes. I let Aunt Carla answer it, assuming it had to be a delivery truck or something. Instead, I heard her yell up the stairs in an excited voice.

"Krissy—there's someone here to see you. It's a boy!"

My heart skidded to a stop in my chest, and my first thought—a hope that washed over me like a tidal wave—was that it had to be Sam. I rushed down the stairs, but even before I saw his face I knew the silhouette was too tall, too rangy.

My face fell.

"Hey, it's me," Darren Kowalski said. "Ms. MacDowell asked if I could take notes for you again. The guidance office added on some stuff from your other classes, too."

I tried to smile, to brush away the crushing disappointment. Darren deserved better than that. "What'd I miss in English?"

"Not too much. Wrap-up stuff on *The Merchant of Venice*—people did their extra-credit scenes."

"Did you do one?"

"Nah. I don't think any of the seniors did, except for Jessica. She did Portia's speech."

The quality of mercy, I remembered.

A blast of cold wind ran through our porch, and Darren stuffed purpling hands into his windbreaker. Feeling the draft, Aunt Carla peeked out of the kitchen and proceeded to bodily drag Darren into our house.

"Kristin Louise Lattimer, are you *trying* to freeze your friend to death? I'm about to make some hot cocoa this very instant, so please do invite this young man who I've never met in, and introduce us like civilized people."

I sighed. Sooner stop a steamroller than halt Aunt Carla once she got the wheels of hospitality going. "Aunt Carla, this is Darren. Darren, this is my aunt Carla."

"Actually, I think we met a long time ago, back when I was in middle school," Darren said. "I'm Anna Kowalski's son."

Aunt Carla brightened. "That's right! The caterer. I always did say that Bob let that one get away."

I couldn't tell if Darren's face was flushed from embarrassment, or if it was the cold, but he came into our kitchen anyway.

Aunt Carla showed him to a counter stool. "Kristin, can you get the sugar for me?"

"You're making it from scratch?" Darren asked. "Can I help?"

"Oh, no, no," Aunt Carla clucked. "Just sit and relax, dear. You're the guest."

"Please," Darren insisted. "Do you know what would happen in my house if I just sat on my butt while the women cooked?"

"He can stir," I volunteered.

"Yes, that is an appropriately basic task for this hapless male." He imitated a caveman. "ME STIR. USE STICK."

For the first time in what seemed like years, I cracked a smile. Darren peeled off his windbreaker, revealing a T-shirt that said DATE A RUNNER. EVERY OTHER ATHLETE IS A PLAYER.

When the hot chocolate was done, and poured into our mismatched coffee mugs with a dollop of Reddi-wip on top, Aunt Carla picked up her paperback book and went to go read in the den.

At first, Darren and I drank in companionable silence. Then the quiet grew heavier and heavier, and eventually he cracked his neck and cleared his throat. "So, you doing okay?" he asked, peering over his New York Rangers coffee mug.

"Yeah," I lied. "I had surgery. For a hernia."

Darren nodded thoughtfully.

Too thoughtfully?

Even when we were in middle school, Darren had always been a fact-checker, the kid who couldn't watch a movie without looking up its historical or scientific accuracy online. I wondered how much searching he'd done on the internet, and what, if anything, he knew about my insides.

I was staring at the dregs of cocoa staining the bottom of my cup when Darren said, "Your dad must be pretty depressed. . . ."

A jolt of pain flashed through my body, laced with disappointment and anger. Why was everyone so fixated on how crushed my dad must be about my diagnosis? I opened my mouth to tell Darren off, but before I could say anything, he continued. "I mean, the Rangers are totally tanking this year. That goalie they have? It'd be more effective if they put pads on a chimpanzee and stuck him in the net."

Hockey! He was talking about hockey. I almost laughed out loud.

"Are you still an Islanders fan?" My relief made me punchy. "Wasn't it the twentieth century the last time they made the playoffs?"

"Hey, it's all part of their grand plan. Suck for a few years, get a bunch of lottery picks in the draft."

"Do you still play?" I had a vague memory of freezing my butt off in a rink or two while our parents were dating.

"Nah. When you get to travel league, it gets pretty expensive. And once my center of gravity got really high I didn't have the speed to be a good defenseman."

We bantered back and forth for a little longer until Darren looked at his watch and frowned.

"I'd better get going," he said, picking up our cups to take them to the sink. "I've got to pick up Becky. I'm sure you've got other plans, too."

I couldn't imagine where he thought I'd be going, dressed

in warm-up pants and an old track T-shirt, with hair that hadn't been washed in three days, but I nodded anyway. "So you're still going out with Jessica Riley's sister?"

"Yeah." Darren blushed a little, and I felt an odd wistfulness.

"Well, have a good time."

After Darren left, I was channel flipping in our living room when Aunt Carla peeked her head in. She had her handbag over her shoulder, and a fresh coat of magenta lipstick that was about three shades too dark for her pale winter skin.

"Well, I'm glad to see you up and about, dear. I wanted to tell you that I have a casserole in the oven that should be ready by the time your father gets home."

I blinked at her, not understanding.

"I've got to get going!" Aunt Carla said brightly. "It's book club night, and I've got to bring the chips and dip!"

"Sure. Have fun," I said. Aunt Carla packed up her knitting, and I decided that I had officially hit rock bottom: my divorced, fifty-year-old aunt had hotter plans for Friday night than I did. I couldn't remember the last weekend night when I didn't have a date, or a party, or some sort of track thing to go to. Being friends with Vee meant you never had to fill your calendar.

Before Aunt Carla left, she gave me a little hug, and whispered, "Maybe tonight you guys can have some father-daughter bonding time!"

That's when I knew I had to get out of the house. After

Aunt Carla left, I went up to my room. Sitting on my bed, dreading the sound of my dad's car pulling into the driveway, I realized I couldn't stand the thought of him having to come up with some awkward, public thing we could do together, like playing miniature golf, or ice-skating.

So I steeled my shoulders, opened my closet, and chose a skirt and top fit for a Homecoming Queen.

My dad must have expected to find me moping around when he came home; he did a double take when he walked in at eight and saw me glammed up and ready to go.

"Faith and I are going out tonight," I lied.

"Oh, okay." I could see the relief in his eyes. "Do you need some money for gas?" It was his favorite way to be a good dad, so I took the twenty that he waved at me.

Walking out of my house into the cold felt amazing, like getting freed from a straitjacket. Never mind that I was freezing my ass off in my miniskirt. I thought about how weird it was that, before, I would never in a million years have gone out alone on a weekend night. It just wasn't something you did when you were popular. You ran with the herd, even if it meant having to argue for an hour about where you were going to go, or who got to ride shotgun, or who was designated driver for the evening.

When you were going out by yourself, you didn't have to deal with all that crap. You made your own decisions, and lived with the consequences. You had to be strong in ways that I'd never thought of back when I believed that not being surrounded by a bunch of friends meant that you were weak.

Instead of turning east out of our development toward Utica, I headed west to Whitesboro, where the restaurants were a little older and the bars not as trendy. Where no one, I hoped, knew about the intersex girl next door.

My heart pounding, I circled around the main strip three or four times before I parked in front of a pub that didn't have a bouncer outside. Sam had gotten me a passable fake ID last summer, but when I saw my reflection in my rearview mirror I worried that I didn't look enough like my picture. Instead of my normal pastels or earth tones, I'd put on the Red Vixen lipstick that I bought for a Halloween costume. I'd deliberately overdone my eyeliner, and had curled my hair instead of putting it in my usual ponytail, praying that even if I did run into someone from my school, they wouldn't recognize me.

After I turned off my engine, I sat in my creaking car as the cold settled in, gathering my nerve. The initial excitement of going it alone had worn off, and I felt suddenly vulnerable. Afraid. For a split second I considered restarting my car and heading home; then I thought about sitting at home with my dad, watching Classic Sports Network while he did sudoku and nursed a Heineken.

I opened my door.

The bar was perfect—cozy and dark, and busy enough

that you could pretend that you were with any one of a number of groups. Noisy enough that if someone wanted to talk to you they had to get so close you could smell the beer on their breath.

I scoped out the crowd. There seemed to be a lot of people who were on their second or third drinks already. Some guys who looked like they were there after work. A bunch of college students watching the game on the flat-screen TV. Not very many couples. More men than women. The odds were in my favor.

When I got up to the bartender I ordered myself an appletini and he barely glanced at my fake ID. While he fixed my drink, I smiled at the boy waiting behind me, a twentysomething guy with a buzz cut. He was wearing a blue pinstripe shirt with the sleeves rolled up like he was getting ready to change the oil in his car or something. He was around my height, but stocky, and built like a wrestler. You could tell he went to the gym. I paid for my drink and I could see out of the corner of my eye that he was checking me out.

Back when I was with Sam, I used to hate the meat-market looks I would get at clubs. Strange, that I had been so ungrateful when guys thought I was sexy.

This time, when I turned to Pinstripe Shirt and saw his gaze slide down my body, I felt a surge of pleasure headier than any booze.

I still had the power.

Leaning just the slightest bit toward Pinstripe Shirt, I sucked on the tiny straw in my appletini, pursing my lips the way I'd practiced when I was twelve and learning how to flirt from TV shows. A little voice in my head whispered, *What if he finds out that you're a boy?*

I'm a girl, I shouted back. *I'm a girl.*

I didn't have to wait long for his pickup line. "Haven't seen you around here before. You here with those guys?" he said, pointing toward the college kids.

"No," I said, laughing like I was insulted. "I'm out of school." It was easier to lie when you were wearing makeup. Like you were in costume or something.

"Nice. I don't do college drama." Someone crowded in to buy a drink and he moved away from the bar, still facing me. "What's your name?"

"Lara," I said, giving him the name of a foreign exchange student from a couple of years back. "What about you?"

"I'm Josh," he said, holding out his hand. He didn't give a last name. I didn't need one.

"Nice to meet you, Josh." I shook his hand, but lingered an extra second. Long enough to see the spark light up in his eyes.

I put back my drink so he couldn't see my smile, and when I set it down he nodded his head toward an empty table.

"Let me buy you another drink," he said.

Vee would have been proud.

An hour later, I was deliciously buzzed and Josh had his hand under my shirt as we made out in a back hallway.

"You are so hot," he murmured, and it should've been a turn-on but instead I just thought about how he was only saying that because he wanted to get laid. Because he was drunk. Because he didn't know about my fucking chromosomes.

It was just what I had wanted. But as Josh's thick fingers roamed down my back and up my miniskirt, the panic at what he would find cut through my Absolut haze. I blurted out the least sexy thing I could think of.

"Shit, I've gotta pee so bad. I'm so sorry." I untangled myself from his arms and ran to the bathroom. All the stalls were full, and there was a pair of girls smoking by the hand dryer. They stared at me with heavily lined eyes as I leaned against the side wall, suddenly overcome with shudders. I could still feel Josh's fingers sliding into the dimple in my tailbone, and the sickening fear that he'd discover what I was.

When I went back out, I half expected Josh to be gone. Instead, he sat slumped on the ground by a free-travel-brochure rack.

"Hey," I said.

"Hey," he said, looking like he was about to enter the sad drunk phase. I had wanted to break the mood, but I felt guilty about it, so when he asked me for my number I gave it to him.

After I left, I took a couple of circuits around the block to clear my head before driving, and to process what a near miss it had been. I passed huddles of giggling girls, a trio of guys smoking and telling jokes outside a club. Everyone seemed to understand that strength came in numbers and identity came as part of a group.

I wouldn't make the same mistake again.

CHAPTER 23

Monday morning I didn't bother setting an alarm. My dad poked his head in before he left for work.

"I don't feel up to school today," I mumbled into my pillow. "I think I have a fever." I'd had another bad night, and my sheets were on the floor from where I'd tossed them.

"Honey, you need to see someone." My dad's eyebrows tilted with anxiety.

"Tomorrow," I promised. "If things aren't any better."

"I'll call for an appointment right now, just in case."

"Fine." At least Aunt Carla worked at Boscov's on Mondays and I wouldn't have to worry about her bugging me to rise and shine.

At around ten, my cell phone chirped. Faith, of course.

U feeling any better?

No mention of Facebook, or of what she did the rest of the

weekend—had she gone out with Vee on Saturday? I knew I could never answer her text the way she wanted, with a cheery "Oh, everything's fine, don't worry about me." The last thing in the world I wanted to do was burden her with something else to worry about.

Faith's brother had been diagnosed with bipolar disorder the summer he turned cute, which was right before his senior year and our freshman year. He was on medicine now, and was at a local college, living just fine on his own, but in the bad years Faith had become a total Pollyanna. She still went through each day as if she wanted to supply the whole world with happy juice. No sad faces allowed.

I lay down on my bed with my head nestled in my pillow, mind racing, wondering how I could ever be in a relationship, how I would ever be able to go back to school, and if I would run competitively again.

I stared at my phone, and deleted Faith's text without responding.

Underneath it, there was one more text that I'd ignored: Josh had messaged me late Sunday night, but I hadn't had the guts to answer him, either.

Hey, Lara. Wanna hang this Fri?

I couldn't imagine what a date would look like now. Before every big track meet, at the point where everyone's nerves were beginning to fray, Coach Auerbach always made us lie down and visualize our races. "'What the mind of man can conceive and believe, the mind can achieve,'" she told us. Some of the other girls rolled their eyes whenever it was time to do our psychosomatics drill, but I always ran smoother and lighter after running the cadences of a race in my head.

So I closed my eyes and pictured a date with Josh. A movie, maybe, was his style. Some superhero movie with a convenient romance. I saw us making out in the back row of the theater, saw his hands move downward. . . .

I shuddered.

The best thing to do was ignore him; if I messaged him back it would only encourage him. But then I thought of his dejected look when I came back from the bathroom, and threw him a bone.

Things R crazy busy this weekend. Will call you when things R less insane.

Somehow, that seemed better. The ball was in my court, and I had no intention to ever send it back.

Ms. Diaz called the next day and left a message on our answering machine. I didn't pick up, of course. She'd heard that I had missed a few days of school and wanted to know how long I thought I would be out. And could I or Mr. Lattimer please give her a call back within the next hour to discuss a few options?

What "options," I wondered, as I deleted her message.

When I got back to bed I found a voice mail on my cell

phone, also from Ms. Diaz. I was almost certain that if I checked my email I would see a message from her there, too, but I didn't ever want to open that email account again.

When our doorbell rang at three o'clock, I hauled myself up from my bed and answered the door. It was—you guessed it—Ms. Diaz.

"Hello, Kristin," she said. "Your father said that you were at home." Her glasses fogged up when she came inside, and I felt guilty for making her wait in the cold for so long.

"Do you want something warm to drink?" I asked automatically.

She took in my pajamas and hair, and shook her head. "You look exhausted. Maybe I should be making *you* a cup of tea?"

I made a noncommittal sound and led her over to the living room. Standing up took too much energy, so I slouched onto the love seat.

Ms. Diaz moved slowly, but her eyes were sharp as she followed me, taking in our family pictures and the books on our shelves.

"So, you were in the neighborhood?" I finally asked.

"Oh, nothing that casual." She smiled. "It's just I noticed that you weren't in school the past few days, and as you had surgery recently, we wanted to make sure that you hadn't had any . . . complications that might require you to take a leave of absence."

"No real complications," I said. "I'm just not bouncing

back as fast as I thought."

"It's a lot to go through," Ms. Diaz said, and I could tell that she wasn't just talking about the surgery. She clasped her hands and leaned forward. I stared at the ground.

"Kristin," she said as I counted the flowers on our living room carpet. "One of your friends came to my office today and told me about some disturbing things that were posted on Facebook. He couldn't show me the actual links, because it appears that they were taken down, but what he described sounded like cyberbullying."

Fifteen. There were fifteen flowers on the border of the carpet.

"Kristin?" Ms. Diaz said softly. "Were you aware of anything questionable on Facebook? Do you know who may have done it?"

Interesting way to put it: "anything questionable." I nodded wordlessly. I could feel my face turning red. I wondered who had told her. It was bad enough that all of my "friends" had seen, but teachers and counselors, too? At the thought, my stomach started to cramp, a dull twisting ache. It wasn't my incisions, but something deeper.

"The administration is working on contacting the company to see if they have any archived images that they can trace. If the person who did that to you is in our school, we will make certain that they are punished appropriately."

"No," I blurted out. "Please don't make a big deal out of all this. It was just a prank." If they did a whole investigation, my dad would find out for sure.

"There's a fine line between pranking and bullying," Ms. Diaz said, her voice sharp. "The person who made that profile crossed it."

I shrugged, and curled my legs into the fetal position. I laid my cheek against my flannel pajamas and closed my eyes, but even then all I could see was a photo of myself with naked boy parts pasted on.

"Kristin, I'm concerned about you." Ms. Diaz's voice was soft again. The kind of voice that brought tears to your eyes even when you thought that you'd cried them all out.

Ms. Diaz reached into her pocketbook and brought out a pack of tissues.

"I can't go back to school again," I said. "I can't see those people again. My 'friends.'" I made quotes in the air with my fingers.

Ms. Diaz sat back in her chair and crossed her legs. "We do have a temporary home-instruction option," she said. "It requires a doctor's note, of course."

She handed me a pamphlet, and I stared at her as if she'd just told me that she believed in immaculate conception. "You mean I don't have to go back?"

"Not right away. Technically, there's a six-week limit to home instruction. But that is flexible if your physician requests more time."

I hiccupped, and the tears slowed down. I couldn't believe it. "Thank you," I whispered. "Thank you so much."

At that point Ms. Diaz got out of her seat and sat next to me. She put her hand over mine, and spoke softly but firmly. "Kristin, you do have to realize that this is a temporary solution until things . . . settle down."

I barely heard her. All I could hear was that I wouldn't have to go to school the next day. Or the day after that.

Ms. Diaz went on. "The one requirement you still need to meet, Kristin, is your community service project. You still need sixty more hours to graduate. I understand that you were working with Big Brothers Big Sisters?"

I froze in the middle of blowing my nose. Vee and I and a few other people had been working on a benefit race for the program. "I'll have to switch to another project," I said, trying to keep the panic out of my voice.

"Do you have any idea where else you'd like to volunteer?"

Wherever Vee wasn't. Or Sam, or Bruce, or . . . anybody.

I shook my head, scrunching my Kleenex into a tight little ball.

"A number of organizations are still looking for students to help out." She handed me a stapled list. "Why don't you look at that and get back to me? I'll start the paperwork for your home instruction. We'll need to have a formal meeting with your father present, and a doctor's note as well."

"We have an appointment in a few days," I said.

"Well, then." Ms. Diaz stood up and put on her coat. "Take care, Kristin. Give yourself some time to heal. We hope to have you back at school soon."

As I showed her out, I wondered who "we" was.

CHAPTER 24

"So, um, have you been checking your email?" Faith asked a couple nights later. She was trying to be casual and all, but even over the phone I could sense an undercurrent of anxiety.

"No, why?"

"Well, Vee wanted me to tell you she sent you an email," she said. "About Big Brothers Big Sisters, now that you're not doing it. She just needed to know about some logistics, but hasn't heard from you."

"Why didn't she just call me herself?" I asked.

"I don't know. Probably because she thought you wouldn't pick up?"

"I would've," I said. Just to see if she said she was sorry.

"Well, anyway, she wanted me to tell you."

When I opened my email I ignored the Facebook notifications, and scrolled down to Vee's message, sent the day after Ms. Diaz's visit. It was four measly lines:

Subject: BBBS

Hey.
Faith said you had surgery. Hope you're okay.
So, I hear from Ms. Diaz that you're not doing BBBS anymore. Can you email me all the info on the sponsors you've gotten so far?
-V

The absence of an apology hit me as hard as any blow. I read the email twice, as if I could've missed something. It was almost worse that she had asked if I was okay, because that implied that she cared. Except if she had given a rat's ass about me, she would've said she was sorry.

I searched through my files to find my sponsor spreadsheet, and sent it to her without bothering to write anything in the message field. Then I slammed my laptop shut, hands trembling.

"You okay?" my dad asked. He put his palm on my forehead. "You look flushed."

I *felt* flushed, and vaguely sick to my stomach. My heart was pounding so hard I could feel it in my fingers.

"Well then," I said, "good thing we made that appointment for tomorrow."

"I don't think there's anything wrong with you," Dr. Cheng said.

"Oh, thank God," said my dad.

Unlike my dad, I wasn't relieved. "Then why do I always feel like I have a fever?"

Dr. Cheng sighed. "It's not clear. Your temp's normal today. Your incisions are healing perfectly well, and you're having bowel movements." That had been the highlight of my visit so far, having to talk about what my poops looked like— and how often I had them—in front of my father. "How's your energy level been? Have you been sleeping?"

My father snorted. "A little too well."

"I've been really tired," I said defensively. "Yeah, I've been sleeping a lot, but that's because I've been tossing and turning because of the fevers."

"Hmm." I could feel Dr. Cheng's eyes on me, could hear the wheels turning in her head.

"And how are you doing with the hormones?" Dr. Cheng asked.

I stared at my boots. After my surgery, I'd gotten a prescription for some estrogen pills. Dr. Cheng had said that I needed to take them for my bone health, now that my body—my testicles—didn't produce hormones naturally anymore.

At my silence, Dr. Cheng raised her eyebrows. "I guess you haven't gotten a chance to pick them up yet. In fact, that might account for your fatigue. It certainly could explain hot flashes. If you're not taking your estrogen, you're essentially menopausal."

As if my body wasn't enough of a yard sale.

"It slipped my mind," I told Dr. Cheng.

Dr. Cheng sighed. "I'll print you out a new prescription. How about the support group? Have you contacted them yet?" She smiled in what I supposed she thought was an encouraging way.

"I talked to one girl," I said.

"Good. You know, they have meetings too, and a mailing list. It's a terrific resource as you go forward with your diagnosis."

Dr. Cheng fiddled on her laptop, and I fixated on what she had said. *Go forward with your diagnosis.* It was nicer than saying "learn to cope with being a freak."

"I'm ordering labs and an X-ray since you've had recent surgery. But you need to take your hormones. And I really want you to think about your fatigue, and whether there may be a psychosomatic element to it."

"What, do you think this is all in her head?" my father asked.

Dr. Cheng held out her hand like she was trying to stop traffic. "I'm not saying anything for sure. But if the X-ray is negative, I would like to refer you to a therapist who specializes in adolescent psychiatry."

Great, I wasn't just a freak. I was crazy, too. The thought of seeing a shrink made me want to cry: Having to tell the whole stupid story all over again. Another waiting room. Another form to fill out where there wasn't a space for "None of the Above." Where there wasn't space for me.

My dad took the referral for the shrink, and I knew that he'd make the appointment.

"You're going to need Dr. Cheng's help if you ever want to go back to school again," he said on the ride home.

"What if I don't ever want to go back? Can't I just get a GED?"

With a screech of tires, my dad pulled to the side of the road. He cut the engine and turned to me, face already getting red. "Are you *joking*? Krissy, what is the matter with you? You'll lose your scholarship for sure."

Suddenly, it was too much, the lies. Trying to be brave for him. "Dad . . . the whole school knows."

"What?" He went pale.

"I . . . I told a couple of people, and you know how rumors spread."

It was a good thing the car was already stopped. My father

put his head in his hands for a moment. "Oh, Krissy. No wonder you don't want to go to school. Why didn't you tell me earlier?"

The helplessness on his face slayed me. So I didn't tell him about the locker, or about Vee and me no longer being friends. Instead, I told him about my talk with Coach Auerbach. To my surprise, his face brightened.

"Well, they have no leg to stand on keeping you off the team, you know. We can take care of that right away."

I stared at him. "Wait, what?"

At the disbelief on my face, my dad's lips curled up, and I thought about how rare it had become for him to smile. "I finally found the right NCAA guidelines," he said, "and people with AIS are considered women for competitive purposes. They *can't* take your scholarship away."

I stared at him. "Why didn't you tell me?"

He shrugged. "I just figured it out last night. You were already sleeping. We know how easy it's been to wake you up lately. And what a peach you are in the morning, too." He muttered the last part under his breath.

I ignored the jab, and swallowed hard, my mind swirling in a dozen different directions. I could still compete, still go to college without my dad having to take out a second mortgage.

I still had a future.

But if I wanted it, I'd eventually have to go back to school.

CHAPTER 25

When Ms. Diaz gave me the list of places I could volunteer, I chose the Caritas Health Clinic, partly because I liked the idea of working with Dr. Johnson, and partly because it was the farthest location from our school, and only two other students had signed up to work there: Darren Kowalski and Jessica Riley.

As I drove up to the health clinic for my orientation, it became pretty obvious why so few people had chosen it for their service projects. The clinic wasn't in the best part of town, and was in the same building as a check-cashing and bail-bond operation. The hallways had a 1970s orange-brown carpet that was matted down with wear and spotted with bits of trampled-in chewing gum.

After a bit of wandering, I finally found a door with a sign saying:

Caritas Health Clinic

Our mission: to administer quality health care
regardless of age, race, gender, or ability to pay.

Just as I was about to press the buzzer to enter, another door just down the hall opened, and a familiar lanky figure came out.

"Hey, Darren," I said. "Your notes were super helpful."

He looked flushed, and blinked a couple of times owlishly. "Um, thanks. So, you're the new volunteer?"

I nodded.

"Cool. I mean, we need all the help we can get here."

"Sure. I'm excited to help. Though, are you doing . . . janitorial work?" I asked, peering at the sign on the door he'd just exited.

He laughed, and opened the door to show me a tiny closet with a computer and a bunch of other whirring equipment with lights. "We call it the Dungeon—it's the main server for the electronic medical records. The desktop is so old you can practically hear it saying 'I think I can, I think I can.' Anyway, it can get pretty hot in there. So I have to come out every so often for air. And to help with orientation." He looked at his watch. "You're right on time. I'll show you the break room."

Darren used his ID badge to buzz me into a waiting room lined with plastic chairs, and brought me behind the front desk to a tiny room set up with a Mr. Coffee, a cube-shaped fridge, and a folding bridge table. Jessica Riley was there, drinking a Red Bull. After the world's fastest double take, she jumped up out of her chair with a smile on her face.

"Kristin! So great to see you here." The look of genuine delight on her face sent an unexpected wave of happiness through me, until I remembered that Jessica had been the female lead in our school play for two years running. If anyone could fake friendliness, she could.

I supposed I should be grateful that she tried.

Dr. Johnson came in, and shook my hand warmly. "Kristin, we're so happy to have you here. As I'm sure you know, we operate on a razor-thin margin and are very short staffed, so every volunteer helps.

"After you get your patient confidentiality training, Darren will get you set up with our electronic medical record system. And Jessica will go over our prenatal-care algorithm. For now, though, we'll just show you how to prepare rooms in between patients and checking people in."

A tiny black-haired nurse's aide named Lisa led me around the back hallways, and taught me how to wipe down the counters in each exam room and change the paper covers on the tables. I tried not to imagine a scared teenage girl lying there, wondering why the lights were so bright, and why the stirrups felt ice-cold, even through her socks.

When I was done, I went out to the front desk to see if they needed any help with mail or copies. The waiting room was starting to fill up with people. All women, which made sense, of course. Dr. Johnson had told me that she only ran her ob-gyn clinic twice a month. The other days, a family doctor staffed the clinic.

I hadn't prepared myself for how many children would be there. Most of the women had kids with them—a majority of them had more than one. A weary-looking woman in a black shirt and jeans had a baby wrapped around her stomach with a beach towel, a toddler in a stroller, and a pair of twin boys that looked to be around four or five. The boys were fighting over a worn copy of *Parenting* magazine. I gave a little laugh when one of the boys finally won the tug-of-war and cried out in triumph. Then I just felt sad, and went back to turn over some rooms.

At dinnertime, Jessica invited me into Darren's Dungeon to eat. The clinic's heating had broken down the night before, and it had only gotten fixed a few hours earlier, so I welcomed the heat coming from the computer's CPUs. I wedged myself onto a bench next to the main computer tower, meaning that I got an earful of the funky soul music blaring from the speaker.

"What band is this, anyway?" I asked.

Darren staggered back and put a hand to his mouth. "You can't say that this is the first time you've been exposed to the genius which is The Concept?"

"Um, yeah."

"Well, prepare to have your life changed," Darren said.

"Just in case you haven't noticed yet," Jessica stage-whispered, "Darren here uses the terms *genius* and *life-changing* very, very loosely. The Concept makes my little sister's garage band sound like the Rolling Stones."

"Hey, Riley," Darren said, pretending to act annoyed. "First of all, don't dis Becky's band. They kick ass. And second: don't yuck my yum. I have my tastes, and you have yours. If you want to listen to something else, you can go back to Antarctica."

Jessica rolled her eyes. "Can you at least turn it down? Not everyone wants to feel like they're at a rave when they're eating dinner."

Darren sighed and moused down the volume. I was surprised that, once I could actually hear the lyrics, the music didn't suck. After the first track ended, the second track was so quiet and introspective that I asked Darren to turn the volume up. He did, grinning triumphantly at Jessica.

I munched on my turkey sandwich and nodded my head to the music. Jessica wolfed down her hummus wrap and took it upon herself to give me the inquisition. "So, I didn't know you were interested in medicine," she said, sounding kind of like a teacher trying to get to know a student better. "It's nice to have more people around, though. There's always work to do somewhere."

"It seemed like a worthy cause," I said lamely. Darren wasn't really involving himself in the conversation, taking bites of his tuna sub in between some work he was doing on the computer. While Jessica crunched on some carrot sticks, I mustered up something polite to say. "How about you? I always thought you were going to end up on Broadway or something. Don't they have a project volunteering at the theater?"

"Nah, I'm planning on nursing school. My mom's a midwife, and I think I want to be one too."

That got Darren's attention. "I really don't get why anyone would want to do that. My uncle said that watching my mom's childbirth video scarred him for life."

Jessica opened her mouth for a rebuttal, but I kicked Darren's chair with my boot. A lecture on the Miracle of Birth would just be more salt in my wounds.

"Don't yuck her yum," I said.

"What?" He stared at me like antlers had just popped out of my head. It felt like the first normal look I'd gotten from him all day.

"Hmm," was all the brilliant Darren Kowalski could think of to say.

But Jessica grinned at me, and despite my suspicions about actresses and their sincerity, I grinned back.

Make that *two* normal looks.

CHAPTER 26

"Thank God you're here," Dr. Johnson's physician assistant said the minute I walked into clinic the next week. "We're going to need you to help with the next two patients. We have two add-ons, and Jessica is coming late today."

Dr. Johnson hadn't been kidding when she said they were short staffed. A maternity patient meant there'd be a pelvic exam. I felt a little queasy. "I haven't been fully trained for that yet."

"All you have to do is give her the instruments she needs." He handed me a bag full of plastic speculums and pointed me toward Exam Room 1, where Dr. Johnson stood reading the patient's chart. When she entered, I followed close behind but hugged the wall when I saw the patient, a tiny Asian girl with long black hair pulled back into a ponytail.

The one-size-fits-all gown hung on her slight frame like a muumuu. She looked about fifteen.

"Kristin, this is Vong," Dr. Johnson said. Vong gave me a tired look, and I stared at the floor.

Speaking slowly, Dr. Johnson introduced me. She asked a few more questions, which Vong answered mostly with nods or headshakes. Then Dr. Johnson went over and started examining her from head to toe. When she moved the gown up to examine Vong's stomach, Vong's knees jerked together involuntarily. The movement caught my eye and I saw the stretch marks making faint white lines on her belly. There was an angry red ridge right at her bikini line. A C-section scar?

I felt a raw ache in my chest and closed my eyes. A minute later, Dr. Johnson called me over. Vong was already in the stirrups. I couldn't see her head anymore because of the drape over her legs.

My gloves stuck to the sweat on my palms. Dr. Johnson asked for a smaller speculum. I stared at the ceiling.

Vong didn't freak out the way I did when the speculum got in; she barely moved at all. After Dr. Johnson positioned the work light and peeked in between Vong's legs, she frowned and didn't ask for a swab like I'd been taught she would. Instead she reached up and pressed on her belly with one hand. She murmured a question that I couldn't hear and sighed at Vong's response.

"Was everything okay?" I asked when we left.

Dr. Johnson grimaced. "As okay as it can be for a girl who's going to be a mother of two before she reaches her sixteenth birthday. Because of her pelvic disproportion, she'll probably need a repeat C-section, which puts her at risk for some scary complications in the future if she keeps having kids."

It took me a while to process. "Can't she . . . can't she have an abortion?" I asked painfully. I couldn't believe I was even suggesting it.

Dr. Johnson shrugged wearily. "Nope. She's Catholic, which is why she didn't get an abortion the first time, even though she was only thirteen and it was essentially a date rape."

I was shaking my head before the words even sank in. I thought of the knobbly knees squeezing together.

"Besides," Dr. Johnson said, "she wouldn't want an abortion even if she weren't Catholic. This second baby is by her new boyfriend." Her voice was flat.

"Maybe things will work out," I said. It was easier to dream up a happy ending than to think too much about Vong's past.

But not exactly realistic.

I was sitting at the front desk, helping with patient check-in, when Jessica and Darren came in laughing. Despite being more than half full, the waiting room was hushed, expectant.

So when the two of them walked in with their cheery outside voices it was jarring, even embarrassing. They dropped their voices almost immediately, but even then their energy buzzed, filled the room.

As he let himself behind the front desk, Darren caught sight of me and tilted his chin in my direction. "Hey. You all right?" he whispered.

I couldn't get Vong out of my head. My eyes flickered out to the waiting room. How many more stories like hers were out there? "I'm fine. Just getting used to how intense things are here."

Darren nodded, understanding. He put his hand on my shoulder and held it there for a heartbeat. It was just a touch, but I shivered at the intimacy.

Later, as Dr. Johnson finished up her charting, I asked her what pelvic disproportion was.

"The term is for when a woman's hips aren't big enough to allow a baby through," she said. "In general, a woman's pelvis is much larger than a man's so it can allow a baby's head to go through. But there's a limit to how wide hips can be before it interferes with your ability to walk—it's called the obstetrical dilemma."

I thought about the pictures I'd seen of Caster Semenya and her stick-straight hips, and grimaced.

Jessica misunderstood my frown. "I know, how messed up

is that?" Jessica said. "To have to choose between having kids and being able to run away from something that wants to eat you? The tyranny of childbirth knows no bounds."

"Hey," said Darren. "What about the tyranny of having your gonads on the outside? It's not like men chose to be one swift kick away from a world of pain."

"Puh-leeze," Jessica said. "Like there's any question that girls have it worse? Menstruation? Labor? PMS? You don't even know how awful it is to have to sit down to pee at rest stops." She turned to me. "Kristin, back me up here."

The two of them turned to stare at me, and in an instant I felt the tomato-and-cheese sandwich I ate for lunch start to come up. With a squeal of metal, I pushed my folding chair back. "Excuse me." I ran to the staff bathroom until the nausea passed. Then I washed my face with cold water and sat down on the toilet seat.

After a few minutes went by I heard a tentative knock on the door.

"I'm almost done," I shouted.

"Kristin? It's Jessica. Are you all right?"

I sighed, and opened the door. Jessica peered in, as if to make sure that I really was done, then walked in and locked the door behind her. She leaned against the sink.

"I'm sorry," she said, looking at the floor. "Darren set me straight on what it means to have your condition."

Darren the Fact-Checker strikes again.

"If all that talk made you uncomfortable, I apologize."

Uncomfortable? I thought. Was that the word to describe what I felt, a combination of wretchedness and hopelessness and revulsion at both what I was—and what I wasn't?

"But to be honest, I'm a bit jealous of you."

I looked up at Jessica, who wasn't smiling, and rolled my eyes. "Seriously?"

"Yes, seriously. You're like . . . Woman 2.0. All of the girl with none of the worry. You never have to stress about getting your period, or about getting pregnant. That's, like, huge. They're the two things I hate the most about being a girl."

I couldn't believe that someone as smart as Jessica was saying these things. "Don't you think that birth control is better than not having a uterus?"

"People always forget their pills, and things happen."

"But at least then you can have a baby someday. I can't."

"I don't mean to sound insensitive, but you can always adopt."

I felt an unfamiliar rumble of anger boiling up inside of me. "It's not the same," I said dismissively.

"No," Jessica agreed. Her voice was cheerful, but her look steely. "It's better. You get to take a child that would otherwise be unloved and give it a home."

Now I felt like the jerk. I looked up at Jessica. Something

about the edge to her voice set off a warning bell: the topic was personal. "You're adopted?"

"I wasn't, but my sister was." I thought back to Homecoming, trying to picture Darren's date. Now that I thought about it, Becky and Jessica couldn't have looked less alike. Becky was all petite with stick-straight dark hair, while Jessica was tall, almost big-boned, with frizzy dirty-blond hair.

Neither of us said anything for a while.

Jessica broke the silence. "So are you done feeling sorry for yourself?" She smiled to take away the sting of the words, and offered me a hand off the toilet seat.

I gave a choked laugh. "For now, maybe. No guarantees about an hour from now."

That night as I got ready for bed, I wondered what Jessica would think if she found out her Woman 2.0 had to take estrogen pills. I'd been procrastinating about starting my hormone therapy, but my dad had picked up the bottle from the pharmacy, and each night he sent me to bed with a kiss and a "Don't forget to take your meds!"

I opened the childproof bottle and slid a tablet into my hand. It was tiny, round, and pink-colored, as if that would somehow make you feel more feminine when you took it. I wondered if testosterone tablets were blue. Who decided that pink = girl and blue = boy, anyway?

As much as I hated the idea of popping pills, I hated the

idea of hot flashes more. If Dr. Cheng was right, the meds would give me more energy, too.

Before I could change my mind, I put the pill in my mouth, and swallowed.

CHAPTER 27

When I first met the therapist Dr. Cheng had recommended, I was struck by how put-together she was. I had expected someone with frizzled hair and frumpy clothes; Dr. LaForte reminded me more of Martha Stewart, her shirt so perfectly ironed it looked like it had come fresh off the rack, the smile on her face professional and photogenic, but not exactly warm.

"Hello," she said, shaking my hand. "I'm Susan LaForte. So very nice to meet you."

"Hi," I said. Her office was on the sunny side of the street and looked out into a backyard garden. She had a small desk facing the window, three wooden chairs with armrests, and—I almost laughed out loud at the cliché—a couch with an embroidered throw pillow.

I sat on the couch and clutched the pillow against my chest. Dr. LaForte pulled over a wooden chair and sat across from me. She was tall, and the sharp angles of her body made her seem stiff rather than sleek.

"So, what would you like me to call you?" she asked.

The smile drained off my face. I felt the muscles in my shoulders clench. A defensive posture. "What do you mean?" My name was Kristin Lattimer. Not Kristopher. Didn't she understand that I was a girl?

"Oh, sometimes my clients are very picky about their nick-names. Do you prefer Kristin, or Krissy? Or should I just call you Miss Lattimer?"

I forced my shoulder muscles to relax. "Kristin is fine, Dr. LaForte. Krissy, too."

"All right, Kristin. Feel free to call me Susan if you so desire. Now that we've introduced ourselves, how may I help you today?"

God, I was so sick of open-ended questions. "Did Dr. Cheng not tell you why I was coming?"

"She gave me some of the medical details, yes, but I'm more interested in hearing from you what you hope to gain from therapy."

I shrugged. What did people normally want from therapy? "To figure things out," I said. "So I can be happy again." Or, at least, feel less crappy.

"Both very valid goals. Can you tell me a bit about what's making you unhappy?"

"I don't even know where to start."

"How about whatever comes to mind?"

For several moments I didn't speak. I stared at the intricate pattern embroidered on the pillow I clutched. It looked hand-stitched—there were slightly crooked stitches here and there—and I wondered idly how many hours its maker had spent hunched over it with a needle and thread.

"Did you make this?" I asked Dr. LaForte, holding up the pillow.

She didn't seem surprised by my question, but I guess therapists are trained that way. "Not me. A very dear friend gave it to me as a wedding gift. When she passed away a few years ago I brought it here to my office to remind me of her."

Had she brought the pillow in as a conversation starter? Was anything in a therapist's office ever put there without deliberation? A little voice in my head told me not to trust her, that she would use the information to . . . do what? What could she possibly do to me that would make things worse?

Then I looked up, met Dr. LaForte's gaze. Her eyes were green, like my mother's.

I told her about Homecoming. How it led to one doctor, and then more doctors. Then I told her about Vee and Sam, and before I realized it I'd told her about my locker and Facebook, too. Two things I didn't tell her about: Nearly stepping in front of the SUV. Making out with Josh. Before I knew it, half an hour had passed. I hadn't known that my story took so long to tell.

"That must have been so hard for you," Dr. LaForte said

when I was done. "To have your whole world turned upside down."

It was such an understatement that I didn't bother to answer.

"What concerns you the most about your intersex diagnosis?"

"It's hard to pick just one thing. But . . ." *Stay Away.* "I hate it that people don't understand what intersex is. That they think that I'm some sort of transsexual," I blurted. Even as I said it out loud, I realized how petulant and closed-minded I must sound.

"I mean, it's not like there's anything wrong with being a transsexual . . . ," I backpedaled, then sighed. Who was I kidding? "I know that getting upset about their calling me a tranny makes me just as judgmental as the people making fun of me. But it hurts anyway. It's so ignorant."

"Of course it is," Dr. LaForte said. "There are whole swaths of the country that don't understand what it means to be transgender, let alone know what intersex is. So it's not surprising that your classmates' transphobia came out."

"Their trans what?"

"Transphobia. Fear and hostility toward transgender people. And anyone who doesn't fit into the typical gender binary, really."

Dr. LaForte shifted in her chair, and leaned in closer to me. "So, Kristin, tell me about your support system. Have you talked to anyone about what you're going through?"

I shook my head.

"May I ask why?"

"I just didn't think anyone would understand."

There was silence. Dr. LaForte's office was in such a quiet part of town that I could hear the ticking of the old-fashioned cuckoo clock on the wall.

Finally she spoke. "It's hard feeling different, Kristin. I know it's a cliché, but only you could ever truly understand what you're going through. At the same time, there are people who care about you. And you are truly not alone. Have you tried reaching out to any other people with your condition?"

"Once."

"I'm so glad. Because no one is going to relate to you better than someone who has lived through your diagnosis."

I liked that she used the phrase *lived through*. As if AIS was some sort of passing storm. I took a deep breath, and let it out through pursed lips. "So, what's the verdict?"

"Excuse me?"

"Am I crazy?"

Dr. LaForte smiled. A real one this time, with a touch of mischief. "We're all crazy, Kristin. There's no such thing as normal. That said, I do think you may be depressed."

When she said it, I felt kind of stupid that I hadn't real-ized it before. Suddenly, I was relieved, because they could treat depression. I looked up at Dr. LaForte hopefully. "Does that mean I have to go on Prozac or something?"

"It's certainly an option, and it's a discussion that you should have with Dr. Cheng or your primary doctor, but I think that you'll do well with therapy. For now, we can focus on the lifestyle changes you can make to improve your mood. Healthy eating and exercise, for example. I can give you literature with some of the basics."

As Dr. LaForte walked to her filing cabinet to rustle up a handout, I took a deep breath and looked out into the next-door garden. There were still some tomato cages standing up in broken rows, protecting nothing but air. An empty birdbath.

We sat quietly for a little while as I read the brochure she gave me, until Dr. LaForte glanced at the clock. "Well, our time is almost up," she said. "For our next session, I have some homework for you. First, I really encourage you to contact the support group again. You won't regret it, truly. Second, I want you to ask yourself: Who are you?"

"What do you mean?" I asked. "Like what I want to be known for? Or what I identify myself as? Or are you talking about what my hopes and dreams are, or something like that?"

"I don't know," Dr. LaForte said, smiling. "All of the above."

CHAPTER 28

When I straggled into the kitchen for breakfast the next morning, my dad surprised me with freshly made blueberry whole wheat pancakes. Back when she was alive, my mom spent most Sunday mornings volunteering at some church event or another, so brunch was always Dad's chance to shine. He'd make pancakes from scratch and top them with fresh fruit or stuff them with ricotta. He became the king of the perfect crepe flip. And his omelets were works of art.

After Mom died, we didn't need to cook for months—Aunt Carla and the other members of Mom's women's group saw to that. But even after we'd worked through all the casseroles, and thawed the last frozen lasagna, Dad's brunches never came back. I missed that Mr. Mom part of my dad, which was a side of him that few people saw.

I pulled the pancakes out of the oven, where he'd put them to keep them warm. "Thanks, Dad. But you didn't have to do that. Cereal's fine."

"Oh, it's Thanksgiving week, so I just wanted to do something special for my girl."

The roughness of his voice made me suspicious. After my therapy session, I'd told my dad about Dr. LaForte's theory that I was depressed and he'd jumped on the "eat healthy and exercise" bandwagon.

My suspicion grew when my dad said a little too casually, "It's a beautiful day. Why don't we go for a run together?"

I took a bite of a pancake, and a blueberry exploded in my mouth. "Are you sure?" I wasn't even certain my dad owned a pair of sneakers, but he nodded. "Okay, but you'll have to tell me if I'm going too fast," I said, slurping down a glass of orange juice. If my dad thought that I wouldn't back down from a challenge, he was right.

The moment we stepped outside into the crisp, sunny November air, my heart beat faster in anticipation of the run. "Where do you want to go?" I asked, jogging in place as my dad stretched.

"Let's just stay around here."

I frowned. "Can't we go to the park?" I could see some of our neighbors already out raking leaves or walking their dogs. The elliptical sounded good right now, all private in our basement.

"I don't want to cut through the meadow. It'll be all wet from the dew. Come on." He started running. His stance was so bad I almost laughed. He held his wrists super loose and they flopped around like clappers.

"Dad! You run like a girl!" I shouted after him, because it had always been a point of pride for me that I didn't, a fact that made me want to both laugh and cry.

Bracing myself for the stares, I started to run, and caught up with my dad in just a few strides. I kept my eyes on the pavement a few feet ahead, focusing on my breathing. Even though my hands wanted to clench into fists, I willed them to relax. Coach Auerbach would've been proud of my karate chops.

I saw one of our neighbor's kids riding his bike toward us, and I sprinted out ahead of my father and crossed the street. But before we reached the end of the block, old Mr. Mullen came out dragging his garbage can. "Ahoy, Lattimers!" He waved, not fazed at all. He probably hadn't heard the news.

There were four more blocks before the main intersection, and I avoided the one with the most kids. Along my alternate route, though, a few boys were playing street hockey with a ratty orange tennis ball. They took up the entire street, and both sidewalks. I slowed down and was about to turn back when my father puffed up from behind me and kept on straight.

I kept my eyes on the pavement.

"Hey, Krissy!" one of the boys shouted. It was Evan Constantino. I'd been his camp counselor a few summers ago. Taught him how to swim. He raised his hockey stick in the air in greeting. His friends looked at me for a second and decided that I wasn't interesting enough and went back to bickering about a penalty shot.

I was too flustered to do anything but wave back.

After a mile, I entered the zone. My teammates used to call me the Junkie because I got my runner's high really early during a run. You know that old cliché, it's not the destination that matters, it's the journey? That's what it was like with me and running. My body loved action. It craved it.

Halfway through the run, I felt the muscles in my face start to feel funny. They stung, almost. It wasn't until we ran past the evergreens fencing Mrs. Nicholson's yard that I figured out what the sensation was.

I was smiling.

The only thing better was to run with my teammates, maybe doing a single-line pursuit where we'd run in a column and have the person at the end sprint to the front, or Coach Auerbach's crazy fruitcake drill where we'd pass a watermelon back and forth while we were running. We'd get to eat the watermelon at the end of practice.

I wondered if Coach Auerbach knew that the NCAA

allowed girls with AIS to compete. Would she let me back on the team, at least to practice, if I showed her my father's research?

When we got back home, my dad was red-faced and hunched over, but I was barely breathing heavily. I felt taller. Looser. After showering I even put on jeans instead of slipping into pajamas again.

I opened my laptop to try to find the NCAA site my dad had told me about. I copied the paragraph I needed and pasted it into a new email to Coach Auerbach:

A female recognized in law should be eligible to compete in female competitions if she has an androgen resistance such that she derives no competitive advantage from such levels.

But as I was about to hit Send, I remembered Rashonda's look when she walked in on me crying in Coach's office. Rashonda, who had been my Little Sister. Whose hair I had decorated with barrettes in our school colors before each meet.

I thought about how all the other girls would look at me if I ever went back. Would they think that I was a cheat? Even if it was technically within the rules, would I ever win a race again without someone grumbling about my being a man?

I deleted the message, and went back to my browser to find the one page my dad had bookmarked that made me feel less alone: a list on the support-group home page with links to famous people with AIS. One of them was María José Martínez-Patiño, a Spanish national champion. She was a hurdler like me. Back in the old days, they used to do sex tests on female athletes, because of countries that were so crazy about the Olympics that they'd cheat by sending men to compete in women's events. Women had had to get official Certificates of Femininity.

María had failed her sex test. She had AIS, like me. And people had outed her, like me:

I was expelled from our athletes' residence, my sports scholarship was revoked, and my running times were erased from my country's athletics records. I felt ashamed and embarrassed. I lost friends, my fiancé, hope, and energy.

I tried to tell myself that things were different now. They didn't make girl athletes parade naked in front of doctors anymore. The NCAA had rules specifically about AIS. María's and Caster Semenya's cases had led to increased awareness; everything was different.

Except the part about losing friends. The rules may have changed, but people were still afraid of the Other.

How naive I had been to tell Vee. How desperate, how stupid.

Only now, after the damage had been done, did I see the answer staring me in the face.

I needed Another Other.

CHAPTER 29

Maggie Blankman had introduced me to Gretchen Lawrence by email the day after our conversation, after I was first diagnosed. Gretchen responded with a perfectly friendly message telling me to call her anytime, but the first few times I picked up my phone to call, I chickened out. She was a busy college student. She barely knew me. She couldn't have meant it.

The person who finally convinced me to call her back wasn't Dr. LaForte—it was Faith, who sent me a link to an article from *Seventeen* with the headline I'M A GIRL WITH BOY CHROMOSOMES. An article that happened to be written by Gretchen Lawrence.

OMG she seems super nice, Faith wrote under the link. did U know there is some sort of support group?

After that, I really had no choice. I emailed Gretchen, and she got back to me within hours, suggesting that we meet up at a Friendly's in Syracuse the Sunday after Thanksgiving.

The day of our get-together, I stressed so much about what to wear that it was almost like a first date. After trying on two outfits, I decided to go simple with a navy-blue long-sleeved T-shirt and jeans.

I got to the restaurant a few minutes early and burned some time looking through the menu, even though I didn't really need to. Vee, Faith, and I had eaten at the Friendly's in Utica practically every week during junior year, and I had the menu memorized. Vee always ordered the Asian chicken salad and picked off the fried wonton strips. Faith was a quesadilla girl. And I always had the turkey club without the bacon. Then we'd share a Mint Cookie Crunch sundae. Vee would always have the cherry on top, except when I had a meet the next day, when she'd give it to me.

Someone tapped me on the shoulder, jolting me out of my memories. "Excuse me, are you Kristin?"

I turned around to see a girl about two or three inches shorter than me with shoulder-length black hair. She had big brown eyes and an even bigger smile on her face.

Without even thinking about it, I smiled back.

"Oh my God. I'm so glad to meet you," Gretchen gushed. "Can I give you a hug? I know we've just met, but . . ."

But we were AIS sisters. Gretchen enveloped me in her arms and I pressed my face against the scratchy wool of her coat. It'd been so long since I'd hugged anyone but my aunt Carla, who didn't count because what she did was more like suffocating someone than hugging them. Gretchen was a good hugger; her arms were strong, and her hair smelled like green apples.

"You order anything yet?" Gretchen asked. "Want to share an appetizer?" The waitress came, and I ordered a pink lemonade and my usual turkey club and we got some mozzarella sticks to share.

While we waited for the food to come I played with the wrapper from my straw, rolling it up into a tight ball. I wondered when I'd gotten so quiet. Then I remembered: I'd always been a little shy. It was my friends who were outgoing.

"So," Gretchen said finally. "You're a senior, right? Do you know where you might want to go in the fall?"

I told her about State, and track. It was easy to deflect the conversation from there, and ask Gretchen about Syracuse. She was a psychology major, and was minoring in women's studies.

"Isn't that kind of ironic?" I commented.

"What, because we're not 'real women'?" She made air quotes. "Why aren't we real women—because we don't have uteruses? What about women who have hysterectomies? Or mastectomies? One of my favorite AIS quotes ever is from a woman named María José Martínez-Patiño: 'Having had my womanliness tested—literally and figuratively—I suspect I have a surer sense of my femininity than many women.'" I startled in recognition at the name. That was the Spanish hurdler I had read about.

Since I had alluded to AIS, Gretchen seemed to think it was fair game. "Maggie said in her email that you just found out about your diagnosis. How's it been, knowing?"

I shrugged. "Sometimes I wish I'd been one of those girls whose parents just told them they had a tumor on their uterus."

"You think so?" Gretchen asked. "You think it's better being lied to, and not knowing what's really going on with your body?"

"What difference does it make? I would feel less like a monster. I mean, it's better than people knowing I had testicles."

Gretchen looked confused. "Um, how would anyone ever know that?"

I glanced around. The tables next to us were crowded with kids. Was mine really a story for a family restaurant? I swallowed. "I can tell you the whole story later. But, long story short, my entire high school found out."

I'd gotten used to seeing disgust on people's faces. Anger, too, and pity. But in Gretchen's face all I saw were shock and understanding.

"Fuck me," she said.

"Exactly," I said.

"Do you have a boyfriend?" I asked Gretchen. "He must

know because he read the article, right?"

"I don't have a boyfriend." She dipped a mozzarella stick into the marinara sauce and took a bite, her mouth forming a secret smile as she chewed. "But I do have a girlfriend, Julia."

"Oh," was all I said, which sounded kind of lame, but I'd never met a lesbian before. At least not one who was open about it. "I'm sorry I assumed you were straight." Then I did that thing where you go back over your conversation to see if you said anything offensive.

"It's okay," Gretchen said easily. "I get it all the time."

Before I had the chance to filter myself, I blurted, "How long have you known that you were gay? Is it something that only happened after you learned about the AIS?"

"Good lord. Are you afraid that having AIS means that you're a lesbian?"

"Not really," I said, embarrassed. "But sometimes it sounds easier. Like, girls would be more likely to understand. Most guys would probably freak out, knowing about the boy parts."

"Good luck *deciding* to be lesbian," Gretchen said. "And let me tell you, some of the most insensitive people I know are women."

"I know," I said, thinking of Vee. "It just sucks always having to wonder what other people see when they look at me. Don't you ever just want to be normal?"

"Well, yeah, I used to tell my mom that all the time. But whenever I did, she always asked me the same question: 'Do you know what another word for normal is?'" Gretchen reached out for another mozzarella stick and ate it while I racked my brain for synonyms.

I was horrible at this game. The only word I could come up with was *typical.*

"That's not the one my mom always told me," she said.

"Then what was?" I asked impatiently.

Gretchen picked up her glass of water and looked into it. Her lips formed a perfect kiss around the straw as she took a sip.

"Average," she said.

After we paid our bill, we drove over to a half-deserted park and I told her my story.

She was a good listener. The only time she reacted negatively was when I told her about my gonadectomy.

"Wait, you called the urologist asking for surgery?" she asked. "And she let you go through with it without making you see a psychiatrist first?"

"I wanted it."

"But you were still wigging out over your diagnosis. That is so *not* the best time to go ahead with something like that."

"I know, that's what she said too, but I needed them out." I stopped for a second. "Wait a minute. Does that mean you still have them?"

"Have what?" Gretchen asked, smirking.

I blushed, and gestured toward my groin. "You know."

"Oh," she said loudly. "You mean my *testicles*?"

I couldn't help myself. I looked around to see if anyone had noticed, but the nearest dog walker was several hundred feet away.

"Yes," Gretchen said firmly. "I still have my testicles."

"How can you stand it?"

"What is there to stand? Whatever higher being you believe in made me what I am. I heart my gonads." She laughed. "But remember, I had years to come to terms with my AIS. You had to deal with other people's reactions to your diagnosis before you really had time to process it yourself."

We were sitting on a bench deep in the park, next to a pair of empty tennis courts with their nets taken down. A few joggers ran by, then a couple who were walking their German shepherd. They strode by arm in arm, and you could see the air fill with little clouds from their conversation.

"How long did it take you to . . . process it all?" I asked.

"I mean, years. Maybe I still haven't."

"You outed yourself to all the readers of *Seventeen* magazine!"

"That was part of processing it, you know? Coming out on my own terms. Plus, hiding who I was had started to suck my soul."

Hiding who we were sounded like a luxury. "Do you still think of yourself as a girl?"

"Most of us with AIS do, though some identify themselves as 'intersex women.'"

That's what Dr. Cheng had said, and it'd driven me crazy trying to parse out what it meant. "But what does that *mean*, to 'identify' as a girl? Just because you *feel* like you're a girl doesn't mean that you really *are*."

Gretchen cocked her head. "Some people would disagree with you about that. Gender is totally a social construct."

"That's right, you told me," I said. "Women's studies minor."

She laughed. "Guilty as charged. It's all true, though. The biggest difference between boys and girls is how people treat them—what color parents think their kids should wear, and what kind of activities they sign their kids up for."

I thought about the pink estrogen pills as Gretchen went on. "Screw that gender essentialism bullshit. Men have as much of a right to care about clothes as women. Girls can like sports and cars and guns too. So why does it even matter if you identify as a girl, a boy, or as neither?"

"It matters because we live in the real world," I said with a heat that surprised me. "I don't want to be some poster child. I just want to get through high school in one piece, graduate from college, and have a family."

"With a boy?" Gretchen interrupted.

"Yes, with a boy," I said painfully. "And if that makes me repulsively"—I searched for the word that I'd heard one day on an episode of *Dr. Phil*—"heteronormative to you? Well, you can suck it."

Gretchen's eyes opened wide. "That's right! Because you're a hermaphrodite, so you must have a penis!"

We both burst out laughing, and God it felt good. I couldn't remember the last time I'd had a good, old-fashioned belly laugh, the kind where you can barely breathe and your eyes start watering.

"Well," Gretchen said, "that was cathartic."

Catharsis. At the end of that first session, Dr. LaForte had used the same term. She'd said that one of the reasons I was so depressed was that I'd been bottling up my emotions. "You might find it helpful if you shifted from inward repression of your feelings to outward expression," she explained. Then she gave me a little notebook with a Monet painting on the front, and told me to start a journal. "I don't expect you to show it to me, Kristin—I just want you to get things out there—your anger, your fear, your confusion and sadness. The goal is to release your emotions in a structured manner."

So far, the book had stayed blank. But the night after I met Gretchen for the first time, I dug it out of the bottom of my book bag. I tried to write down everything I remembered from our conversation, tried to tease out the tangled web of theories and ideas and come up with something I could live by, in the real world.

One last thing that Gretchen said just before we parted ways stuck in my head:

"I'm not saying that you have to become this Übermilitant Intersex Warrior. I'm just telling you to be careful of letting other people define who—and what—you are."

They were words to live by. Yet, like so many things in life, easier said than done.

CHAPTER 30

I started running in the evenings, mapping out a new route to avoid the park, where Sam ran and sometimes played basketball. There were some woods behind my neighborhood, with a thin trail developed enough so I could keep up my pace without worrying about twisting my ankle.

It felt weird starting up a new routine. Disconcerting. At first, I experimented with the timing of my run to avoid seeing too many people, and it made my workouts seem less about the running itself and more about the path I took. The key was to leave my house at four thirty, well before rush hour, to avoid the strings of cars and after-work dog walkers. Evening patterns weren't as predictable as mornings, though, and it kind of drove me crazy. Then, one day I bumped into Darren.

I had just entered the woods and was so focused on the ground that he was almost past me before I heard him shout my name. I could tell he was near the end of his loop because he had that slump-shouldered gassed look, but he slowed to a walk when I raised my hand at him.

Usually when I pass people I know while I'm in the middle of a workout, I'm a nod-and-wave person. Especially when I've just started my run. But when someone stops for you, the polite thing to do is to chat for a while, and so I did. The motto on his running tee made me grin: I'M TOO XC FOR THIS SHIRT.

"Hey. You always run here?" Darren asked, slightly breathless. "Haven't seen you before."

"Just trying out something new."

"Which path are you taking?"

"There's more than one?" I asked.

"Yeah, this is the perimeter trail. Good for speed. But there's an offshoot that takes you up some hills."

"Really? Where?" Short hills were good for strength. Perfect for hurdlers.

"There's a fork about four hundred yards down. Here, I'll show you." Darren turned around and started to jog back into the forest. I almost protested that he was tired at the end of a run, but I knew no cross-country runner worth his salt would ever complain about having to go an extra mile. So I followed.

It felt bizarre running with a boy other than Sam. We weren't close to being in sync; Darren was so tall his stride was almost a foot longer than mine. The trail was barely wide enough for the two of us, and I had to duck a lot of branches and steer clear of bushes. At one point I stumbled as my sneaker caught on an enormous root, and Darren shot out his hand to steady me. I flung out my arms for balance, and caught on to his forearm, feeling his sinewy muscles tense as he braced my fall.

Our eyes met. His were a shifting hazel, dark and deep. I felt a flicker in my chest, and let go of his arm, taking a long breath before I resumed my run. Darren let me run a little bit in front of him, and I noticed him cutting back his stride to match my post-surgery pace.

By the time we reached the top of the hill, the sun was just above the tree line. I climbed on a rock at a little overhang and looked south over our town: The manicured sea of the golf course. The streetlights lining the way downtown. The criss-crossing roads that were already starting to crawl with normal people living out their happy, average lives.

Darren clambered up beside me. "It gives you some per-spective, doesn't it? To look out there, see thousands of houses full of thousands of people, and know that there are a thousand more cities out there with just as many people. I started writing my application essays, you know, and sometimes I get freaked out: What makes me different from every other schmuck out there who wants to get into their dream school?"

"You're, like, in the top five in our class."

Darren shook his head. "Oh, I know I'll probably get in somewhere good. But sometimes I remember that, in the grand scheme of things, I'm just a little speck of dust in the universe."

"My aunt Carla always says that every person is a unique snowflake."

"Yeah. And let's hope colleges think that this snowflake is more unique than others."

I stopped myself from reminding him that sometimes being able to differentiate yourself wasn't what it was cracked up to be.

The sun dipped below the trees. "It's getting dark," Darren said, sliding off the rock. He put his hand out to help me down, and even though I didn't need his help, I took it. The air was chilly, so his hand was cool, but his grip was strong.

Dr. LaForte had told me to ask myself, "Who am I?" The night before my appointment with her, I sat in my room with my Monet book, staring at a blank page.

Who *was* I? I played so many roles: daughter, friend, babysitter, runner, girlfriend.

I'd been proud when I was elected team captain, but now I wondered who my teammates had thought they'd voted for. And who my classmates had thought they'd elected Homecoming Queen.

Sam had said that I was someone who smiled at people in the hallways. In my birthday card just a month ago, Vee had thanked me for always being there to listen. My junior yearbook had been full of notes using words like *nice* and *sweet*.

But if that was who I was, how had people turned on me so quickly? Take away the people around me, and who was I? Just another smiling face? There had to be more.

In the margins of my Monet book I doodled a set of ten hurdles, and drew a finishing tape at the bottom of the page. Freshman year before tryouts, Coach Auerbach had introduced all the newbies to the different track-and-field events. She told us that each discipline had its own personality. Sprinters were the divas of track, long-distance runners were the patient workhorses, throwers were the loose cannons, and jumpers were the free spirits.

Hurdlers were a breed of their own.

When Coach Auerbach talked about the hurdles, she cautioned us that the event wasn't for the faint of heart. "Hurdling has the steepest learning curve, and probably the most painful. It's all about technique, so there's a ton of practice involved. A lot of hitting your knees and face-planting. They say that hurdlers need three things: speed, flexibility, and courage."

Within the first day of learning how to hurdle, I knew she was right to warn us. I looked at my sprinter friends and was totally jealous of how easy they seemed to have it. But at the same time, I loved being hard-core. That's who I was: a hurdler. And hurdlers were never afraid to fall.

Dr. LaForte was pleased with my homework.

"So, Kristin. Here's the million-dollar question: Have any

of these character traits been impacted by your AIS?"

"No." It was such an obvious leading question that I almost rolled my eyes.

"I ask you this because I want to show you that nothing changed when that doctor told you your diagnosis."

"*Everything* changed," I insisted. "Even though I kept on telling Sam and Vee and all the others that I was the same, everything was different."

Dr. LaForte shook her head. "The world around you may have shifted, seen you in a different light. But the *Mona Lisa* is a masterpiece whether it's in a pitch-black room, under a strobe light, or in the sun."

When I didn't say anything, she reached over sideways to her desk and pulled out a manila envelope. "You may remember that you allowed me access to your school records." It must've been on one of the dozens of release forms that my dad and I had filled out the first day.

"Ms. Diaz's file had several of your recommendations in it. I won't tell you who wrote them, but I will read a couple of excerpts to you. Because the person described in these pages is still there inside of you: 'Kristin Lattimer is a young lady of great character. Hardworking, kind, and unfailingly polite, she is respected by students and faculty alike.'"

"It sounds like a form letter." I grimaced. Of course I had been kind. It was easy to be kind when you were popular, when everyone loved you.

But Dr. LaForte went on. "Here's another one. 'What sets Kristin apart from my other students is her leadership. She obviously leads by example while she competes, but she also takes an active role in nurturing underclassmen. She always has their back and is always looking outward and thinking of others.'"

That was obviously Coach Auerbach. Like she was an objective observer. "So what?"

At first Dr. LaForte didn't say anything. She just looked at me, and I looked away after a second, wondering how I had managed to get her to hate me, too.

"Do you think these people were lying, Kristin?" Dr. LaForte asked gently.

I chewed at the cuticles on my left index finger. "No," I said reluctantly, "they weren't lying. They're just . . ." I didn't know how to say what I wanted to say. I'd fooled them the way I'd fooled my pediatrician. I was a fraud. "They're just seeing what they want to see."

"Have you ever heard the phrase 'Perception is reality,' Kristin?"

"So," I said bitterly, "you're saying that if people perceive me as the Homecoming Hermaphrodite, that's what I am?"

"Not exactly. The idea that perception is reality is flawed on many levels, not the least because it doesn't take into consideration causal effects and self-fulfilling prophecies. More often than not, the child who is labeled as stupid fails because he doesn't *think* that he's smart enough. But more importantly, perhaps, it doesn't make clear that the opposite is also true: reality shapes perception as well. Sometimes the change is slow, a day-by-day evolution." She paused and met my gaze.

"Or, as you know, sometimes perception can change in an instant."

CHAPTER 31

"You should create a new Facebook profile," Gretchen said. She'd been calling me a couple of times a week to check in. It kind of felt weird, like she was my AA sponsor or something. But it was also nice, like I had a big sister. "There's an AIS private group. Don't even bother telling anyone in your high school about the new account, and when you go to college you can use the new one instead."

"I've got to delete my old profile. Or at least stop getting all those stupid notifications." Maybe then I'd start emailing again.

"Make sure you save all the photos and messages you want first."

"It's not worth the hassle," I said.

"Don't be ridiculous. You can't just delete your whole life." She offered to use my username and password to download my photos to her computer, and when I remembered how I'd been tagged in some old pictures that my cousins in California had posted of my mom, I finally said yes.

"Hey," she said after she'd logged in. "You have some really nice messages here."

"What?"

"One from a girl named Rashonda. She says she misses you and hopes you come back soon."

"Huh. It must be Rashonda Glenn." Not that I knew any other Rashondas, but I remembered the look on her face when she saw me crying in Coach Auerbach's office. Though, when I thought about it, shocked disgust looked pretty similar to shocked embarrassment.

"Was it a private message, or did she post it on my wall?" I asked.

"It was a PM."

So she didn't have the guts to say it in public, I thought.

"But you have a sweet wall post from Tamara Leffard: 'Thinking of you this holiday season. I hope to see you next year.'"

Tamara was a student teacher, an adult. She didn't count.

"Then there's another message from a girl named Peggy Shah. She says, 'Miss you, lab partner. Get well soon!'"

Peggy was a good egg. Not popular, but kind. I thought about her and Rashonda, and Ms. Diaz and Ms. Leffard. Darren and Jessica. Faith and Coach Auerbach. Were eight people enough to go back to school for? If not, what number was? Twenty? Sixty? A hundred?

I was three weeks into my six-week leave of absence, and despite Dr. LaForte's best efforts I didn't feel any closer to going back. My dad still thought that to get my scholarship, I had to officially graduate. He'd mentioned it the other day, when he told my tutor that we'd probably only need him for a few more weeks.

"But Ms. Diaz said that we might be able to file for an extension," I'd told him.

"Honey, you can't hide here at home forever."

"No, just until college," I'd said. My dad had sighed.

Gretchen got bored with scrolling through my wall. "Okay, I'm downloading your pics now." I heard a bunch of mouse clicks on her end of the line. "You should join me and my friends some night. Here in Syracuse."

"Really?" I'd almost forgotten what it was like to hang out, and have the biggest stress in your life be what kind of shoes you were going to wear.

"Sure. You need to get out."

But I *had* gone out. I told Gretchen about Josh.

"So what happened after? Did you get his number?"

"Well, he asked for mine."

"Did he call?"

"He texted. But I didn't exactly encourage him."

Gretchen didn't seem to judge. "You know, a lot of girls

have reactionary hookups after their diagnosis. It's a way to prove their femininity. Not that I can relate. The one time I ever let a guy stick himself in me, it didn't make me feel like a woman. It made me feel like I was an electrical socket."

I laughed, and Gretchen went on. "No, seriously. You know when I feel the most feminine? When I'm with Julia."

We were both silent for a minute. And I wondered for the first time whether "feeling feminine" just meant feeling good in your own skin.

"Seriously, come out with me sometime. Do you like The Concept?"

That was the band I'd listened to in Darren's Dungeon. "Yeah, they're great," I said.

"My friends and I are going to see them later this month, a week or two before Christmas. Julia's coming, and a bunch of other people. You can crash at my house if you're worried about driving home."

"Umm . . ."

"I know you're trying to come up with a reason not to. But let me tell you from personal experience: it's exhausting to always have to come up with new excuses. Trust me, you're not going to be able to think of one that sticks."

I believed her. I penciled the date into my calendar, otherwise empty except for doctor's appointments. Then, after Gretchen had hung up, I did something more daring: I traced over it in pen.

CHAPTER 32

The next day, my caller ID brought up an unfamiliar number. A few weeks earlier, maybe I would've let it go to voice mail. But that day, I took a deep breath and answered. It was Darren, asking for a ride to the clinic. Jessica would be missing the next few weeks because she was the lead in *Much Ado About Nothing*.

"I'd drive myself," he said apologetically, "but we only have one car and Tuesdays are my sister's Zumba class. I'd probably end up as body parts in our deep freezer if she can't go. It's her only form of relaxation since Leighton was born, and my mom's looking forward to some quality grandma time." Darren's sister Wendy had gotten pregnant right before graduating.

"Bet your mom's an amazing grandmother."

"Let's just say, if *Iron Chef* ever held a gourmet puree competition, she'd win hands down."

"Should I pick you up at your house?"

"It's in the wrong direction. It's easier to pick me up from school. Say, three o'clock in the east lot?"

I almost said no. I hadn't been on campus in weeks, and the east lot was the parking area closest to the football field. The team had made the playoffs, so they'd still be practicing. But as my mind contorted, sorting through different options and twisting through a maze of ways to explain to Darren why I wanted to pick him up at a different time and place, I realized that Gretchen had been right. Making excuses took way too much energy. So I said, "Three o'clock. East lot. I'll be there."

Before I picked Darren up, I emptied my car of all my old drugstore receipts and put up a new air freshener. Not that guys usually cared about things like that, but what did I know? I'd never driven a boy around before. Whenever we went anywhere, Sam would pick me up in his Scion so I wouldn't have to drive my twelve-year-old Honda Civic, which had been my mom's.

When I pulled into school, I breathed easier when I saw that the football team was safely assembled on the far side of the field, so far away they looked like little blots of orange and blue. The parking lot had pretty much cleared out, too, and Darren sat alone on one of the benches with a book and a pad of sticky notes.

"Sorry about the sardine-can car," I said as he squeezed in. Even with the passenger seat pushed back all the way, Darren's knees were almost up to his chin.

"Hey, I'm just glad that I didn't have to hitchhike my way to the clinic. I would've had to borrow my sister's rape whistle."

"Yeah, doesn't she need it for her Zumba class?"

Darren snorted. It was lovely to make someone laugh.

I turned the radio on as I navigated through town. "You care what we listen to?"

"Anything, as long as it's not by someone who rose to fame on a Disney Channel show."

"Please." I gave him the stink eye. "Give me *some* credit."

"No judgment. I'm just giving you my trigger warnings, that's all."

I couldn't remember the last time I'd been relaxed enough with a person to actually banter. Even conversations with Faith were awkward—she skirted the big issues like they were land mines, and I fell all over myself to not seem like a pathetic depressive.

With Darren, though, it was as if the undercurrent of our past history as almost siblings smoothed everything over. Or maybe it was just that I knew that he carried as much baggage as I did. The funny thing was, because our families had spent so much time together, I knew stuff like Darren's favorite soda (Dr Pepper) and way to eat eggs (poached, with A.1. sauce), but I didn't know a lot of nonsuperficial stuff, like where he really wanted to go to college (Columbia).

"Wow, Ivy League," I said.

"It all depends on whether I get good financial aid. Though my dad said he'd help."

"How's he doing, anyway?"

"He's fine," Darren said in that automatic tone that you used when people asked questions you didn't really want to answer. I knew that tone well.

"My dad is starting to go back to his bachelor ways," I said, to fill up the space in our conversation. "He hasn't seen anyone practically since your mom. Every weekend night is a date with the La-Z-Boy. If he's lucky, he'll go out for a poker night with his buddies, but lately he hasn't even been doing that. I don't know what he's going to do when I go to college. Start eating frozen dinners every night, probably."

"Hey, my mom has a healthy-frozen-dinner service."

"Yes, better that than condemn him to Aunt Carla's casseroles."

There was only so much you could say about casseroles, and Darren changed the subject. "So, you've been running again?"

"Yeah. I liked your trail. Is that your usual run?"

"Yup. Every day except Wednesdays."

"What's on Wednesday?"

Darren grimaced. "Promise you won't judge?"

"Why would I judge?" I asked innocently.

"Okay, now I *know* I'm not going to tell you."

"Come on!" I laughed. "What could be that bad?"

He turned and raised his eyebrows. Then he coughed in his hand while saying, "Science Olympiad."

I smiled, more at his embarrassment than anything else. "That's nothing to be ashamed of."

"Yeah, because it's rated ten out of ten on the high school coolness scale."

"Come on, what girl can resist an Olympian?"

"Actually, that *is* where I met Becky."

"See? Smart is sexy." I was happy for him. Really, I was. But I couldn't help feeling a little bit sorry for myself, too. Being single sucked when everyone around you was pairing up like it was Noah's ark.

Later, when we were in the clinic break room eating our dinner, Lisa, the nurse's aide, poked her head in.

"Mikey's here for his infusion," she said.

Darren stuffed down the remaining half of his sandwich, grunted an apology in my direction, and scrambled out. I looked at Lisa. She grinned. "When you're done eating, go to the procedure room to check out Mikey's setup."

It didn't take me long to finish my leftover lasagna. About halfway to the procedure room, a rat-a-tat that sounded like a machine gun filtered down the hall. Seconds later I heard a few explosions, and a boy's voice shouting, "No! Bring your guys in from the south!"

When I pushed open the door to the procedure room, I saw a skinny, bald African-American kid wearing black plastic glasses and an I ♥ BOOBIES T-shirt sitting in the infusion chair. He had one of the clinic laptops sitting on a metal instrument stand and was clicking away at his mouse and keyboard so vigorously I was afraid he'd pull the IV right out of his arm.

Darren sat across from him pounding away at his own laptop. "Don't worry, I've got reinforcements. But you need to get those upgrades soon!"

"Nice way to fulfill your community service requirement," I deadpanned.

Darren didn't bother looking up, but raised his middle finger behind his back so Mikey wouldn't see it. "It's only a sixty-minute infusion. I consider it back pay for all the lunches I've worked through."

I craned my neck to peek over his shoulder. "StarCraft Two, huh?"

At that, Darren froze for a second and looked at me. I heard Mikey scream as one of his buildings blew up. "What, you know how to play?"

"One of the kids I babysat for was obsessed with it." I shrugged. "I know the basics." I squinted at his screen. "Enough to know that you need some Vespene gas *stat*."

"Crap!"

On the ride home, Darren told me that Mikey had been coming in for infusions every three weeks for the past two months. "They're trying to treat his bone cancer with chemo before surgery. Hopefully they won't need to amputate his leg."

If I hadn't been driving, I would have closed my eyes. Instead, I just stared ahead, and counted the dotted lines on the highway median to keep my shit together. As awful as chemo had been for a woman with a ten-year-old child, how horrible must it be when it's the ten-year-old who's sick?

"Mikey's mom can't afford a computer, so I try to game with him as often as I can."

"The clinic could be a lot better for kids," I said. "Is there any budget to stock the waiting room? They should get a subscription to *Highlights*." I had loved those when I went to appointments with my mom.

Darren shook his head. "The clinic barely even has a budget for basic medical stuff. Most of the supplies are donated, which is why there are, like, five different brands of exam gloves and none of them ever fit properly. That's one of the awesome things Jessica's doing—she's organizing a supply drive through the local hospitals."

At the admiration in Darren's voice, I felt a pang of jealousy. It surprised me, because I wasn't normally the kind of person who did things to impress other people. My mom had drilled it into me that doing the right thing was its own reward. But after I dropped Darren off, I spent most of the ride home trying to figure out why his opinion of me suddenly mattered so much. I respected how smart he was, for sure, and I couldn't imagine a more stand-up guy. But after our parents broke up, I never went beyond the occasional small talk when I ran into him. It wasn't like it was normal to hang out with the son of your dad's ex-girlfriend, right?

It was a new thing, having to go out of my way to make friends. Before, they'd just fall into my life, whether through Vee and Faith, or track. The last time I'd had to work to make friends was probably before my mom died, when I first started going to Sunday school. I dreaded the hour after the service, because the three other girls my age all went to school on the same bus and, as Aunt Carla would put it, were thick as thieves. It wasn't that they were mean to me—they just weren't exactly inclusive. When I mentioned it to my mom, she told me I should try to compliment their clothes, or invite them to a movie, or somehow impress them with a joke. In the end, after a couple of variations on "Wow, what a cute dress," I gave up.

But now? I wanted to impress Darren.

Just a few blocks away from home, I took a little detour and went to Colonial Plaza. I wormed my way through the mostly empty lot, and parked by the used bookstore.

"We're closing in fifteen minutes," barked the crusty old owner when I walked in. "No sales after eight p.m."

"I'll be quick," I assured him. And I was. I made a bee-line back to the children's book section and picked up a set of Eric Carle books, an old copy of *The Snowy Day*, and a few Dr. Seuss classics. I almost whooped for joy when I found a Spanish translation of *Oh, the Places You'll Go!*

The magazine section consisted of four milk crates filled

to the rim with a hodgepodge of titles, but eventually I found a dozen copies of *Highlights* that had barely been touched, a bargain at ten cents apiece. I added a couple of copies of *Seventeen* for the older girls.

When I got home, I crawled up into our attic and brought out the heavy artillery. The summer before sophomore year, when I had started babysitting hard-core, I'd found a big rolling suitcase from Goodwill and filled it with coloring books, stickers, Legos, and the occasional box of fruit snacks in case of emergency. I added in the books and magazines I'd gotten.

It seemed like a small offering, when I thought about the big-picture perspective that Darren had talked about that day we'd run up to the top of the hill. But then I thought of a different perspective—that of a ten-year-old girl sitting in a doctor's office, waiting for her mother to get called in. And I remembered how from that point of view, the right magazine or a good book was as large as the world.

CHAPTER 33

The next Monday I timed my run perfectly and reached the woods just as Darren was jogging in.

His face lit up when he saw me, and he pulled his earbuds out. "You heading in?"

I nodded, trying to play it cool.

We fell into step. Under the canopy of trees, it was dark and chilly, and it was comforting to have someone beside me, to have someone else's footsteps echoing my own.

"Were you listening to The Concept?" I gestured toward his iPod.

"Nah, they're not really running music, you know? Too slow, too many tempo changes."

I shook my head. "I never really listen to music when I'm working out." It was too hard to set my pace when I did—I always wanted to match my stride to whatever song was playing.

And besides, I never used to run alone. "What *is* good to run to, then?"

"Depends. Did you know there are websites out there that tell you how many beats per minute there are to a given song? So you can choose what to listen to based on how fast you want to go."

Surprisingly, I didn't.

"Lemme show you," Darren said, flicking through his iPod. "We're on pace for what? A ten-minute mile? I've got a playlist for that. Here." He stopped for a second and unwrapped his earbuds, handing me the left one. I slipped it in and he started the song, a poppy, happy tune that we fell into step with right away. Tethered by his earbuds, we ran close—almost as if we were dancing our way through a three-legged race.

It felt both comfortable and slightly disconcerting. I was aware of Darren's every breath, of the moments when he reached up to wipe sweat from his forehead. Now and then he'd shake his head to get an unruly brown curl out of his eyes, or pull out his CamelBak to take a sip, and it was as if his headphones amplified not just the music, but how attuned I was to his every movement.

The playlist brought us to the top of the overlook, where we stopped for a breather. I took out the earbud and dropped it into Darren's open hand, suddenly shy. Then I walked up to the view point and did a couple of quad stretches, turning back to watch Darren from a distance. Even though the physical thing linking us was gone, some part of our bodies' understanding remained. I knew that, from that point on, I would never have a problem recognizing him from a distance.

We ran back down, and when it was time to part ways I hesitated.

"See you on Tuesday, then? East lot?"

"Yeah," said Darren. He fiddled with his headphones for a bit before tilting his head back toward the woods. "So, anyway. If you end up running tomorrow, or Thursday, just send me a text. Maybe I can find something a bit more up-tempo for you. Jeez, did you even break a sweat?"

"You're too sweet," I said, looking down as I scuffed the curb with my sneaker.

I ran home wearing a silly little grin.

The good feelings lasted until I checked my email, and found a message from Coach Auerbach. My dad had forwarded her the relevant NCAA guidelines, and she'd been able to convince the school board to reinstate me to the team. Would I like to come to practice starting tomorrow?

I was coming off a great run. I'd started taking my hormones and seeing a therapist. And still I felt blank, like the feeling you get in your leg after sitting on it the wrong way, just before the pins-and-needles pain comes rushing in with your circulation. But I didn't delete her email, either.

Would I like to go to practice tomorrow? Even now, my gut said no.

I replied back, and lied. I told her that Dr. Cheng hadn't wanted me to do any vigorous physical activity for ten weeks.

Maybe in a month I'd be ready.

I was *almost* there.

CHAPTER 34

On Tuesday, I got to the east lot early, well before the after-school activities started to let out. Despite everything, I couldn't help staring out at the football field once the blue and orange dots began to emerge. Usually, I could spot Sam from a mile away, but that day I couldn't pinpoint anyone with his height and running stride. Was he injured, or in detention? Could he have quit the team? I thought about logging onto Facebook to see if he'd posted any updates, and then I remembered that he'd blocked me, and I felt that old sickening feeling, like someone had stomped on my heart.

My phone alarm went off at four, and I looked for Darren among the clusters of kids scattered across the sidewalk. With his height, I spotted him in no time, leaning over a slim girl almost a foot shorter than him that I recognized as Becky Riley. He faced me, so I could see his animated motions, and his surprising smile.

I found it *surprising* because I'd always thought of Darren as a serious guy. He had a sense of humor, yes, but most of the time he'd deadpan, or if he was really pleased with a joke, he'd smirk. The smile he gave Becky was a genuine, 24-karat grin, unironic, unfettered by insecurity, and true. It was the kind of smile that transformed a perfectly ordinary, likable boy into a boy a girl could *like.*

I felt an unexpected twinge in my chest. I rolled down the window of my car, which was suddenly way too stuffy.

Eventually, Darren peeked at his watch and scanned the row of cars until he found mine. He said something to Becky, who glanced in my direction. I caught a glimpse of her heart-shaped face, and her long black hair. A smile lingered on her lips, a reflection of Darren's own.

Darren leaned over for a kiss, and I looked away for a second. But I couldn't keep myself from looking back; they were cute together. A Science Olympiad power couple. Good for him. Good for her.

I pulled out my copy of *Beloved* and pretended to be surprised when Darren finally opened the door to my car.

"Sorry, I lost track of time," he said.

"Oh, I was a little late too," I said, not knowing why I lied.

At the clinic, Darren did a double take when I popped the

trunk to unload my suitcase.

"You going somewhere afterward?" he asked.

"It's my donation to the clinic." I went to lift the suitcase.

"What? Cool. Let me help you get that thing out," he insisted, reaching in at the same time.

My hand brushed his wrist.

He yanked his hand away as if I'd scorched him.

I was unprepared for the flush in my face, for the stab of pain right over my solar plexus. Darren didn't look at me. "Sorry," he mumbled. "I know you can take care of yourself."

"Sure can," I joked, trying to mask how rattled I felt. "I can bench-press ninety-eight pounds."

We didn't say much else as I rolled my suitcase into the clinic. Darren walked an arm's length away from me, and checked his phone the entire way. Probably texting Becky.

When Darren peeled off to go to the Dungeon, I took a deep breath. I reminded myself that volunteering at the health clinic wasn't about me and Darren. It was about the patients and their families. I went back to the doctor's office to show Dr. Johnson what I had brought.

"Is it okay for me to set up a little kids' play area in the waiting room?" I asked.

Her face lit up as I showed her my setup. "That'd be brilliant, Kristin. I'll bet the parents would love that."

So I went back to the waiting room and climbed up to one

of the light fixtures. I used an old sheet and some string to make a play tent. Underneath, I laid out a second sheet with the Legos and a DVD player from the Stone Age. I set up the craft supplies on one of the folding chairs, and scattered the *Highlights* and *Seventeen*s throughout the waiting room.

By then, I had an audience. Four little kids couldn't take their eyes off of me, though they dutifully stayed sitting under the watchful stare of their mother. One of the girls, bolder than the rest, picked up a magazine, but looked longingly at the pompoms and googly eyes on the folding chair every few minutes.

They reminded me of myself. So polite. Conditioned not to put anyone out.

I looked at the mom. "Is it okay if they come to play?" She'd barely nodded before they ran over. The younger boys cranked up the DVD player right away.

"What's your name?" I asked the bold girl, who hovered over the craft area.

A pair of bright brown eyes peered up at me from under a mop of dark curls. "My name's Lucinda. It's spelled L-U-C-I-N-D-A," she recited.

"Wow, Lucinda. You are a terrific speller. Do you want to do coloring, painting, or puppets?"

"Puppets, please."

We were hard at work on a Popsicle-stick family when I

felt eyes on me. I looked up, and saw Darren jerk his head back toward the charts in his hand. I could see the tips of his ears coloring pink as he grimaced.

I knew that look.

My face burned. Was he thinking of my wrongness? Breaking down the width of my shoulders and the narrowness of my hips, comparing them to Becky's willowy perfection? Or was he imagining that my boobs weren't real? Tears sprang up unbidden.

I drew deeper into the play tent as Darren carried the charts back to the Dungeon. I wiped my hand across my eyes and dried it on the sheet, and turned back to Lucinda.

"Tell me again what you wanted to make? A girl puppet or a boy puppet?"

"Oh, please please please a girl puppet."

"What color should her hair be?"

"Brown, like yours," she said with utter certainty. "With green eyes."

My eyes misted again as I helped Lucinda cut some yarn, and she pasted it in an unruly pile above two green sequin eyes. She frowned, and picked at the eyes.

"It doesn't look right," she said.

"Are you kidding? I have brown hair and green eyes. It's perfect."

"Okay," she said doubtfully. Then she smiled up at me,

sunlight and apples. "It's for you!"

"Thank you, sweetie." I laid the puppet gently onto another folding chair. I blinked, and forced a smile in return. "Now let's make one for you."

CHAPTER 35

"Wait until you get to college and meet some real boys," Gretchen told me a couple of days later.

"Yeah, about that." I paused. "I've actually been thinking about taking a year off."

"What?"

"To keep my scholarship, I have to go back to school, which I'm not sure if I want to do in the first place. But even if I do end up at State, there are ten people from my class going there, too. It'll be like I've never left."

"Are you fucking kidding me?"

"Taking a year off would be perfect—I could reapply to some places that are farther away. I don't have to run Division One, I've decided that. And I can definitely get a Division Two scholarship. Some of the smaller schools, maybe they'd be fun. Be a big fish in a little pond. There are thousands of colleges—"

"Kristin, listen to me." Gretchen cut off my babbling. "You can't hide from your diagnosis for the rest of your life."

I crumpled up the piece of paper I was doodling on and sighed. "I know. But don't blame me for trying?"

"Whatever. You're still coming with us to Club Eternal a week from Saturday, right? Because if you don't show up, I will personally hunt you down and drag your ass out."

"Fine," I said, but only because the club was in Syracuse, and I knew Gretchen probably would resort to bodily harm.

"Good. And the next thing you need to do is come with me to one of the national AIS-DSD meetings," Gretchen said. "You'd be surprised at how normal and well-adjusted people are, once they settle into their diagnosis."

I snorted. She made it sound like getting used to having AIS was like moving into a new apartment.

"Sure, everyone has issues at first," she said. "People fall apart. Some people start drinking. One woman did heroin for a little while after she was diagnosed. But that's what those meetings are for. You realize that no matter what they've gone through, people can heal, as long as they have someone to show them the way.

"The meetings are like a big reunion, with lots of food and mingling. In the evening there's drinking. There was this woman one night who'd had a couple of glasses of wine. She got up on a cocktail table and yelled, 'I am intersex—hear me roar!'"

Gretchen laughed, but I shuddered. How comfortable would someone have to be with herself to do that in front of strangers?

"Was she old?" I asked.

"Dunno—maybe in her forties?"

"So I've got twenty years to get used to it."

"Now that's just crazy talk. There's a teenage support group too. Not just in the US. I'm sending you a link to some of the stories on the UK website. Add that to your homework list. Required reading, due next weekend."

I groaned. "What, am I going to have to write a book report?"

"No, but class participation counts."

CHAPTER 36

Now that the play was over, Jessica and Darren resumed their normal carpool routine, though they offered to have me join them.

"No, it doesn't make sense," I said, back to excuses. "I've always got doctors' appointments and things to rush to afterward. Thanks, though."

The clinic had been thoroughly Christmasfied, though the decorations were low on the Santa-and-elf scale, being more heavily weighted toward Nativity scenes and lambs.

"Can't they diversify a little bit and put up some Hanukkah stuff?" Jessica complained at lunch.

"Why do you care? You're as Jewish as the Dalai Lama," said Darren.

"It's the principle of it. Don't impose your religion on other people."

"So let me get this straight." Darren leaned back in his chair. "You're saying that if I got your sister a present for Christmas, I'd be imposing my religion on her? That'd save me a mint."

"Don't be an asshole. By the way, Becky's not into diamonds. She's more of a sapphire girl."

"Yeah, I'll keep that in mind if I win the lottery," Darren muttered.

The tips of his ears turned pink. I couldn't tell if he felt embarrassed talking about Becky, or about money. Maybe both. Jessica's eyes flicked over to me.

All of a sudden I became acutely aware of being an intruder, a last-minute interloper into *their* clinic. I didn't want to be a doctor, or a nurse. I was just looking for another place to hide. After one last bite of my turkey sandwich, I packed up.

As I got up to leave, Jessica looked at her watch. "We've got another twenty minutes for lunch."

"I'm just running to the bathroom," I said. And I did go to the restroom, but instead of going into a stall I stood at the sink and looked at myself. I stared at my Adam's apple. My jawline. I held up my wrist and examined the bone structure. I wondered if Caster Semenya ever got questioned for using women's restrooms.

Staff filtered in for the end-of-lunch rush, and I left. Instead of going back to the break room, I went to the waiting area, which was just starting to fill up. No older kids yet, just a baby in a car seat. So I picked up a bit. From inside the play tent

I watched for a pair of Converses. Only after I saw them go by and exit into the hallway did I head back to the exam rooms to help with turnover.

I did a quick calculation on the way there. I'd worked the clinic two full Saturdays, and five weekday nights. That gave me almost thirty of the sixty hours I needed for my community service requirement. If I just pushed through and volunteered like crazy during the holidays, when Jessica and Darren were less likely to be there anyway, I would fulfill my requirement and get out of everyone's hair.

I grabbed my coat to go home as soon as Dr. Johnson saw her last patient. Jessica, who was helping Dr. Johnson finish up her paperwork, waved me down as I went by.

"Hey, Kristin. A bunch of us are going to see the new James Bond movie and maybe hang out afterward. Quincy. Darren and my sister, some other people too. Wanna come?"

It was nice of her, but every bone in my body screamed no. I wasn't ready for something that public. And if I was perfectly honest with myself, I would rather eat iron filings than spend a night watching Darren Kowalski making out in the back row of a movie theater with his adorable girlfriend.

"Sorry, but I've got plans with my dad. Rain check?"

"'Kay." Unlike Gretchen, Jessica took no for an answer.

I trudged out in the December chill and sat for a while in my car while it warmed up. My evening stretched out in front of me like a desert, not an oasis in sight. My stomach rumbled, and I dug out an old PowerBar from my glove compartment.

The thought of having to cook dinner depressed me, so I called in some pizza. One meat lover's for my dad, one broccoli and spinach for me. You can tell something's a true comfort food when you feel better just having ordered it.

There are probably dozens of pizzerias in Utica, but Tony's Pizza had always been my mom's favorite because she had gone to high school with the owner's son. She was loyal like that, even though Tony's pies were a little more expensive and had fewer topping choices. Once she passed away, my dad and I kept ordering from Tony's because to switch to another pizzeria seemed a betrayal of her principles even greater than buying 1 percent milk instead of skim, or not going to church.

It being Saturday, the pies weren't ready when I swung by Tony's on the way home. So I stood reading the ads and business cards posted on a corkboard by the front door, marveling that Utica could support so many dog walkers and tarot-card readers. As the minutes passed, more and more people came trickling in and I moved closer to the dining room to give them space. Okay, I'll be honest—to give *me* space.

Just as I went to the counter to ask how much longer my pizza would take, a loud crash and an even louder curse burst from the dining room. Along with everyone else, I rubbernecked, and saw Rashonda Glenn sprawled on the ground in a shower of broken glass.

I knelt down to help her round up the shards.

"Shonda, you okay?" I asked, even though I knew she would be. Rashonda wasn't a hurdler, but she was a long jumper, which made her almost as tough.

"Sh . . . sugar." She grimaced. "Hey, Krissy. I'm fine. It's my paycheck that's gonna be hurting when I have to pay for these glasses. That's *if* I'm lucky and my manager didn't hear me yell the *F* word in his family restaurant."

"You could just tell him you were yelling *fork*," I offered.

"Yeah, if he buys that I'll get you a drink." She shooed me away when she heard the pickup people call my name. "Go. Your order's done. I'm fine here. Thanks, and get your butt back to the team soon."

I felt a flush of warmth, and stood up smiling.

That's when I saw Sam.

He saw me too, and his eyes darted away like he'd been burned. And I felt like I'd been scorched by his gaze as well. Was there a hint of guilt when he looked at me? Despite how much it hurt, I couldn't avert my eyes from the sight of Sam sitting at a cozy two-person table with Stephanie Peterson, head of the football boosters club. The only thing that would've been more cliché was if she were a cheerleader.

Sam mumbled something into his drink and Stephanie swiveled around in my direction, her eyebrows raised in a perfectly plucked arch. If Sam's eyes seared, then Stephanie's gaze chilled me with its detached curiosity. I could've been a zoo animal, or a fish in an aquarium—she didn't see *me*, and really only bothered staring for a few seconds before she smirked and turned back to her salad.

Rashonda stood up after picking up the worst of the glass. She took my arm gently, angled me away from Sam's table, and nudged me toward the front door. "Your pies are ready, Krissy. You know they aren't any good once they get cold."

I closed my eyes and held them shut, as if I could press the restart button on my brain, and nodded.

It shouldn't have been a shock. Sam was too hot and too popular to be single for long, even with the stigma of having done it with a freak. It still hurt, though, in the way that I suppose a phantom limb hurts. I knew that the person I loved wasn't there anymore, yet I still felt the hope for him, the memory of his touch.

The worst thing, though, was the fear that I would never be able to fill that void again.

When I got home, I thumbed through my phone for Jessica's number to see if I could take her up on her offer. My call went to voice mail, and in desperation I actually left a message. I had to. Something about the house around the holidays made me want to go out in the worst way. Maybe it had to do with how my dad played his *Home for the Holidays* CD in a constant loop. Or maybe it was the silent loneliness of the dead bulbs on our Christmas lights, which Aunt Carla insisted on hanging on our windows "to guide the angels to our house."

Either way, I had to escape.

It was too cold for a skirt, so I dug up my red pleather pants, knee-high boots, and a black top. The minute Dad came in and saw me all made up, he asked if I had plans, nodding happily when I told him yes, and handing me another twenty. "Say hi to Faith for me," he said.

I headed out to Whitesboro again, and trolled the strip looking for a club that seemed likely—not too popular, but not too empty either. I had decided on a club called Bliss and was looking for parking when I saw them, standing in line, shivering adorably in their miniskirts while they laughed, not a care in the world.

Vee and Faith.

CHAPTER 37

It was the first time I'd seen Vee in a month. The gut-punching sense of betrayal wasn't shocking, nor was the sense of loss. We'd been friends for eighteen years; of course part of me missed her still.

The anger, though, surprised me.

I am not a vengeful person. But one look at Vee, with her perky, queen-of-the-world head tilt and her careless, self-absorbed smirk, and it was all I could do to prevent myself from slamming on the gas and turning her into a very unattractive hood ornament.

Instead, I jerked into a parking space and turned the engine off. As the cold seeped into my car, I thought over my options. Much as I wanted to, I wasn't going to run her over. But I wasn't going to let myself drive away like a powerless victim, either.

I wanted answers.

How could she live with herself after ruining my life? Without even apologizing? Did she feel *anything*? I wanted her to see me. If I could make her feel a speck of guilt, disrupt her happiness for just a fraction of a second, it might be enough. I wasn't going to make a scene. If I knew that she felt sorry for what she did, for the friendship that she'd flushed down the drain, I'd be able to let go.

My hands shook as I unlocked the door. Stepping out, the soles of my boots skidded on a patch of ice, but I righted myself. Took a deep breath. And walked up to face my former BFF.

Faith saw me first. "Oh! Hi, Krissy!" she said too brightly, glancing at Vee. She always did turn to other people for cues about how to behave.

"Hi," I said, following Faith's gaze to look at Vee, who had taken a sudden interest in her cell phone. When I didn't move on, Vee put her cell phone away and made a show of raising her eyebrows as if just noticing me.

"Hey." She nodded coolly. "Long time no see."

If I had wanted to see remorse, I wasn't going to get it. I felt like a fool. Had I really expected her to beg for my forgiveness?

"Um, excuse me?" a blue-haired girl behind Vee said. "No cutting. We've been waiting forever to get in."

"Nothing to worry about," Vee drawled. "She's not with us."

She spoke the truth, but it still hurt. Faith tried to intercede.

"Come on, Vee, why don't you just talk? You guys are better than this."

"Better than what?" Vee snapped. "*She's* the one who called me a jealous bitch and then ignored me for a fucking month."

"*You* were the one who told my boyfriend that I was a hermaphrodite!" The words came out before I remembered where we were. A couple of Blue-Haired Girl's friends giggled nervously, and I could feel their eyes on me. I wanted to shrink from their scrutiny, but there was no going back now. "Like I could forget about that? Ever?"

"I told you," Vee said with gritted teeth. "I didn't tell your precious Sam-I-am."

"Oh, please. No one else knew!"

"Not true," she said. Her eyes darted toward my other best friend, who was staring down at her sparkly gold high heels. "Why don't you ask Faith how Sam found out?"

The world spun, then contracted. Around us I sensed people shuffling forward in line. When it was clear we were going nowhere, Blue-Haired Girl stepped around us. I barely noticed, my eyes fixed on Faith, whose face wore the guilt that I'd hoped to see on Vee's.

She was still looking at her shoes.

"Faith, is she telling the truth?" I asked shakily. I didn't know why I asked, though. I already knew the answer.

"Krissy," she said so quietly I could barely hear. "When I found out, I called Sam to see how he was doing." Her voice trembled. "I didn't realize that he didn't know."

I closed my eyes. Opened them again. Faith had finally looked up from her feet, and I recognized the expression she'd worn around me so many times since my diagnosis. Now, at last, I realized it was guilt.

"Why didn't you tell me?" I asked. My voice sounded childish, bewildered.

"I was going to try to make it right. And I did try to tell you once, but I didn't want you to be mad at me. . . ." Her upper lip trembled and she started to cry.

"Oh, Faith." I put my hand to my forehead, suddenly disoriented by the backlash from my misplaced anger. "Please stop crying."

"Are you going to hate me forever?"

I let out a long, slow breath and watched it billow in the cold night air. "Of course not. You know it's impossible for anyone to stay mad at you."

It was true, had always been true, but my saying it only made her sob louder.

"Jesus fucking Christ." Vee sighed. "Come on. Both of you." She put one arm around Faith to guide her and gestured at me to follow. When we got to her car, she put me in the driver's seat and made Faith take shotgun. Then she planted herself in the middle of the backseat and watched us: Faith sitting hunched up, still weeping quietly. Me staring out of the window, unable to look at either of them.

"All right, get on with it, guys," Vee said after a minute of silence.

"Get on with what?" I asked, finally looking at her.

She closed her eyes, and grimaced. "Faith, stop crying and tell Krissy you're sorry. Krissy, stop moping and tell Faith you forgive her. And while you're at it, would you get on with your life already?"

"What are you talking about?"

"I'm talking about you *getting over yourself*. It's been weeks since you've been at school. The other day my mom and I ran into your aunt Carla at ShopRite, and she was going on and on about how concerned she was about you. Krissy, it's time to *move on*."

Even as I cringed at the thought of Aunt Carla accosting the Richardsons, I was furious. "Oh, that's right! My boyfriend dumps me, the whole school thinks I'm a man, and I'll move on, just like that! To think that all I needed to solve my problems was the great Vanessa Richardson telling me to snap out of it."

Then Faith spoke up, her voice stuffy and pathetic. "She's right, you know."

I stared. "Why are you taking *her* side?"

"There's no side taking here," Faith said. "I'm the one who screwed up, remember? Anyway, I'm really worried about you. You've become, like, a hermit or something."

The windows were starting to fog up, and I traced a circle

on the cold, wet glass. Suddenly, the car felt suffocating. I could feel both Vee and Faith staring at me. I was so sick and tired of people telling me what I should do with my life: My dad. Ms. Diaz. Dr. LaForte. And now the Dynamic Duo.

"You guys don't understand," I said stubbornly. "The whispers. The looks."

"Listen to us, Krissy," Vee said. "How long have we been friends?"

"Eighteen years, if you include playdates before we could talk," sniffed Faith.

"Right. So we've known you for almost two decades. What would your—" She cut herself off, as if aware that she was going too far.

The air in the car grew heavy. I felt a familiar ache blossom in my chest as the muffled sounds outside receded into the distance. I stared at Vee, who looked down at her hands.

"Go on," I told her. "I know what you wanted to say. What would my mother think if she saw me like this?"

That's when I lost it. I've never been a pretty crier, not like Faith. I was ugly cry all the way: bloodshot eyes, red nose, snot everywhere. Because what would my mother think? That I was a quitter? That I was weak? Would she just shake her head at the mess that I had become?

"Come on, Krissy," Vee said roughly, handing me a tissue. "I don't think I have enough Kleenex for you and Faith both."

I sob-laughed. "I'll just have to use my sleeve, then."

"Um, gross," Vee said.

"Be nice, Vee," Faith said. She dabbed at her eyes and reached out to me. "I'm so sorry, Krissy. How can you ever forgive me?"

What a question. In all the years I had known Faith, I couldn't remember a time when I'd been truly angry at her. Whatever things she did to irritate me, her intentions were always true. I slid into her hug and closed my eyes. "Of course I forgive you, Faith."

I was too tired to hate. And too guilty.

In the backseat, Vee's phone rang, but she silenced it. A moment later, it vibrated at the same time Faith's phone dinged.

"I hate to break up the lovefest," Vee said after checking the message, "but the others are inside Bliss, wondering where we are. We should go soon." She turned to me and paused just a second before adding, "You should come."

My heart wanted to, but my mind said no. I shook my head. "Thanks, but I'm going to go home. It's not that I'm running away," I added quickly. "I just need some time to pull myself together. I mean, look at me, right?" I gestured toward my post-sob face.

"Okay." Vee gave me a searching look. She got out of the backseat and opened the door to let me out.

As I slid out of the car, I grabbed hold of Vee's coat. "Wait," I said quietly. "I'm sorry I accused you of telling Sam."

Vee shrugged. Started to say something, but stopped. I

could have been the wind, but I thought I saw tears in her eyes, too. "Apology accepted."

We walked back toward my car huddled together to shield ourselves from the cold, and I thought about my new reality. It would take a while to sink in. Then again, all good changes did.

CHAPTER 38

As I fumbled around in my purse for my car keys, I noticed my cell phone blinking. There was a text from Jessica that must've come through while I was in the bathroom at home.

Got UR message. We're catching the 8:10 show at Sanger-town. CU there.

It was like a time capsule from the past. I almost didn't remember that I had called Jessica out of loneliness. I hadn't known, then, that I was partly to blame for my isolation. Now that I had let the weight of my self-pity go, I felt strangely adrift.

On my way home, I passed by the Sangertown Square Mall. I glanced at the clock—it was almost ten—and found myself turning in to the mall, and heading toward the movie theaters in the back lot.

Maybe Vee had been right. It was time to move on.

When I got to the theater, the movie was letting out in ten

minutes. So I sat in the lobby next to a giant cardboard cutout of a cartoon monkey, trying not to look too stalkerish.

As people poured from the theater, I saw Jessica first, arguing with her boyfriend, Quincy, also a debater. A couple of other Honors kids trailed after them, and then Darren came out with Becky. They were holding hands, cute as ever, and I was struck once again by how petite Becky was. I felt like an Amazon next to her.

Darren did a double take after he saw me, and the two of them parted.

"Hey," Jessica said as the group gathered in front of me. "We missed you."

"Sorry, I didn't get your text until just now. But you guys were going out afterward, right?"

"That's the plan. Meet you at Carmella's?"

At the restaurant, the seven of us squeezed into a booth. Jessica and Quincy sat on one side with Jorge, who I knew from AP English class. Becky slid into the opposite side after her friend Miranda, and Darren and I followed. I took the outside seat.

It'd been weeks since I'd been out with a group, and I couldn't believe how *loud* they were. Everyone talked over each other, angling for laughs and groans instead of saying things that actually mattered. Mostly, I listened. I was the seventh wheel, the one who disturbed the balance of the table.

I was aware of Darren's every move next to me. When he

talked, I could actually feel the vibration of his baritone. When his sleeve brushed my arm as he reached for his Diet Dr Pepper, it sent a little quiver down my spine.

Jessica was going off about the Bond girl. "Next time, they should just use an inflatable vagina, instead of bothering an actual actress with the part. Those roles are so fucking degrading."

"What, you didn't think that one scene when she jabbed the guy in the eye with a nail file was an example of a strong woman?" Darren quipped.

"Sadly, yes. That was her best moment. At least she saved her own ass."

I excused myself to go to the bathroom. In the stall I slumped on the toilet, breathing in the silence, letting it restore me so I could go back out again. Maybe I should've stayed at the club. It would've been noisy, but it would've been *moving* noisy. I tried to close my eyes and visualize myself laughing with the others. Real laughs that bubbled up from the belly, not forced ones that felt pumped out.

When I came back our nachos had arrived and were already half destroyed. "You okay?" Darren asked me.

"I'm fine," I said, so it would be true. I touched my nose, wondering if it was still red. "Is there something wrong with my face?"

"No," he said hastily. "You just looked worried, that's all."

"Way to stress a girl out, Darren," said Becky, giving him a little shove. "Haven't I taught you *anything*?"

"Shit. I knew I should've taken notes." He gave me a panicked look and stage-whispered, "Don't tell anyone, but I think I'm gonna fail Boyfriend 101. My teacher's a total hard-ass."

Becky punched him. A giggle bubbled up from my belly, despite myself.

Jessica and Darren's friends were easy to hang out with. Maybe it was because they were from different grades, but they hardly mentioned any other people from our school except in passing. Mostly they talked about movies, and music. They talked about Jessica's play, and where they were thinking of going to college.

Becky frowned when Darren mentioned Columbia. "Cornell's an awesome school, too," she reminded him. "And it's so much closer."

After the nachos had been reduced to a puddle of scraped-over cheese, we sat for over an hour, until our waitress pointedly brought our check. I trailed the others out of the restaurant, and saw Darren say something to Becky before dropping back to talk to me.

"Mind if I hitch a ride home with you?" he asked. "I rode with Quincy, but you're a lot closer."

"Sure, I guess." I gave a fleeting thought to what Becky would think of him riding home with me. Though I wasn't exactly competition.

The passenger seat was still pushed way back from the last

time we'd carpooled to the health clinic, and Darren slid in.

"It was fun hanging out with you guys," I said as we pulled out of the parking lot.

"Well, it was cool to have you there," Darren said, his voice strangely stiff. I looked over at him. Where had the ease of our carpool and running conversations gone? It was like he was suddenly treating me like someone he'd just met.

I didn't want to be someone he'd just met. "Was it really? I only ask because I know I haven't been good company lately."

I paused, weighing my next words, wondering if I really wanted to go there. I decided that I did. "Someone told me tonight that I needed to get over myself, that I've been so caught up in my . . . my diagnosis that I've basically been a shitty friend. And paranoid too," I added. "I can't forget the paranoid part."

"Did you tell them to go screw themselves?"

I smiled. "No. Because I think they're right."

"Well, I wouldn't go that far," Darren said after a bit. "It takes a lot of hard work to be truly, top-notch paranoid, and I'm afraid you don't quite make the cut. Sorry."

"Really?"

"Yeah, I have to say you're kind of an also-ran in the shitty friend department, actually."

"I don't know about that." I sighed, and flexed my grip on the steering wheel. "I basically accused my best friend of telling the whole school that I was a hermaphrodite. I wasn't wrong. But I was blaming the wrong best friend."

"Oh. Crap."

"So, shitty friend."

"Okay, so maybe you're in the ballpark. What did you do when you found out you were wrong?"

"I apologized."

He made a game-show buzzer sound. "Sorry, you're out of the running again."

"But I was a jerk. Do you know how much it sucks to be the jerk?"

"That's kind of personal, isn't it?"

I groaned, even as part of me warmed at the banter. "It was a rhetorical question."

Darren stretched in his seat, and ran his hand through his hair. "Rhetorical or no, the answer is yes. When my father first came out, I was a total asshole."

"Weren't you, like, ten?"

"That doesn't excuse me. Nor does the fact that he ran off with a guy who'd been my student teacher in fourth grade, leaving my practically suicidal mother in sole custody of me and my hormonally challenged older sister."

"God. That must've been awful."

"Yeah, my life pretty much blew. Anyway, I blamed it all on my dad. Not on my mom, who, it turned out, actually knew that my father was gay. Or at least bi.

"The thing I hated the most was that he had played the

straight guy for so many years. Couldn't he have just kept his dick in his pants, or at least waited until I'd gotten through the hardest years of my life before taking off? Don't answer that question. I know it wasn't the most mature thing to think. But like you said, I was ten. So I threw tantrums whenever I had to go to his house. I deleted his emails without reading them. In other words, yes, I know what it's like to be the jerk, and to have to deal with the suck when you realize that you've been in the wrong."

"Oh, Darren." I tried to imagine how a ten-year-old could've handled the betrayal and guilt. "What helped?"

"Several thousand dollars of therapy."

"Well, I'm working on that, at least."

"Time. Chocolate. And more therapy. But you know what? All those sessions with a shrink really only taught me one thing: To not be too hard on myself. Or my dad."

When we pulled into Darren's driveway, the light in his kitchen was still on. "Your mom's up late."

"Yeah, she's got a big event tomorrow, and she said she'd be up late experimenting with different éclair fillings."

"Oh my God, your mom's éclairs," I said wistfully. "Worth killing for."

"You aren't kidding," Darren said as he opened the door to get out. "Come on in. She's always up for some taste testers."

"I can't," I protested. "It's too late. What would your mom

think?" More importantly, what would Becky think?

"Bull. Shit. My mom loves you. Come on, I don't want to be held responsible if you resort to justifiable homicide to get one of those éclairs tomorrow."

Darren walked around to open my door, so how could I refuse?

CHAPTER 39

Darren's house was pretty much like I remembered it, with the exception, of course, of the baby paraphernalia that had infiltrated every room. We took our shoes off next to the stroller by the door, and walked through the living room strewn with burp cloths and soft toys. Even the kitchen had been compromised by a huge bottle-drying rack. Ms. Kowalski sat at the center island with an icing bag, surrounded by pastry shells.

"Hey, Mom," Darren said. "I brought you a set of taste buds."

"Kristin!" Ms. Kowalski exclaimed when she saw me. She got up and gave me a handless hug, careful not to get any sugar on me. "It's been ages. My, you've become such a gorgeous woman."

I glanced at Darren, who nodded his head ever so slightly. His mom knew. I closed my eyes and leaned into her hug, breathing in the scent of flour and butter.

"You came at the perfect time," she said. "My client is a horticulturist, and wanted a floral theme for the reception. I'm trying some new lavender and rosewater fillings, and I need to know if they're too overwhelming."

She held out an éclair for each of us. I closed my eyes as I bit down, savoring the delicate explosion of flavor. "Wow," I said. "It's like edible aromatherapy."

"And that's a good thing?" she asked anxiously.

My mouth was too full of éclair to answer so I nodded instead. "Mmm hmmm."

Ms. Kowalski beamed. "Here, try one of the rosewater ones."

"Can I help you fill them? It's the least I can do." I reached for the other icing bag and plopped myself down by a tray of shells.

"Kristin," Ms. Kowalski protested, "I'm sure this isn't how you want to spend your Saturday night."

"Actually, I can't think of a place I'd rather be." Aware of how cheesy I sounded, I didn't dare look over at Darren. But I heard a metallic screech as he pulled over a chair, picked up a pastry brush, and began putting a chocolate coat on my finished éclairs.

After a couple of minutes, the baby monitor went off. "Oh, dear," Ms. Kowalski said. "Wendy's in the shower. I'll be back in a bit."

"Okay, now's your time to jet," Darren whispered as his mother's footsteps faded. "You've paid your dues. Éclair points earned. I'll tell my mom your dad called or something."

"No need for excuses." I smiled as I filled another shell. "It's kind of soothing." There was a rhythm to baking, a surety of repetition that was as satisfying as running. The brightly lit kitchen and fantastic smells were just what I needed after a roller-coaster night.

Then it occurred to me. "Unless you want me to leave." I put down the icing bag and slid off my chair.

"No, of course not!" Darren reached out to stop me, but only managed to paint my arm with chocolate. He swore, and ran to get a wet washcloth.

"I'm so sorry."

"Don't even worry about it," I said. I ran my finger across the offending chocolate and licked it off. "See? All better. Getting messy never tasted so good."

Darren sighed, but he was smiling. "My mother is such a bad influence. Let me at least get the sugar off so you don't get all sticky." He took my hand in his and gently wiped down my arm. My skin tingled.

We were so close I could hear Darren's tiny gasp as my fingers tightened around his. A strand of unruly hair fell out from behind his ear and I had to restrain myself from reaching out to tuck it back. Outside, a motorcycle zoomed by, setting off a chorus of dog barks.

We both stared down at our clasped hands.

"Kristin," he said quietly.

Darren's cell phone went off, shrill and jarring, breaking the spell. He pulled his hand from mine as he reached for the phone, and when he saw the caller ID he turned around so his back was to me.

"Hey, babe," he answered.

I picked up the icing bag again, pretending not to eavesdrop. But of course I heard every word.

"Yup, I got home okay." Was it me, or did Darren's voice sound just a little too casual? He was silent for a while as Becky monologued, nodding his head once.

"Yeah, I remember him. . . . Okay. . . . I'll check it out."

After what seemed like forever, he finally wrapped things up. "Well, thanks for calling, babe. I gotta go. My mom needs my help with some last-minute catering stuff. See you on Monday?

"That was Becky," he said unnecessarily after he hung up. He didn't look me in the eye.

"Yeah, kind of figured," I said. I could still feel the echo of his hand on mine.

"She was telling me about her uncle who went to Cornell and loved it," he said with an eyeroll.

"Oh," I said. I filled the last éclair, and set it carefully on Ms. Kowalski's lacquered tray. I stood and picked up my keys. "Well, that's the last of the lavender batch. Tell your mom thank you again?"

Darren gave me a halfhearted grin. "You already know what she'll say: anytime."

"You guys are too awesome," I said.

And I meant it so intensely that it hurt.

CHAPTER 40

The next morning, it was clear that Faith was ready for the Three Musketeers to be back together again.

Faith: So. U want V and me to pick U up 2morow?

Me: No not quite ready

Faith: Srsly?

Me: Im almost there

Faith: Okay fine. But gonna keep bugging you.

She wasn't the only one breathing down my neck. That afternoon, Ms. Diaz called to "check in," reminding me that I only had a week's leave of absence left.

"It's really close to the end of the semester. Wouldn't it make sense to have a fresh start at the beginning of the year?" I asked. That'd give me until after winter break to pull things together.

"Well, the district has strict criteria for extended leaves.

We'll have to get some paperwork from your physicians, and you'll need to be evaluated every two weeks."

I hated the idea of another visit to Dr. Cheng's office. After I got off the phone with Ms. Diaz, I paced around my room, then lay down on my bed. I pretended I was in the middle of a track field, and imagined Coach Auerbach's voice leading me through her visualization exercise:

Focus on the area under your belly button, and breathe in using your abdomen, as if you're pulling the breath out with a string. Relax your shoulders. Reach out. Now draw a picture in your mind.

I visualized myself getting out of Faith's car and entering the doors of Ralph Perry High with Vee by my side. As we walked through the hallways, people stopped and stared, and I imagined myself standing tall and ignoring them. Good people were there, too: Jessica and Darren, and maybe even Jorge and Quincy.

Then I remembered the heaviness in Darren's voice while we were filling éclairs. The moment Becky called, he had started to say something. I had a hunch that he had been about to let me down easy. Thank God he hadn't had the chance.

I deleted Darren's face from my visualization and put in Rashonda Glenn and Peggy Shah. Once classes started it was easier to see how I could fall back into the routine, the machinery of school.

Maybe I was ready, after all.

But as I pictured myself walking into the cafeteria, Bruce

appeared. And he did more than stare. He taunted, and got some of his buddies to follow me into the hall as I fled. He cornered me in a stairway, pushed me up against the wall, and unzipped my jeans as I flailed. . . .

I opened my eyes, my heart pounding.

Leaning up against my bookshelf, half hidden from view, there was a picture board that Faith and Vee had put together for me on my sixteenth birthday; I had taken it down one day after things fell apart, and hadn't rehung it yet. My gaze settled on one picture of the three of us hugging in front of a church. We were all wearing black.

My mom had been sick for almost a year before the cancer finally took her. She died in the summertime, and on the morning of the funeral I went out with Aunt Carla and some of my mom's friends to collect wildflowers—her favorite.

I remember Aunt Carla bawling behind me as I bent over to pick a daylily. "What is Bob going to do with a motherless child?"

"Shhh," Mrs. Wu whispered. "It'll be okay, Carla. Kids are resilient. Look at how poised and strong Kristin's been today."

Poised, I thought, when they poured dirt over my mom's casket. *Strong*, I told myself that night when I hugged my father as he sobbed.

Six years later, I realized I was neither. How poised could I be if I was sitting in my room, trembling at the thought of Bruce Torino bullying me? How strong was I if I couldn't even envision a place or a time when I could stand up and confront my diagnosis, rather than fleeing from who I was?

Except, according to Gretchen, such a place existed. People with AIS found ways to live and thrive, ways to be loved. And some of them had shared their stories. I turned my computer on and found the link she'd sent me to the support-group website. I expected maybe a couple of testimonials or links to magazine articles, maybe even a video or two.

I didn't expect 146 personal stories, ranging from a few paragraphs to a few pages. Written by women who'd found out about their AIS when they were as young as twelve and as old as thirty-five, and by a few men with partial versions of AIS that sounded even more confusing and mind-messing than what I had.

Then there were links to information on other types of intersex, including conditions that were nowhere near as cut-and-dried as AIS was. Syndromes like 5-alpha-reductase deficiency, where you start out looking like a girl but then "virilize" when you hit puberty.

For the first time since my diagnosis, I felt like I'd gotten lucky. Only *lucky* didn't completely describe my feelings: *humbled* was a better word for what I felt reading the honesty on that webpage. Truth stripped naked for the entire internet to see.

The common thread from all those stories was that talking

helped, and listening, and time. One day I would find my own place. I couldn't run there, though, because it didn't exist yet; I had to build it myself, out of forgiveness, truth, and terrifying gestures of friendship.

CHAPTER 41

Before I left to go clubbing the next Saturday, I came up with a story for how I met Gretchen just in case her friends asked how we knew each other. Once we got there, though, I relaxed, because it turned out to be one of those clubs where the bass was so intense you could feel it in your cheekbones. It was the perfect way to hang out with four people you barely knew, because we couldn't have had more than a five-word conversation if we'd tried.

Gretchen introduced me to her girlfriend, Julia, as we waited outside in line, and I liked her instantly, even if I was intimidated by how glam and gorgeous she looked in a black sheath with a gold belt and fishnets. Inside the club, we met up with their friends Jenn and Leslie at the coat check. We'd barely exchanged words before I was half deaf from the pounding music and strangely amped up, itching to move. We plunged into the strobe-lit chaos.

For the first time since my surgery, I danced. Not the single-girl dance, all flirty and mussing my hair around, but the girl-friend dance, in a little circle with the others. I danced until I could feel the sweat soaking my top. Once in a while one of the other girls would take a break to go to the bathroom or get a drink, but I kept going even when I didn't like the music, as if I were running a race. I just moved and enjoyed the feeling of being lost in a crowd.

Then the music stopped, and an emcee came onto the stage and chatted us all up. The crowd started to make that restless, get-on-with-it murmur, and we slid off the dance floor to get a better view of the stage. As I did, I saw a familiar lanky figure standing against a wall.

"Darren!" I yelled. I ran over, still high from dancing, and gave him a hug. Of course he was there—he was the one who had introduced me to The Concept, after all. I looked around for other kids from our school. "Are you here with Becky?" It was an eighteen-plus club, and Becky was a couple of years younger than we were. Club Eternal was notorious for kicking out kids with fake IDs if there was any suspicion that they weren't legit.

Darren looked uncomfortable. "Um, no. Quincy and Jessica." He fiddled with his ticket stub. "Who are *you* here with?"

"Oh, just some friends," I said vaguely. I'd already forgotten my made-up story about Gretchen.

Quincy saved me, butting in to tug at Darren's shirt. "C'mon, we scored a table over by the bar. Oh, hi, Kristin." He brightened when he saw me, and glanced over at Darren before asking, "Wanna join?"

I looked at Darren. He didn't say anything or meet my gaze, and I felt myself coming down from my dancing high. "Thanks," I said quietly, "but my friends are over there."

"Who was that?" Julia asked when I rejoined them. "He was cute, in that confident nerd way."

I gave a pained smile at the description. "Just an old friend."

"An old friend . . . that you have a thing for?"

"I don't—" I stopped. Who was I kidding? I did. "He has a girlfriend."

"Don't see him with one tonight," Julia pointed out.

"Well . . . he's not into me, then," I said.

"His loss. Plenty of other fish in the sea."

Were there, in my sea?

Leslie misinterpreted my silence. "If you're shy, I'll be your wingwoman. It'll be perfect. Come hang out with me at the bar. You don't have a stamp, so they won't serve you, but you can at least mingle."

The opening band started its set, and things got loud again. I joined Leslie in the sweaty press around the bar. As we waited to be served, she nudged me. "Hey, that dude is totally checking you out."

I turned, scanned the crowd, and saw him. It was Josh.

Pinstripe Shirt from my night out in Whitesboro. My heart did a triple jump in my chest.

"Lara, right?" He slid over, leaning in until I could smell the Pabst on his breath. "What's up? You never called me back after that one text."

"Hey!" My mind raced to find an excuse. "I'm sorry. Things have been super busy. And I had surgery."

His eyes widened with real sympathy. "No shit? Well, it must've been minor because you're looking pretty fine now," Josh said, his gaze drifting down from my face for a moment. Leslie tapped me on the shoulder and I watched out of the corner of my eye as she slipped away after a smiling "See ya later, Kristin."

After a second of panic, I allowed myself to be flattered that Josh wanted to come back for more. Wasn't this what I wanted? To be swimming in the sea? We shouted at each other for a little while, to at least pretend that we were there for the conversation, but I was glad when Josh led me back out onto the floor.

It was so crowded that we were practically glued to each other. Right away, Josh put his hands on my waist. Then they snaked up my back, and his hips were moving and I could feel his hard-on rubbing against me as we gyrated. It felt gross and amazing at the same time, raw and real.

In between sets, Josh pulled me behind a decorative curtain hiding a little nook in the wall. We could still hear the noise of the club, but we were hidden from view. In the tiny, enclosed space I had a moment of doubt, until I reminded myself that this was what I had come for.

Josh kept on whispering how hot I was, and I closed my eyes to get beyond the terror of being found out, and to focus on the feel of someone touching me, desiring me beyond any doubt. His hand slid up my skirt and under my panties, and I willed myself not to flinch.

Behind the curtain it was like a sauna. My hair was a mess, my neck sticky with sweat, so I put it up in a ponytail. I stripped down to a tank that I had layered under my top, and reached a hand up to wipe my forehead. And that's when Josh truly looked at me for the first time.

"Shit," I heard him say. I glanced through the slit of the curtain, thinking that there was a bouncer coming around.

"Are you that . . . ?" Josh was staring at me. The lighting was all wrong for me to see the expression on his face, but I sensed the shock of his recognition. And heard the disgust creeping into his voice.

I recoiled, my heart pounding so hard I could feel it in my fingertips. "No," I said, so desperately it sounded like a whimper. He couldn't even say what I was out loud.

"You said your name was Lara, but that girl called you Kristin. You're . . . whatshername. Kristin Lattimer." Josh's voice started to rise. "I remember seeing you at a track meet last year with my sister. She was saying at dinner the other night that she might have a chance at State because you'd been DQ'd because you were . . . a man." He spat the last word.

I wanted to crawl into a hole and never come back, but the shame paralyzed me. When I didn't say anything, Josh shook his head, running his hands through his hair over and over.

"Jesus Christ. *Jesus Christ,*" he muttered, so close to me that I could feel his breath on my face. "Why didn't you say something?" At first, it was almost like a plea. But then the cap came off his rage, bursting like a shaken-up soda bottle.

"Why didn't you tell me?" His voice filled the curtained nook. I reached up to cover my ears, but my quick movement must've startled him, because he reached out to grab my left wrist so hard I could feel my bones rubbing against each other. I screamed, partly in pain and partly in fear.

"What the fuck kind of freak are you?" Josh shook my wrist.

"I didn't . . . I'm not . . ." *I'm a girl,* I wanted to say. But nothing came out of my mouth except sobs. Then all of sudden Josh started tearing at my clothes with his free hand, pulling at my miniskirt. There was no room where we were, nowhere to back up, and I could feel the unfinished concrete of the wall pressed against my bare skin.

"Where'd you hide it?" His fingers were thick, and they groped at my waist, gouging into my flesh.

"What? What?" I finally got out between the tears. "I'm not hiding anything!"

"Where's your dick? Did you, like, tie it back or something?"

"I don't have one, I swear."

"You're lying." He let go of my wrist to go at my skirt with both hands. I scratched at his fingers.

"FUCK!" Josh yelled.

My eye lit up with an explosion of pain and I jerked at the curtain, pulling us into the flashing lights of the club. It was so noisy that my cry for help got absorbed into the chaos. I scrabbled toward the dance floor, but Josh grabbed me in a rough embrace and backed me toward an emergency exit.

He growled in my ear. "Scream again, and every person in this club is going to find out what you are."

Behind us, people cheered even louder as the emcee came onstage.

"All right, my friends, time to get this party started! Let's have a hand for The Concept!"

The strobe lights came on again as Josh led me outside. In the alleyway, he shoved me through the piles of garbage and broken-down boxes. After the stifling heat of the club, the cold air and the silence almost felt like a relief.

"What are you going to do?" I whispered, my breath barely frosting the air.

Josh spun me against a wall so we stood face-to-face. In heels I was taller than him, though he had more bulk. I knew I should be terrified, but I'd been expecting hatred and violence since the first text message and the vandalism to my locker.

Now we'd come to the natural conclusion of my story. The worst-case scenario.

I watched the sinewy muscles on his neck for the first sign of a blow. My fists clenched in anticipation.

Then the back door to the club clattered open, and a hoarse voice shouted out, "Hey, you! Hey, Neanderthal!"

I stiffened. I didn't want an audience. Josh swore, and turned. "What the fuck do you want?"

I looked past him. Saw a scrawny figure in a light-gray band T-shirt. And my heart sank.

CHAPTER 42

In an eerily calm voice, Darren held up his hands palm out. Despite the chill, I could see a thin layer of sweat on his forehead. "Look, is this about money? Because . . . here. I've got some cash on me. And a phone. Take it." He bent over and laid his wallet and phone on the ground.

Josh ignored Darren. So he didn't see how Darren had pressed one of the numbers on his phone a little more deliberately than most people would during a supposed mugging.

"Mind your own business, will you?" Josh said.

There was no way I wanted Darren to get involved. He was tall, but Josh had at least fifty pounds on him. I still held out a crazy hope that I could talk Josh down. "It's okay, Darren," I called out. "We're just trying to figure some things out. You should go back inside—I don't want you to miss the concert."

"Nah, those guys suck," Darren lied. "I just wanted to get

some fresh air." I almost laughed at the thought of him coming out to breathe in the smell of stale hops and old puke.

Josh turned to take a closer look at Darren. "I told you. Get. The fuck. Out of here." He let go of me and took a threatening step in his direction.

Still, Darren didn't go.

Instead, he turned to one side, like he was a fencer getting into a ready stance. He curled his hand into a fist, and I felt a sinking sense of impending doom.

Josh threw the first punch, but Darren managed to dodge it. They circled each other a couple of times, but before Darren could even get a punch in, Josh rushed him, swept his ankle up in a vicious circle and kicked Darren's legs out from under him. I winced as Darren dropped to the ground with a thud. I thought I heard a shoulder crack. Josh looked around grimly, and picked up an empty bottle lying in the alleyway.

I couldn't run for help because they were blocking my way to the club. Desperately, I scrabbled through the debris on the ground next to me. No rocks. No bottles. Then my fingers curled around a can of spray paint left behind by a graffiti artist.

I hauled myself up. Josh leaned over a half-crouching Darren, the bottle raised high. The light from the streetlamp made the brown glass glitter. With all my strength, I slammed the spray paint down onto Josh's head with both hands.

The can dented with the impact.

Josh's head didn't. He turned on me. A vein stuck out in his forehead. His breaths came out in huge puffs of steam. He reached for me.

And I brought my leg back in my best hurdler leap, and kicked him in the balls.

It turned out that David Letterman's gender-verification test had something to it, after all.

CHAPTER 43

Josh toppled over with a garbled moan. On the ground, Darren let out a faint whoop of relief. Then the back door slammed open and someone shouted, "There he is!"

"Darren, Kristin, are you okay?" Jessica ran out, trailed by Quincy.

An older, red-haired man ran out and made a beeline for me and Josh. He stopped about a foot away. "What's going on here? The cops are on their way!"

There was a dull thud as Josh dropped the bottle. He got to his feet, grimacing. He was so close I could feel him tremble as he struggled to gain control over his emotions.

"No, Mr. Sanderson," Josh said. Clearly the guy was a manager of some kind. "It was just a misunderstanding."

"A misunderstanding?" The red-haired man looked at me, and frowned. "Did someone hit you, miss?"

"Yes." I pointed at Josh.

The red-haired man's frown deepened into a scowl. "So you're the type of guy that likes to hit women?" he growled.

Josh reddened, then looked at me. Suddenly he grinned. A crowd had gathered at the door. "Actually, sir, that's not a *woman* over there."

I froze. *No, no, no. Not here.*

Josh looked through the crowd and found the bouncer who'd been at the entrance. "Hey, Pinky, did this one pay the chick rate?" The bouncer nodded and Josh's grin widened. "Then she's guilty of fraud. She's a man."

I crossed my arms to cover my chest, and kept on squeezing as if I could pinch myself right out of existence.

"You're a tranny?" a bouncer asked, bug-eyed.

"Actually, the technical term is intersex," Quincy said. I knew he was trying to be helpful, but I was mortified.

"What, are you her . . . his . . . boyfriend?" the red-haired man asked. He was still trying to put the pieces of the puzzle together.

"Oh, no," Quincy said, making a point of putting his arm around Jessica. "Just a friend."

Josh's laughter made me wince. Left unsaid was the question: What kind of freak would date someone like me?

A few of the girls huddled in the club doorway giggled, and I stared at the ground. A gust of wind blew through the alley. In the distance I could hear the emcee trying to get people back into the club, and some of the curious heads disappeared. I heard the red-haired man enlist Pinky to get Josh inside.

Within minutes, the cops that policed the clubbing district arrived. One of them, a stout older man with graying temples, took a statement from me, and asked if I wanted to press charges.

I thought of police stations and depositions and having to tell my dad, and shook my head. "There'll be a report of everything, right? In case anything else happens?" Though I doubted it. Josh wasn't stupid. He knew that he could never do anything now, after having fifty witnesses.

"We'll have a record, miss. And if you change your mind . . ." He handed me a business card, which I clutched tightly like a talisman. I tried to get out a thank-you, but all I could manage was a shaky smile.

After the cops left, I sat down against a pile of broken-down boxes, too drained to move and too raw to go back inside. In the blessed silence after the last group of people filed out, the burn of my shame faded to a dull ache.

But I had done it. My worst-case scenario had occurred, and I was still here.

The last surge of adrenaline had come and gone, and I felt hollowed out inside.

Darren limped up, rubbing his shoulder. He sat down next to me, picked up the dented spray paint can, and flipped it around and around.

"You okay?" he asked me.

I nodded, and forced an unconvincing smile. "Thanks for . . . intervening."

"It's not like I did anything but distract him. You delivered the knockout punch." He let out a puff of a laugh. "Remind me to donate to a sperm bank before I ever pick a fight with you."

I smiled. Then I burst out crying.

All the anxiety and guilt and self-loathing that I'd been holding in for weeks came out in the catharsis Dr. LaForte had been hoping for since I started therapy. But it wasn't fear that pushed all my emotions past the tipping point; it was the realization that I was kind of in love with Darren Kowalski for making me laugh minutes after I'd survived a potential hate crime. I cried like a baby, and as embarrassing as it was to have a meltdown with the object of my affection sitting there patting me awkwardly on the arm to get me to stop, the release was so liberating that I didn't care.

When the torrent had subsided, I leaned my head back to gaze up into the midwinter sky. The air was so clear and cold that you could see the stars even through the city lights.

"Wanna get in out of the cold?" Darren asked. He had his hands tucked deep into his pockets.

"You should go inside. I just need another second or two out here."

"No, I'll stay and keep you company," he said, trying to pretend that he wasn't freezing. Though I could have stayed out there all night, I took pity on him and went inside.

The minute we stepped back into Club Eternal, Gretchen came running. "There you are, Kristin! Are you okay? We heard there was a fight."

"I'm fine," I said. "I just want to get home."

"Are you sure you're up to driving all the way back to Utica alone?" Leslie asked. "You could always crash in my dorm."

"I can drive with her and walk home," Darren said behind me. "If that's okay with you," he added, suddenly shy.

Julia flashed me a quick smile. I blushed, wondering what Becky would say about Darren driving home with me again.

"Okay, then," Gretchen said, jangling her keys. "I'll call you tomorrow."

"Tomorrow." I nodded.

CHAPTER 44

After Darren sardined himself into my car, we didn't talk much. I fiddled with my stereo and settled on a classic rock station, not sure what to say, not daring to start something that Darren might not be willing or able to finish. As we neared my neighborhood, he pressed some money into my hand to pay for the toll on the Thruway. I waved him off.

"No, please," I said. "It's the least I can do for dragging you into that situation."

"Whatever; it was nothing."

"No, seriously. What would Becky have thought if you'd gotten hurt defending me?"

Darren winced. "Well, if I go by what she said when she dumped me last weekend, she'd probably think I deserved it."

"Oh no!" A thrill went down my spine, and my cheeks flushed. "What happened?" I worked to keep my voice steady.

"It's not that big of a deal; I mean, it was kind of doomed from the start. She's a sophomore, and I'm going to be leaving for college. She really didn't like the idea of me being in New York City. Besides . . ." Darren paused, and I watched him struggle for a second before he turned to give me a swift, shy glance. "I think she knew that I might have feelings for someone else."

Suddenly, I found it hard to breathe. There was an ache just below my right collarbone; it was the wrong side of the chest to be my heart, really, but close enough. Darren started to say something. False-started. Finally, he asked me:

"You know that I've had a crush on you since our parents dated, right?"

"No," I whispered. I'd always assumed that he was just shy, and nice. I shook my head, unable to think of anything remotely crushworthy about me during middle school.

We turned off the main drag onto my street. All the traffic signals had switched to flashing yellow; it was getting to be the witching hour. How else to explain what Darren was telling me?

"Why me?" I asked.

Darren laughed, incredulous. "Because you're probably the only Homecoming Queen in the world who would ever wonder why someone would like her."

I grimaced. "I'm also probably the only Homecoming Queen who's intersex."

"True enough. But you can run me into the ground and aren't snotty about it. Your idea of a fun Saturday-night activity is filling éclairs with my mom. And you make a mean Popsicle-stick puppet."

I remembered the day at the clinic when I'd caught him staring at me under the play tent. I'd thought he'd just been ogling the freak. "Aren't you afraid of what people will think?"

I pulled into my driveway, and cut the engine. For the longest time, he didn't respond. My nerves roller-coastered as we listened to the tinkling creaks of the cooling engine.

When he finally spoke, his voice was quiet but clear as glass. "If there's one thing I learned from my dad leaving my mom, it's that love isn't a choice. You fall for the person, not their chromosomes."

The knot in my chest had been present for so long I'd forgotten it was there. But with Darren's words I could feel it loosening. I made a little noise that could've been a laugh, except I was crying again.

"Shit." Darren fumbled around in his coat pocket for a tissue and came up with a crumpled Carmella's napkin. "I'm so sorry," he said. "This is, like, the most unromantic object ever offered to wipe away someone's tears."

I gasped a laugh as Darren dabbed at my face, then shivered as he ran a finger along my cheek. I closed my eyes and leaned into the warmth of his palm, sensing rather than seeing him pull closer to me, his breath growing ragged. I caught the faint scent of Dr Pepper and Old Spice.

When our lips touched, I could taste my own tears.

Our kiss was tentative at first, as if this thing between us was made of spun glass, liable to break if we moved too quickly. When Josh and I had kissed, it'd been furtive and rushed. With Darren, though, I knew instantly that we had all the time in the world.

I'd been running for so long, trying to escape from who I was. Here in the steady circle of Darren's arms, I was finally ready to stand still.

CHAPTER 45

It was almost three before I got home, but I was wide awake. My dad had left the front porch light on, and I crept in as silently as I could, the door making only the barest whisper. I was unwinding my scarf in the dark when the foyer lights flickered on.

Footsteps creaked down the stairs and my father squinted at me. "Kristin, that you?"

"Sorry to wake you up, Dad."

"Thank God you're all right." Rough with sleep, his tone was accusing, which I thought was odd because the last couple of times I went out, my dad had been so excited that he didn't bother setting a curfew.

"You could've texted me if you were worried," I reminded him.

He sighed, and rubbed his hand across his stubbled chin.

"Didn't want to cramp your style," he said finally. "Well, glad you're home all right." He started to go back up the stairs, and for some reason the sight of the frayed cuffs of his flannel pajamas made my eyes prickle.

"Dad?" I called out, just wanting him to be close.

He turned around and squinted at me again. But at first I couldn't get the words out. Finally: "You know that I love you, right?"

He rubbed his eyes with his fists, and then blinked rapidly a few times. "You know I love you too, sweetie. Forever and ever, until the sun fades."

I blinked too, as my vision blurred. "Forever and ever," I repeated, and my dad walked down the last few steps and wrapped me in his arms. I burrowed into the soft, Irish Spring scent of his shirt.

"Dad," I said, "remind me to make an appointment with Dr. Cheng on Monday."

I felt him stiffen, but I went on. "She needs to fill out some paperwork so Coach Auerbach will let me start practice again once I go back to school."

My father collapsed into himself with relief, hugged me tighter. I led him back up the stairs and kissed his salt-and-pepper cheek before going into my room.

But I couldn't fall asleep.

So I turned on my computer and created a new Facebook profile using my high school email, instead of my middle school one. For my profile picture I chose a picture of me when I was ten years old and making valentines with my mother. I friended Gretchen, Julia, Darren, Jessica, and Quincy right away. Then I added Vee and Faith, remembering to forgive and be forgiven.

My blank timeline stared back at me. It was beautiful.

AUTHOR'S NOTE

I was a fifth-year surgical resident when I met my first intersex patient, and she haunts me still.

Like Kristin, my patient had AIS. Like Kristin, she was a teenager when she found out. After I helped with the operation to remove her gonads, I saw her postoperatively. She came from a very poor and disadvantaged background, and I think I was the first person to really talk to her about her condition and what to expect in the future. During our office visit, she was remarkably stoic—uninterested, almost. She had come to our clinic alone, so I worried about her support system. I also knew there were questions she would only think of after the appointment, so I made sure to give her information about the AIS support group. In retrospect, that was probably the single most important thing I did for her.

After that clinic visit, I never saw my AIS patient again, but she stayed in my thoughts. I've always wondered what became of her, and how she came to terms with her diagnosis. Did she have a boyfriend? What happened the first time she tried to have sex? Who did she tell—if anyone—about her condition?

It was early 2009. I was pregnant with my first child, a daughter. Just months later, Caster Semenya's story hit, and it became clear to me that intersex was a perfect jumping-off point for a discussion of tolerance, feminism, and gender essentialism. It begged so many questions: What does it mean to be a woman? What happens when you don't fit perfectly into the gender binary? And what role does your biology play not only in who you love, but who loves you?

As I began researching my story, it became clear to me that the great challenge of writing about intersex is that it encompasses so many different variations of biology and personal experience. There is no one intersex story. That said, it became clear that there were two controversies within the intersex community that I needed to address if I hoped to contribute responsibly to intersex awareness.

The first is the question of naming. While some in the medical community advocate use of the term Disorder of Sex Development (DSD), this phrase has been criticized because the word *disorder* suggests something inherently "wrong," so it has been replaced by many with the term "Differences in Sex Development." In *None of the Above* I chose to use the term *intersex*. I also made the difficult decision to have some of my characters use the word *hermaphrodite* in the pejorative sense because intersex awareness isn't widespread enough to have eradicated the term. In recent years, though, some intersex people have reclaimed the word *hermaphrodite* in much the same way that gay men and women did the word *queer.* While this usage isn't for everyone, it gives me hope that someday in the future the term will be freed from its stigma.

The second issue is that of surgery. Until the early 2000s, intersex children were operated on with some regularity, often as infants. There are countless stories of intersex children whose genitalia were "corrected" in a way that caused irreparable harm and suffering, all in the name of relieving parents' stress by "normalizing" their babies' anatomy with what is essentially a cosmetic surgery.

These days, due to the efforts of intersex-awareness organizations, including Accord Alliance (www.accordalliance.org), Organization Intersex International (www.oiiinternational.com), and Advocates for Informed Choice (www.aiclegal.org), the strong recommendation is to hold off on surgery until the child is old enough to a) have formed a gender identity and b) consent to surgery knowing the full risks and benefits. Unfortunately, despite these recommendations, some intersex children are still subjected to unnecessary surgeries, underscoring the urgent need to educate physicians and parents on changing guidelines.

If there is anything I know as a surgeon, it's that every surgery has risks. So I struggled when I came to the part of

Kristin's narrative where she opted for a gonadectomy. In the end, with her family history of cancer, and the psychological space she was in, it was the right choice for her; importantly for me, she went in with her eyes wide open.

I couldn't have written *None of the Above* with a whit of authenticity without the incredible support of the AIS community. I can't thank Jeanne Nollman (president of the AIS-DSD Support Group for Women and Families: www.aisdsd.org) and Margaret Simmonds (director of the UK Androgen Insensitivity Syndrome Support Group: www.aissg.org) enough for reading early drafts, and providing me with the kindest insight and encouragement. Dr. Arlene Baratz read a later iteration, and her suggestions added considerable nuance and accuracy to *None of the Above*. Any and all errors of representation are mine and mine alone.

Finally, my deepest admiration goes to Pigeon Pagonis and Sean Saifa Wall for their courageous work with Inter/Act (http://inter-actyouth.tumblr.com) and Advocates for Informed Choice. You are my heroes. In Saifa's words, they speak "for the many who cannot speak, including those living with the shame, isolation, and secrecy that surround people with intersex conditions." It's my fervent hope that Kristin's story resonates not only with readers who are intersex, but with any teenager who has ever felt that they were different, struggled with intimacy, or wished that they were "normal."

RECOMMENDED READING

Works of fiction featuring intersex characters

Middlesex by Jeffrey Eugenides

Golden Boy by Abigail Tarttelin

Nonfiction

Fixing Sex: Intersex, Medical Authority, and Lived Experience by Katrina Karkazis

Hermaphrodites and the Medical Invention of Sex by Alice Domurat Dreger

Articles and websites of note

Accord Alliance. "Learn About DSD." www.accordalliance .org/learn-about-dsd/faqs

Dreger, Alice Domurat. "Media Advisory on Sex Verification in Sports." www.alicedreger.com/media_ advisory_01.html

Inter/Act: A Tumblr "for young people with intersex conditions or DSDs to come together, express themselves, and unite their individual stories to develop a voice for a new generation." http://inter-actyouth. tumblr.com

Kinsman, Kat. "Intersex Dating: Finding Love across the Intersection." April 15, 2014. www.cnn.com/2014/ 04/15/living/intersex-dating-relate

Organization Intersex International. "The Real Michael Phelps Girlfriend Story." www. oiiinternational.com/3110/the-real-michael-phelps-girlfriend-story

ACKNOWLEDGMENTS

There's a special place in paradise for the agents and editors of debut authors. This book would not be in your hands were it not for Jessica Regel's faith in the first sixty pages of this story—I couldn't have asked for a better advocate and friend. More important, Jess matched me with an editorial dream team that at times understood my book better than I did. I'll be forever indebted to Alessandra Balzer, Sara Sargent, and Kelsey Murphy for helping me to kill my darlings and inspiring me to write new ones; for knowing when to be merciless and when to be kind; but most of all, for believing that Kristin's story was one worth telling. Thanks to the entire B+B editorial team—Donna Bray, Kristin Daly Rens, Jordan Brown, and Viana Siniscalchi—for making me feel so welcome.

Thank you to the crackerjack managing editorial team of Bethany Reis, Mark Rifkin, Josh Weiss, and copyeditor extraordinaire Kathryn Hinds, for catching countless embarrassing mistakes in my draft; any errors that are still in the book are mine and mine alone. A round of applause for Alison Donalty, Jenna Stempel, and Barb Fitzsimmons, who designed a cover that is both visually stunning and true to the story.

To Caroline Sun and Booki Vivat, the best publicity team a girl could hope for, I say "Bravo." Mad love to Nellie Kurtzman, Jenna Lisanti, Stefanie Hoffman, Megan Barlog, and the whole Harper marketing team for their enthusiasm for this book. In particular, a shout-out to Patty Rosati and the School and Library team for making *None of the Above* a Common Core focus title, and for tangibly increasing intersex awareness in our schools. I heart you, Molly Motch, Preeti Chhibber, Stephanie Macy, and Robin Pinto! Thank you to the many people in the sales department who championed my book, including Bernie Moran, Kim Gombar, Ashton Quinn, and Ronnie Kutys.

Huge tackle-hugs to my talented critique partners Abigail Hing Wen and Sonya Mukherjee, who have been there from the very beginning, cheering me when I got things right and setting me straight when my efforts went awry. It's not an overstatement to say that I may never have gotten published without them, and I can't wait to see their own books on my shelf.

My undying gratitude to the beta readers whose fresh eyes kept me on the right path as *None* went through revision after revision: Libby Copeland, Eliza Jones, Stacey Lee, Karen Akins, Marieke Nijkamp, Anna-Marie McLemore, Katia

Raina, Natasha Sinel, Dianne K. Salerni, K. M. Walton, Evelyn Ehrlich, Amy Garvey, and Kelly Lyman—you rock. Jazz Tigan, Christine Danek, Jeanne Schriel, Kevin P. Sheridan, and Joanne Fritz also offered valuable insight as I worked out Kristin's voice. Super-special props to An-Lon Chen for both beta reading and designing my amazing SWAG, and to Elena Gregorio, Vince Grim, and David Aversa, who very kindly gave me incredible insight into the worlds of social work, counseling, and psychiatry.

Thanks to the numerous publishing peeps whose keen insight steered Kristin's story in the right direction, particularly Jennifer Laughran, Brett Wright, Marie Lamba, and Amy Tipton.

Sometimes I joke that taking out someone's bladder tumor is a walk in the park—it's the writing life that's stressful. I owe whatever sanity I have to the We Need Diverse Books team, the Fearless Fifteeners, the Class of 2k15, and the Diversity League for helping me navigate this sometimes tortuous journey. Shout-outs also to the Hopefuls, the Milestones critique group, and the members of the SCBWI (née Verla Kay) Blueboards.

Long, long ago in a galaxy far, far away named New Hartford, New York, Robert Evans and Marilyn Morgan nursed the fragile writer within me. Thank you to Bridget Madsen for never doubting that I would see my words in print. At Penn, Karen Rile was an inspiration, and at Yale, Richard Selzer allowed me to believe that someday I really could mesh my writing with my medical career. A million thanks to Jacqueline Woodson, Beth Kephart, and Kristin Elizabeth Clark for alleviating my blurb anxiety, and for modeling the types of writers (and people) I want to become.

Thank you to my parents and my grandparents for instilling a passion for reading in me when I was very young. Thank you to the Gregorio and Roberts families for giving me my pen name, and for supporting my craft with food, babysitting, and a general love of literature. Thank you to Olivia and Gabriel for putting up with Mommy on days when she had to lock herself into her office, coming out only for hydration and trail mix.

And then there's Joe: my first reader, my copyeditor, my publicist, and my best friend. Thank you for rooting for me every second of this crazy ride.

Last but most certainly not least, thank you to the intersex women of the AIS Support Group and Inter/Act Youth for embracing me so warmly as I told their story. I hope that I did it justice.

Stealing their signoff:

XOXY